Beatrice said a

Nicholas gave a little shudder to shake off the haunting memories, then looked down at her and smiled. "Owen now calls me Papa. Mayhap his aunt should take his example and learn to call me Nicholas. Will you say it for me?"

The flickering shadows of the midsummer twilight lent an air of unreality to the scene. Beatrice's eyes were inscrutable as she paused, then moistened her lips and said, "Nicholas."

The word seemed to stir a wave inside him. As it intensified, he suddenly recognized the familiar sensation. With a feeling akin to panic, he tried to tell himself that he was a changed man. Yet as Beatrice swayed ever so slightly closer to him in the shadows, he could not deny his feelings.

He wanted her....

Dear Reader,

This month our exciting medieval series KNIGHTS OF THE BLACK ROSE continues with *The Rogue* by Ana Seymour, a secret baby story in which rogue knight Nicholas Hendry finds his one true love. Judith Stacy returns with *Written in the Heart,* the delightful tale of an uptight California businessman who hires a marriage-shy female handwriting analyst to solve some of his company's capers. In *Angel of the Knight,* a medieval novel by Diana Hall, a carefree warrior falls deeply in love with his betrothed, and does all he can to free her from a family curse. Talented newcomer Mary Burton brings us *A Bride for McCain,* about a mining millionaire who enters a marriage of convenience with the town's schoolteacher.

For the next three months, we are going to be asking readers to let us know what you are looking for from Harlequin Historicals. We hope you'll participate by sending your ideas to us at:

Harlequin Historicals
300 E. 42nd St.
New York, NY 10017

Q. What are your favorite historical settings?

_____

_____

Q. Which Harlequin Historicals authors do you read?

_____

_____

Whatever your taste in reading, you'll be sure to find a romantic journey back to the past between the covers of a Harlequin Historicals novel. We hope you'll join us next month, too!

Sincerely,

Tracy Farrell,
Senior Editor

Ana Seymour

The Rogue

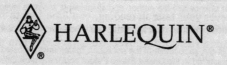

HARLEQUIN®

TORONTO • NEW YORK • LONDON
AMSTERDAM • PARIS • SYDNEY • HAMBURG
STOCKHOLM • ATHENS • TOKYO • MILAN • MADRID
PRAGUE • WARSAW • BUDAPEST • AUCKLAND

ISBN 0-373-29099-3

THE ROGUE

Copyright © 2000 by Mary Bracho

This edition published by arrangement with Harlequin Books S.A.

® and TM are trademarks of the publisher. Trademarks indicated with ® are registered in the United States Patent and Trademark Office, the Canadian Trade Marks Office and in other countries.

Visit us at www.romance.net

Printed in U.S.A.

Please address questions and book requests to:
Harlequin Reader Service
U.S.: 3010 Walden Ave., P.O. Box 1325, Buffalo, NY 14269
Canadian: P.O. Box 609, Fort Erie, Ont. L2A 5X3

With affection and thanks to my wonderful fellow Harlequin Historicals authors, especially the team who brought the KNIGHTS OF THE BLACK ROSE to life— Suzanne Barclay, Shari Anton, Lyn Stone, Sharon Schulze and Laurie Grant. And special thanks to Margaret Moore, who started us all down this path.

Chapter One

"I'll not be able to sit straight on my horse if we continue," Gervase of Palgrave said, shaking away the tankard being pushed at him by the smiling barmaid.

The knight sitting across the table from him frowned, gave an exaggerated blink and stopped the girl's retreat with a heavy hand on her arm. The tankard clattered to the floor.

"By the saints, Nick, you're swoggled!" Gervase cried, jumping from his stool. He swatted at his legs where the liquid had splashed his clothes. "I'll smell like a brewmaster."

His companion kept his seat but cast a look of remorse at the indignant serving girl. "I beg pardon, sweetheart," he mumbled, then punctuated the apology with a smile.

Immediately the anger drained from the girl's round face. "'Twas an accident, milord," she said, her eyes fixed on the handsome knight. Even masked by the grime of many weeks' travel, Nicholas of Hendry's strong features caused most who saw him to take a second look.

As the girl stooped to retrieve the mug and swipe at the spill with her skirt, Gervase seated himself again with a grunt of disgust. "What ails you, my friend?" he asked. "We're but half a league from Hendry Hall, yet you insist on tarrying here in this sorry excuse of an inn like a bashful bridegroom. Are you not eager to see your family?"

The two knights were the only customers in the tiny inn, which was really just an ale shop, nothing like the bustling establishments they had visited on the long road home.

Nicholas put both elbows on the table and stared into his empty tankard. "Aye."

"Then, let's be off, man. I warrant there's a lady or two who'll be anxious to see your pretty face again." He glanced at the serving girl, who had not taken her gaze off Nicholas. "Mayhap more than one or two."

Nicholas offered the girl another smile and she turned scarlet. She bobbed up and down, holding the tankard in one hand and her sopping dress in the other. "Would the gentlemen, ah, my lords, ah…shall I draw another flagon of ale?"

Nicholas sighed and pushed himself back from the table. "Nay, sweetheart. My friend is right. 'Tis past time for me to reach home." He stood. "You will accept the hospitality of Hendry Hall this night before traveling on, Gervase?"

Gervase nodded. "I'd like to meet your father. He'll be a proud man to welcome back a hero son."

Nicholas gave a humorless laugh. "Surviving makes us heroes, is that it?"

Gervase reached for his gloves and stood. "All returning Crusaders are heroes, Nick."

"We've won nothing, accomplished nothing more than sending a few poor heathens to their own heathen hell. But we've struck a blow for Christendom and lived to tell the tale. Aye, you may be right. It might be enough to make my father proud of his son. If so, I don't know whose will be the greater astonishment—his or mine."

The two knights started walking out of the inn, Nicholas weaving the first two steps until he gained his equilibrium. "Surely not," Gervase protested, steadying his friend with a hand on his elbow. "How could a father not be proud of a son like you—a superb horseman, deadly with a sword, quick-witted, not to mention that devil's countenance that has melted the hearts of half the maidens between here and Sicily?"

"There's the rub, precisely. My father was always disappointed that I neglected those first attributes you mentioned in favor of the last."

"He disapproved of your female conquests?"

Nicholas squinted as they walked out into the sunlight. "'Twas a vacillation between disapproval and disgust, I believe. He claimed I curried trouble by what he called my 'irresponsible attachments.'"

His companion gave Nicholas a sideways glance. The lean, blond Gervase was only a couple of years older than Nicholas, but his expression was much less world-weary. His blue eyes were clear and innocent.

"There were many, then?" he asked, his voice softly curious.

"Aye. Many."

They'd almost reached their horses when the girl who had been serving them in the inn came running out the door and called to them, "Begging yer pardon, my lords."

They turned toward her. "What is it, girl?" Gervase asked.

Her eyes on Nicholas again, the girl, shuffling her feet in obvious discomfort, said, "The master said ye was to pay fer the spilled ale, my lords. I'd not ask it meself, but he said ye was to pay."

Gervase looked toward the inn, then at Nicholas. "Do you know the owner, Nicholas?" he asked.

Nicholas shook his head slowly, as if trying to clear it. "It's been nearly four years. I don't remember. Who's your master, sweetheart?" he asked the girl.

"Master Thibault, sir," she said. "I'd not ask it myself," she repeated with another nervous bob.

"Thibault the brewer?" Nicholas asked. "Phillip Thibault is master of this place?"

The girl bobbed in confirmation.

"You did spill the drink, Nick," Gervase said. "Pay the chit and let's be on our way."

But Nicholas shook his head. "Tell Master Thibault we'd speak directly with him."

"Very good, milord." The girl turned and ran into the inn.

"I'll give you the coin," Gervase offered, "if it will get us on the road."

Nicholas didn't answer his friend. His eyes were fixed on the door of the inn, but the person who emerged was obviously not Thibault the innkeeper. It was a woman, tall and slender. As she marched toward them, Nicholas could see that her features were finely chiseled, her nose straight and narrow, her cheekbones high.

"Might this be one of your conquests, Nick?" Gervase asked under his breath. "Because methinks the lady has had a change of opinion since your departure. I see daggers in those blue eyes."

"I know her not," Nicholas answered, puzzled himself by the woman's obvious animosity.

She didn't speak until she was practically on top of them. Then she said, "So 'tis truly you. I didn't believe it when they told me. We'd thought you dead. I'd *hoped* you dead." As she finished speaking, she set her feet apart, rocked up on her toes and spit square in his face. Then she whirled around and stalked back into the inn.

The two knights looked at each other in astonishment, Nicholas wiping the spittle from his face with the back of his hand.

Finally Gervase broke the silence with a shaky smile. "My friend, I've had second thoughts about asking your instruction in matters of the heart."

"I swear, Gervase, I never set eyes on her," Nicholas insisted as the two knights rode side by side along the dusty road to Hendry Hall. After the young woman had disappeared inside the inn, Gervase had argued Nicholas into continuing on their journey at once, rather than waiting to see if the innkeeper shared the lovely spitfire's hostility. "Do you think I'd not remember a woman like that?"

"She seemed to know you right enough."

"Aye. And I'll have an answer to that mystery, but now I'm for Hendry Hall."

"Am I seeing at last a glimmer of eagerness to be home?"

Nicholas shifted in his saddle. "They said at the inn that they'd thought me dead. No doubt my arrival will be a surprise."

"We six were all counted among the departed when we didn't come back directly at the end of the fighting."

Just six. Of the two hundred knights who'd ridden off four years before proudly flaunting the banner of the Black Rose, only the six comrades-in-arms had returned. Level-headed Simon, the natural leader of the group; Nicholas, the charmer; Bernard, battle-hardened from humble squire to deadly conquerer; Guy, the outlander who was rightfully the lord's son; Gervase, the innocent who'd taken a vow none of the others would dare; and Hugh, whose soft-hearted manner disguised a warrior's strength.

"I thought the news of our miraculous survival would make our welcome all the merrier," Gervase continued when Nicholas remained silent.

"Hendry Hall is not a merry place, Gervase, which is perhaps why I was wont to seek friendlier diversions away from home."

"By the saints, Nicholas, if all your diversions were like the one we just met, I'd say you'd find friendlier ground back fighting the infidels."

Nicholas shook his head. "And still you refuse to believe me. The lady was not my lover." He stared ahead at the gray stone manor house that had come into view around the bend in the road. He'd always favored buxom maids with pleasing smiles and easy ways. The woman at the inn had had a strength to her, no matter how willowy her form. And there'd been steel in her gaze. "Trust me, Gervase," he said softly. "I'd have remembered such a one as she."

Beatrice crooned softly as she rocked the sleeping boy in her arms. *"'twas in the merry month of May, when green buds were a-swellin'…"*

She enjoyed these quiet evening times with her little nephew, though she knew that he would soon be beyond such attentions. Over three years old now, he seemed to grow bigger daily.

The door to her bedchamber creaked open. "Do you think to sit here the rest of the night, daughter?" Phillip Thibault asked softly, taking one step into the room.

"Flora was right, Father," she answered, still rocking, and rubbing her hand lightly over the child's dark curls. "Handsome as the devil himself, she used to say. Dancing black eyes that can melt the innards of whatever woman they light upon."

"You should come down to sup, lass. You've taken nothing since this morning, and that was before dawn."

Beatrice's glance slid to her father. Her blue eyes were icy without a hint of tears. "As handsome as the devil and twice as wicked, I trow."

Phillip shook his head sadly. "Put little Owen in his bed and come downstairs with me. Gertie left a leg of mutton that's fair charred on the spit while I've waited for you."

"You should have supped, Father. I've no taste for food this night."

Phillip walked across the room. His daughter's bed-chamber was large, encompassing half the upper floor of the Gilded Boar. It had once been the master's quarters, but when Beatrice had come from York to care for her sister, Phillip had insisted on moving to the small room at the rear of the inn. He'd stayed there now that the big upstairs chamber served as both sleeping quarters and nursery. The big bed Phillip had shared years ago for too short a span with Beatrice and Flora's mother was pushed up against one slant-ing wall. The rest of the room was devoted to the child's needs.

"You'll be a fine nursemaid to the lad on the mor-row after a day of fasting," Phillip said sternly, reach-ing for the child. "He'll be awake with the cock's crow, running every which way and begging to be off to the meadow while you slump over your porridge."

Owen murmured as his grandfather lifted him, but remained asleep. Beatrice watched nervously as her father carried the child across the room. Phillip was not strong these days, and at times the shaking made it difficult to keep his balance. She let out a little sigh of relief as her father placed the boy successfully on his pallet.

"I cannot stomach the thought of food while that blackguard's face still dances before my eyes," she said.

"Then banish him from your mind, Beatrice. You need not have any contact with Master Hendry."

"With Sir Nicholas Hendry, you mean," she corrected bitterly. "You forget he's a hero now, returning from the Holy Crusade."

Phillip took her hand and pulled her out of the chair. "Ah, you see. He couldn't be such a devil after all if he's spent the past four years on the Lord's work."

Beatrice let her father lead her out of the room. "'Tis more likely that he's spent the past four years seducing every maid between here and Jerusalem."

Phillip shook his head again slowly and pushed gently on his daughter's shoulders to start her moving down the narrow stairs to the tavern room. "Put him out of your head, lass. With any luck he'll be so busy over at Hendry Hall that we won't soon see his face again."

Nicholas bit his lip as he gave Gervase a full forearm grip. The younger knight's free hand went to Nicholas's shoulder. "We'll meet again, my friend," he said, his voice thick.

Nicholas nodded without speaking.

"I'll stay on a few days if you need me, Nick. If you need help with...you know...settling your father's affairs."

"It appears they've been well settled without me," Nicholas answered with a shake of his head. "Though I can still scarcely credit it. I'd thought my father too tough to ever let death catch up with him."

"'Twas not the homecoming you'd planned."

"Nay."

The two knights let their hands drop and Gervase moved toward his horse, saying, "You'll give my thanks to your lady mother for the night's lodging?"

"Aye."

Gervase mounted his big stallion. "We've a brotherhood, you know, Nick, the six of us. Knights of the Black Rose. We're the only ones left to tell the stories."

Nicholas ventured a wan smile. "I know. Forgive this melancholy farewell, Gervase. I count you as a brother and always shall."

"There's nothing to forgive, Nick. You've come back to find a house of mourning. It will take you some time to get used to the idea that you're the new master of Hendry Hall."

Nicholas shook his head once again. He'd not told Gervase the true extent of the bad news he'd learned from his mother last night after the rejoicing at his safe return had subsided. "Aye, it will take time," he said simply. He gave the horse a gentle slap. "Now off with you, my friend, to put your own affairs to rights. You, too, return to a house much altered."

Gervase gave a sad smile. "You know me like a brother as well, Nicholas. I'll send word when I'm settled."

Nicholas nodded and forced a smile to his lips as his friend rode off. Saying goodbye to the last of his comrade knights put an end to the adventure that had at times seemed part of a four-year-long dream. Now it was time to awaken. Past time. Gervase's horse disappeared around the bend. His shoulders set, Nicholas turned back toward the house where his newly widowed mother waited.

"That's the third time you've invoked the name of Baron Hawse in the past five minutes, Mother,"

Nicholas said wearily. "I care nothing for the baron's thoughts on the matter. I want to know yours."

The mistress of Hendry Hall was a tiny woman, totally dwarfed by her strapping son, but her gaze did not waver. "Baron Hawse has been my savior, Nicholas. I'd likely have perished without him, thinking both you and your father dead."

"I grant you it must have been difficult, Mother, but now I'm back and Hendry Hall can be restored to its rightful master. I mislike the idea that the ghost of my father has been chased away by the presence of our neighbor to the south. If I recall, Father thought little of the man."

Constance turned away from her son's gaze and walked a few steps to sit on the low stoop by the small fireplace that had been a recent improvement to the spacious master's chambers of Hendry Hall. When alive, Nicholas's father, Arthur, had been constantly rebuilding the stone house that had started as a much more humble abode shortly after the days of the Conquest.

Nicholas looked down at his mother. At twoscore years, she was an old woman, yet in the flickering firelight her face was devoid of lines, her eyes clear. After a long moment she turned her head back to him and said, "As I recall it, you and your father were too often at odds for you to know much about what he thought."

Nicholas hesitated a moment, then crossed the room to drop down beside her directly in front of the fire. "Aye. 'Twas the principal thing that I was determined to change. I've thought of little else this year past as we struggled to make our way home."

Constance reached out to her son and gently brushed an unruly lock of hair from his forehead. "I know. 'Tis a bitter pill that you two were never reconciled. But, Nicholas, in my heart I know that your father truly did love you."

Nicholas looked away from her as he said, "Aye. He loved me so much that he signed away my birthright to a man he didn't even like."

"He thought you dead, Nicholas. And he respected the baron's position. To him that was the most important thing. He was trying to protect me."

Nicholas leaned toward the flames and felt the welcome heat on his face. The house had not entirely given up the chill of the long winter months. "I still can't believe it—Baron Hawse as master of Hendry lands and Hendry Hall." He looked up at his mother. "And of the mistress of Hendry Hall as well, from the way you speak of him."

"The only man who has ever been my master is dead, Nicholas. And I've no desire to lease myself to a new one."

"Yet the baron is in want of a wife. 'Twould be a natural match." Nicholas finally voiced the thought that had been in his head since his mother had told him how his father, on his deathbed, had signed over his estate to Gilbert, Baron Hawse.

"Mayhap. But 'tis not a match I seek. And I'd mourn your father this twelvemonth before I'd even consider such a notion."

Though her words were a denial, something in her tone told Nicholas that the idea of marrying the baron had, indeed, occurred to his mother. The thought made the back of his mouth taste sour.

His bad leg had gone stiff. He untwisted it and rose awkwardly to his feet. "By the rood, Mother, you deserve happiness after enduring my father all those long years. But I intend to fight Hawse on this matter of the Hendry lands. I'd hoped you'd not let your heart get in the way. Women are ever soft on these matters."

Constance gave a sad smile. "Before you went off to the war, the rumor was that you were something of an expert on the subject of women's hearts, my son. I confess I'd hoped that the years away would have taught you something about their heads as well."

"The Crusades taught me many things, Mother. You'll not find me the reckless philanderer who fled here four years ago. I've grown up."

"I'm glad to hear it." The firelight caught the brightening of her eyes.

"But the Crusades also taught me to fight my own battles. Hendry Hall belongs to me, in spite of the documents my father signed." He rubbed his thigh where the old wound nagged.

"The baron will be here on the morrow," his mother said. "He has made no move to implement the change in title, and has promised not to act until the mourning year is over. Mayhap we can come to a peaceful resolution."

"Mayhap." He bent to plant a kiss on the top of his mother's head. "Don't fret yourself, Mother. You've had too many worries since my father's death. Now that I'm home, I'd see the smile back on your face."

She obliged him with the broadest smile she'd

given since he had arrived on the previous day. "My prayers have been answered by your return, my son."

He turned to leave, moving gingerly as the feeling came slowly back into his leg. As he reached to open the door, he was startled by a knock that sounded from the other side. He pulled it open to reveal his mother's handmaid.

The girl was breathing heavily, evidently having just run up the steep stairway to the upstairs bed-chambers. "Visitor's awaiting, Master Nicholas," she puffed.

Nicholas looked back at his mother. "I thought you said the baron was coming tomorrow."

"'Tis not Baron Hawse," the girl said. "'Tis a lady. Not a fine one, but not common neither."

"One of your former admirers, no doubt, son," said Constance with an air of resignation. "I thought it would not take them long to discover your return."

Nicholas frowned and turned to follow the servant girl downstairs.

Chapter Two

The news that had awaited him upon his arrival home had almost made him forget the incident at the Gilded Boar Inn. But even before he entered the great hall and saw the tall woman waiting for him at the opposite end of the hall, he somehow suspected that his surprise visitor might be her.

Oddly enough, the thought rather pleased him. For one thing, it would give him the opportunity to solve the mystery of her dramatic response to his visit to the inn the previous noon.

She looked up as he approached. Once again, her eyes were like skewers. However, this time he had ample opportunity to observe that they were also handsome, as was the rest of her. "Mistress," he said in acknowledgement. When she didn't speak at once, he decided to be direct. "You have the advantage of me. You seem to know who I am, but I remain in ignorance of your identity."

Her chin went up a notch. "I did not come here to make your acquaintance," she said.

Her voice was musical, he noted, in spite of the

frost. "Then you admit that we are not acquainted, mistress. Yet it appears that you must bear me some ill will." He rubbed a hand across his chin. "I'm quite sure that when I left this country 'twas not the custom to greet perfect strangers by expectorating in their faces."

Beatrice felt unexpectedly shaky. She hadn't thought it would be this difficult to face the monster. Her father had argued against this visit, and perhaps she should have paid him heed. But she had a reason for wanting to be sure that Nicholas Hendry would never again set foot anywhere near the Gilded Boar. The sudden memory of little Owen strengthened her resolve.

"The gesture was spontaneous," she said. "But I offer no apology. And you may believe that the sentiment behind it was genuine."

Nicholas's dark eyes warmed to the edge of a smile. "I believe you, mistress."

His lack of anger made her task more difficult. "Be that as it may, I've come to be sure that the message was received."

Nicholas merely tipped his head, questioning.

"You're not welcome at the Boar," Beatrice continued.

Now he frowned. "Who are you, mistress? And how is it that you are warning me away from an inn that, if I calculate correctly, is on lands leased from this very estate?"

Beatrice felt her face grow warm. If she were to accomplish her mission, she had to tell him that much. "The master of the inn, Phillip Thibault, is my father."

Nicholas blinked as though a sudden memory had shifted in the back of his head. "You're not Flora," he said, his voice low.

"So you *do* remember her?"

"Aye. The brewer's daughter, Flora. But you are not she."

"Flora was my sister." Her voice held steady.

"Was?" He looked stricken. She'd give him that much, at least.

"Flora's dead these three years past."

Nicholas looked down. "It grieves me to hear it." Lifting his eyes to his visitor's face, he asked, "What happened to her?"

Beatrice swallowed the lump that threatened to erupt from her throat. It was anger she wanted to show this man, not grief. "You killed her," she said finally.

Nicholas's shock was more acute than on their earlier encounter when she had spit at him. He remembered sweet Flora vividly. She'd been his last light o' love before he'd set out on the Crusade. They'd had but a few short meetings before he had to take leave of her. He remembered her tender farewell, had tasted her tears all the way across the Channel.

You killed her, the woman had said, hate dripping with each word. He shook his head to clear it, and felt the beginning of anger. He may have taken unfair advantage of Flora Thibault, as he had too many other women in those wild days. But he'd never harmed her, of that he was certain.

"She was in perfect health when I left England," he said stiffly.

"She died of a broken heart."

Nicholas shook his head. Broken hearts were the stuff of minstrel songs. People did not die of them. Perhaps this woman, however intelligent she appeared, was of weak mind. The notion made him speak more gently. "Flora knew from the onset that our time together would be short. I can't believe that my departure caused her such distress."

"If you'd truly known my sister, you would have seen that she was in love with you."

"We loved each other, Mistress Thibault, but we both knew 'twas a fleeting pleasure. I swear your sister understood this as well as I."

"Yet she is dead," Beatrice said, delivering each word as if it were a judge's sentence.

"Did she have no disease, no wound?"

Beatrice ignored his question and continued in her deliberate tone. "I can do nothing to prove you accountable, Master Hendry, but listen well. I've come to ask you civilly to honor my father's grief and my own. Do not show your face anywhere near the Gilded Boar."

"I'd speak with your father, mistress. I want—"

Beatrice held up a hand to stop his speech. "We have many friends in the village, sir. If you'll not heed my words, you might find your welcome home much less warm than you had hoped."

Nicholas shook his head in wonderment. What kind of woman was this to come threatening the master of the estate, ordering him to stay off a portion of his own property? Or what *should* be his property, he amended. Perhaps it was already known throughout the territory that Baron Hawse was the new master at Hendry.

He took a long moment to consider his reply. Finally he said, ''I've returned determined to heal old wounds, mistress, not to open them. But your father looked upon me kindly once, and I'd have him know that I had nothing to do with his daughter's death.''

Beatrice's shakiness had subsided, but her head was feeling muddled. She'd prepared herself for an angry confrontation with her sister's former lover. She'd rehearsed the words she would hurl at him. But she was finding it hard to rail against his measured tones and sad countenance.

Her fingers moved restlessly at her sides in the folds of her overskirt. ''I speak for my father as well as myself,'' she said. ''''Twould be a kindness to a grieving family if you would stay away.''

His nearly black eyes were steady and grave. There was not a hint of the playful charmer her sister had talked of with such incessant longing. ''Then I'll honor your wishes and his, Mistress Thibault. But please tell your father that I share your grief. I'll mourn sweet Flora as I do my own father.''

It was all Beatrice could do to make her way across the big room and out the door to the courtyard. Nothing about the interview had gone as she had planned. She'd thought to feed her three-year long anger on his arrogant words. Instead, she'd found herself feeling almost sorry for the pain she'd brought to him with her news.

The crisp spring air helped. She took a great gulp of it and willed herself to slow her pace as she walked along the gravel path to the unfenced stone pillars that marked the entrance to Hendry Hall. She'd accomplished her mission. She had his promise not to come to the Boar, and that was all that counted.

The village of Hendry was small. When Owen grew old enough to run about on his own, he'd no doubt cross paths with the master of Hendry Hall. But if her luck held, Sir Nicholas would never suspect his connection to the boy.

Amazingly enough, it had not even occurred to him that Flora's death might have been the result of giving birth to a child he had left planted inside her. Just like a man, Beatrice thought, relieved to feel her anger returning.

She reached the pillars and looked to the left at the sound of a horse approaching. Even from a distance, she knew the rider. Baron Hawse was a familiar sight in the neighborhood. His lands surrounded the Hendry estate and he'd never been shy about venturing onto Hendry lands as if he and not the Hendry family were the overlord.

She stopped and waited. She'd not bow her head to him, but neither did she want to be so rude as to turn her back and walk away.

"Mistress Thibault, is it not?" the baron called as he approached. "Did you have some business with the lady Constance?"

Beatrice gave an inconclusive murmur. She couldn't see how her business was any of the baron's affair, no matter if he was the most important man in the shire.

"Meself, I've come to see the returning prodigal— young Nicholas, home from the wars, hale and hearty, in spite of all the accounts to the contrary. 'Tis somewhat of a miracle, hey?"

"Aye," she answered simply.

The baron pulled his horse up and peered down at her, squinting. "Mayhap 'twas Nicholas you came to see. He always was a one for the ladies."

The baron was a big man, overspilling his small saddle, but his size was solid bulk, not fat, and his proportions were manly. The only signs of his age were the fine veins that crisscrossed his somewhat bulbous nose, giving his face a florid appearance against the contrast of his snow-white hair. Though he had never said anything improper to her, his glances always made Beatrice feel as if something cold was creeping over her skin.

"Good day to you, milord," she said, continuing to ignore his questions.

She turned to head in the opposite direction from which the baron had come, but he danced his horse forward a couple of steps, blocking her path.

"So it *was* Nicholas you came to see," he said. "I'd thought the boy preferred lasses with soft curves and empty heads. I'd evidently not given him enough credit."

His eyes watched her, bright with speculation.

"Excuse me, Baron Hawse. I'm just on my way back to the inn, where I warrant my father will be missing me."

"As I recall, you've not lived here long, mistress. You were raised by an aunt in York, I believe? You came only shortly before your sister's death. Was it on a prior visit that you made Nicholas Hendry's acquaintance?"

Beatrice was astounded at the extent of his knowledge of her family's affairs. She'd often heard that the baron knew in intimate detail the comings and goings of all the neighborhood inhabitants, no matter how lowly. But she hadn't realized the truth of the statement until now.

"I have nothing to do with Nicholas Hendry," she said bluntly. "Nor do I expect that I ever shall. Now, forgive me, Baron, but I really must be on my way."

This time Hawse did not prevent her from turning down the road toward the village. The baron sat still on his horse for several moments, watching her leave. Beatrice Thibault was a rare woman, as spirited as she was beautiful. How convenient that with his acquisition of the Hendry lands, she was now one of his very tenants.

It was not widely known in Hendry that he was to be their new master. He'd refrained from taking active control of the lands in deference to Constance. But her year of mourning would soon be past and she would be his wife at last, after all these long years.

Then he'd have no compunction about exerting his lordly rights over the people of Hendry. And he might just start with the haughty Mistress Thibault. The notion turned up his lips in a sly smile of anticipation.

The great hall of the manor occupied the entire rear half of the bottom floor. It had fireplaces at each end, another of Arthur Hendry's improvements, and a raised dais along the west wall so that the members of the family and their guests could eat at a table raised from the trestles set out for the servants and lesser visitors.

Nicholas had just helped his mother mount the single step to the long table when there was a commotion at the huge double doors leading into the big room. He turned to see the larger-than-life form of their neighbor, lumbering across the room toward him, arms outstretched.

"I found I could not wait another day to see you, Nicholas," Baron Hawse said, engulfing the younger man in a hearty embrace.

Nicholas tried not to wince. He'd never liked the baron, even as a boy, but for his mother's sake, he was determined to be civil. He allowed the embrace, then stepped back. "'Tis kind of you to trouble yourself, Baron."

"Not at all, boy. With your father gone, I feel it's my place to be here to welcome you. Back from the dead, hey? Not often a man has a chance to welcome someone back from those nether regions."

The motley assortment of household retainers who had been milling about finding their places at the lower benches stood uncertainly, not wanting to be seated while their new master remained standing.

"I never counted myself dead, Baron," Nicholas answered dryly. "Though I felt the spectre's breath a time or two. You'll join us for supper?"

"Of course, lad," the baron boomed. "I should have been here last night for your welcome home meal." He turned a reproving glance on Constance, who also remained standing by her chair. "You should have sent word, my dear."

Nicholas frowned as his mother bit her lip in embarrassment.

"As you can imagine, Baron," he said stiffly, "the tidings that greeted me upon my arrival did not exactly put us in the mood for company."

The baron gave Nicholas a hearty clap on the shoulder and stepped past him up on the dais. "Precisely, lad. I should have been here to deliver the news of your father's death. Women are over-maudlin about these affairs. No doubt you had all manner of tears and carrying on to contend with." Once again he looked at Constance, who dropped her gaze to the floor.

Nicholas struggled to keep his temper, reminding himself that the baron had cared for his mother in her bereavement. "My mother's heart is too tender not to mourn her husband's passing, Baron Hawse. I do not count that as a fault."

He followed the baron up on the dais and began to motion him to the bench on the other side of his mother, but the older man stopped at the center of the table, pulled out the lord's chair and sat. Nicholas's mouth fell open in astonishment. The previous evening when his mother had urged him to be seated in the master's place, it had felt sad and odd, but to have his father's old chair occupied by a stranger seemed nearly intolerable.

He looked at his mother. Her soft brown eyes pleaded with him not to create a scene. Baron Hawse had occupied this chair before, Nicholas realized. As the baron pulled a trencher forward to share with Constance, Nicholas wondered exactly how much of Arthur Hendry's former life had already been taken over by his neighbor.

Giving his mother a smile of reassurance, he took a seat on the bench to the baron's left and pulled his own trencher forward. He'd not share a board with this man.

Once the head table was seated, there was a sudden bustle in the room as the other diners sat and the serving girls began to move among the tables with dishes of stew and plates of roasted rabbit with wild berries.

Nicholas ate in silence, speaking only when the baron asked him a direct question. He scarcely noticed the carefully prepared dinner, which his mother had been supervising in the kitchen much of the afternoon. Watching the baron carve off succulent bits of rabbit and offer them on his knife to Constance's mouth was making Nicholas lose his appetite.

"I'm sure he'll be pleased to, won't you, son?" His mother's soft voice broke through his gloomy thoughts.

He looked from Constance to the baron, who both appeared to be waiting for him to speak. "I beg your pardon," he mumbled. "I would be pleased to *what?*"

"To visit us at Hawse Castle two days hence," the baron supplied. "If you've fully recovered from your journey."

"I'd thought to begin seeing to the estate here. I've a meeting with the steward on the morrow to go over the accounts and—"

"Well, then, that's perfect," the baron interrupted. "You can join us at Hawse the next day and we'll see where we stand on this matter of the estates. I have all the papers your father signed before his death, of course."

Nicholas's eyes narrowed. "Papers that he signed thinking me dead."

The baron's hearty voice did not waver. "Of

course. Which is why we have much to discuss, you and I. We'll discuss your father's plans for this place.''

Nicholas pushed away his board, leaving the rabbit mostly untouched. "My father's plans for Hendry were to pass it on to his only son. No amount of discussion will alter that."

Hawse smiled. "Indeed." He reached out a big hand and gave a painful squeeze to Nicholas's forearm. "I have some plans of my own to discuss with you, lad. I believe we can work our way out of this unfortunate tangle. Come see me the day after tomorrow."

"We'll both go," Constance said quickly. "It would be churlish to refuse my lord's hospitality after all you've done for me."

Hawse turned toward Constance and gave her a smile that even to Nicholas looked almost tender.

"'Tis not within your power to be churlish, Lady Constance," he told her, his voice softening.

Nicholas pushed back his bench and stood. "In two days hence, then. We'll attend you at Hawse Castle. Now if you'll excuse me, I am still, as you say, fatigued from my journey."

Without taking further leave of them, he turned and made his way out of the room.

He sat in the dark looking out the deep window of his bedchamber into the moonlit yard below. It was early for sleep, but he didn't feel like talking to anyone, not even the servants, so he had retired to his room and had not lit the wall torch near his bed.

The knock on his door was so soft, he almost didn't

hear it. For several moments, he resolved to let the caller go unanswered, but then he thought that perhaps his mother needed him, so he reluctantly got to his feet and crossed over to open the door. The visitor was a woman, but definitely not his mother.

Mollie had changed little in the four years since he'd last seen her. If anything, her breasts spilled even more voluptuously from the scanty, thin blouse. Her sparkling green eyes glinted even more wickedly with invitation.

"So, ye've come back, ye naughty boy," she laughed, twining her arms around his neck with such energy that it pushed him back into the room.

In spite of himself, Nicholas felt a flare of desire course through him as the serving maid's soft contours wriggled against him. He dropped a light kiss on her lips and gently pried her hands loose. "Hallo, sweetheart," he said.

She took a step back and thudded her small fist into his chest. "For shame, Nicky. I'll not listen to yer 'sweethearts' after ye ran away like that without so much as a farewell buss."

Mollie had been one of the most good-natured of his lovemaking partners. A full five years older than Nicholas, she'd had a string of lovers herself and understood that their friendship was nothing more than the mutual satisfaction of shared passions.

Nicholas grinned at her and captured the hand that continued pounding him with little effect. "You'll always be my sweetheart, Mollie. You know that."

She pulled her hand out of his and laid it tenderly along his cheek. "Aye, Nicky. We were fair eager for it in those days, weren't we?"

Unexpectedly, Nicholas was suddenly eager once again. He put a hand at Mollie's waist and pulled her toward him, but she pushed away. "Aye, we were," he murmured.

"Ah, Nicky. I've not come for that." She pushed him away. "I'm a proper goodwife now."

Nicholas dropped his hands from her as if he'd been burned. "Wife?"

"Aye, these three years past. Got meself two young'uns."

He blinked in astonishment. "Babies?"

Mollie laughed and gave him a friendly pat on his chest. "What did ye think comes of all that gallivanting in the corn, Master Hendry? Ye were always a careful one, but not all are like that." A brief shadow crossed her face, but then she giggled and added, "I knew I'd end up round as a herring barrel some day."

Her words added to his gloom. Merry, passionate, carefree Mollie. A wife and mother. It was hard to believe. "Are you happy, Mollie?" he asked finally. "Is your husband a good man?"

She smiled and nodded. "Aye, Nicky, he is. Ye do know him. 'Tis Clarence, the baker."

Nicholas had a vague memory of a big, quiet man, perhaps twenty years his senior, who ran the bake shop at the edge of the village and sent fresh bread to the manor each day. A pleasant yeasty odor always seemed to cling to the man.

"Then I'm happy for you, Mollie. You deserve a good man and a good life."

"As do we all, Nicky," she agreed softly. "Well,

I'd best be getting back before the wee ones start howling for their mum.''

Nicholas shook his head, still trying to reconcile the picture of Mollie caring for two youngsters. "I'm glad for you, Mollie," he told her.

"And I to see ye back here and not a ghost, ye great lug." She grinned. "I said a mass for ye, now there's a tale'll spin yer head."

"A mass?"

"When they said ye was dead. I went into the church, proper like. That and me wedding are the only two times I've ever gone inside."

Nicholas smiled. "I'm obliged to you, Mollie."

"Take care, Nicky," she said quickly. She stretched up on tiptoes to kiss him full on the mouth, and she was gone.

It was late. All activity in the yard below had long since ceased. But Nicholas was still not ready to stretch out on his pallet and sleep. Mollie's visit had left him even more restless than before. Jovial, generous Mollie. Married and a mother. At least she was happy, and to all appearances her dalliance with Nicholas had not done any damage to her life. Some of the other women he'd loved and left might not be so forgiving.

How would Flora have greeted him, he wondered, if she were alive? He could not imagine that her reception would have been anything like the one given to him by her sister. Flora had been the soul of sweetness.

He sighed and paced the length of his room. When he'd thought all was lost on the Crusades, he'd sworn that if he ever got back to England, he'd lead a better life. He would make it up to the women he'd wronged. He would show his father that he was the kind of son Arthur Hendry had always wanted. Now his father was dead. At least one of his lovers was happily married and had all but forgotten about him.

But there were still amends to make. And he intended to begin the process immediately. He'd start on the morrow. With Flora.

Chapter Three

No one knew the origins of the little village formerly called Hendry's Lea and now simply Hendry. The old ones told tales of ancient times when spirits walked about and the druids held ceremonies out on the wide meadow to the north. The name predated the current Hendry family, they claimed, and certainly was around long before Hendry Hall. But since there had now been several generations of Hendrys connected to the place, ending with the returned-from-the-dead heir, most of the villagers took it as natural that it was to Nicholas that they owed allegiance.

There was little resentment over the system. The Hendrys had always been magnanimous landlords. If a family found itself a bit hard-pressed when it came time to collect the twice yearly rents, it never occurred to them that they would be turned off their lands for nonpayment. Indeed, it was not unusual for the Hendrys themselves to see that a few extra coins appeared at the needy household.

After Arthur's death, there had been some consternation in the village as the rumors spread that some new land baron from the court would appear and undo several generations of Hendry generosity. However, as the months went on with no apparent change, the rumors subsided.

Nevertheless, the sudden appearance of Nicholas was a cause for rejoicing in the village, at least in the households where there was no irate father waiting to nail Nicholas's hide to the door for having enticed his willing daughter.

Nicholas had awakened before dawn with his head throbbing from the ale with which he'd finally drunk himself to sleep the previous evening after Mollie's visit. But the bright spring day and the villagers' hearty greetings as he rode through town lifted his spirits. He was pleased that he remembered many of their names. Little by little the life he had left four years ago was returning to him. Only this time, he would live it more honorably than he had in his thoughtless youth.

The stone church at the far end of the village had not changed. No doubt more graves had been added, but the mossy ground of the churchyard covered the new as well as the old, camouflaging any recent arrival.

He tied his horse to a newel on the sunny side of the church and walked the worn path around the building to the graves. The stone column in the center of the yard said Hendry, but Nicholas gave it only a passing glance. The monument was old. Recent generations of the family, including his father, were buried in a small crypt at the back of Hendry Hall itself.

The morning sun didn't reach this place, and Nicholas shivered as he walked among the headstones, scanning the names. He knew Phillip Thibault would not have seen his daughter laid to rest without proper marking.

He saw her mother's first. *Laurette, beloved wife.* A smooth, unmarked stone stood beside that, no doubt awaiting Phillip's arrival. It was the kind of gesture he would expect from the man. And beyond the blank stone was the one he'd been seeking. *Flora, beloved daughter.*

Nicholas walked the edge of the three graves and knelt at the far end. His hand traced the inscription on the stone. *Flora.* Such a cold, hard memorial for the warm, loving young woman he had known. Over and over he traced it, his eyes closed. He tried to picture her face. It had been alive and vital, he recalled, but the memory was dim. He knew that her eyes had danced when he'd lifted her onto his big horse. She'd loved to ride. Once in the Holy Lands he'd seen a girl on a pony and he'd thought to himself, *When I get back to England I'm going to get Flora her own horse, a little mare as sweet and gentle as her owner.*

His eyes prickled, then burned under the closed lids. He'd shed no tears for his father, but they came, unbidden, for Flora. Little Flora, whose pretty face he could no longer clearly remember.

He opened his eyes, blinked rapidly and gave an unmanly sniff. His old leg wound was telling him to change from his kneeling position, but he hesitated a moment, feeling as if he should do something more. He should have gathered some spring wildflowers from the meadow before he'd come, he thought. Flora had loved flowers. She'd made him a garland one afternoon and had hung it around his neck, laughingly proclaiming him King of the May.

He took a deep, ragged breath, then, impulsively, pulled the silver chain from around his neck. It held a tiny cross. He'd worn it all through the years abroad and it had come to be a talisman to him. He weighed it in his palm for a moment, then gently tucked it into the mossy grass just at the base of Flora's tombstone. "Rest in peace, sweet Flora," he whispered.

His head bowed, he didn't see the woman coming around the corner of the church, but he heard her gasp plainly.

"What are you doing here?" she asked, her voice shaking.

Nicholas rose awkwardly to his feet, resisting the urge to rub his bad leg. His mental image of the sweet, departed Flora was replaced by the real life vision of her sister, face flushed with anger. "I come on the same mission you do, I'd suppose, mistress. To pay my respects to Flora."

"'Twas more than you paid to her when she was alive." Beatrice was carrying the wildflowers he'd neglected to bring. She brushed past him and scattered them equally over her sister's grave and her mother's.

Nicholas watched her distribute the flowers, then said, "I'll not fault you for your words, since you no doubt are grieving your sister sorely. But I'll tell you again that I never held Flora in disrespect. I was greatly fond of her."

She dropped the last flower, then straightened up. Their faces were mere inches apart, her eyes glacial. For a long moment neither said a word.

"I'll not argue the point standing over her grave," she said finally. "But perhaps you will do *me* the respect of allowing me to mourn in private."

Still their gazes held, and Beatrice was certain that Nicholas Hendry had more that he wanted to say to her. But after a moment, he nodded and said only, "As you wish." Then with one final glance at the carved stone name, he turned and walked away.

She stood for several minutes until he had disappeared behind the church. His appearance there had left her feeling shaky. Could it be true that his eyes had been rimmed with red? she asked herself. It simply did not fit with the picture of Nicholas Hendry she'd been holding all these years to think of him weeping over her sister's grave.

She gave herself a shake and sank to her knees beside the grave. Then she cocked her head as she noticed something glinting near Flora's tombstone. Picking the object from the ground, she looked at it. It was a silver cross, suspended from a chain. Beatrice's eyes widened. On her visit to Hendry Hall the previous day, she'd seen this very cross hanging from Nicholas Hendry's neck.

She sat back, stunned. Could this be the callous knight she had pictured—this man who wept at his former lover's grave and left his necklace as tribute?

Tears welled in her eyes. "Ah, Flora," she said in a low voice. "Do you know that your knight has returned from the Crusades at last? Did you see him here, little sister? He's left you a holy cross."

She leaned over and pressed her warm cheek to the cool, mossy ground. "Help me not to hate him, Flora.

Help me to understand why Nicholas Hendry came back from the dead and you never shall.''

Then she lay against the softly mounded grass and wept.

Owen was playing in his special cave. Phillip had made it from an old ale barrel that he had cut so that it rested on its side and made a perfect hiding place for a three-year old. Beatrice kept one eye on the child while she carefully poured hot tallow into the candle molds.

There were no customers in the inn that afternoon, which was not an unusual occurrence, and she'd sent the barmaid Gertie home early.

"He killed your daughter, and yet you defend him," she said to her father, who watched her from his bench on the other side of the fire.

"I'm not defending him, lass, but neither did he kill Flora." He looked over at the barrel where two protruding shoes were the only evidence of the child inside. Lowering his voice, he continued, "'Twas the childbirth that killed her, just as it did your mother. Both were too frail for birthing."

"Flora would never have been birthing if it hadn't been for Nicholas Hendry."

"And your mother would not have given birth if it hadn't been for me. Does that make me a murderer, too?"

His voice cracked with long held pain, and Beatrice felt a stab of remorse. Setting aside the mold, she crossed over to her father and dropped to her knees beside him, and put her arms around his shoulders. "Forgive me, Father. Let's not speak any more of

Nicholas Hendry. I'd be happy never to hear the man's name again.''

"Now, that's not likely. He's our landlord and our neighbor." Phillip pulled out of his daughter's embrace and turned to her, his aging eyes watery. "This bitterness will solve nothing, Beady. What's more, resentment works like a wicked little worm inside a person, gnawing away until you're left with a rotted hole where your heart should be."

A ghost of a smile crossed her lips at his use of her old childhood nickname. "'Twas my mother first gave me that name, was it not?" she asked.

Phillip smiled and stroked the hair back from her forehead. "Aye, our little Beady. What I wouldn't give to have her see you now, a woman grown, proud and beautiful."

His hand shook as he withdrew it from her hair. The palsy grew worse with each passing week, Beatrice noted with the familiar mix of sadness and fear. What would she and Owen do when her father was no longer around?

She gave him another squeeze, then got to her feet as the barrel across the room began rocking furiously back and forth. A small head poked out the entrance.

"Bear!" the child proclaimed, his dark eyes dancing.

Beatrice walked over to the contraption and hunched down at the mouth. "Did a bear come into your cave, Owen?" she asked.

Owen nodded, giggling.

"A big one?"

"Aye, fearsome big." Bears had been Owen's number one preoccupation since his grandfather and

aunt had taken him to see one dance at the May Day
fair. It had been a motheaten, sorry creature who
could barely lift itself onto its hind legs, much less
dance or look fierce, but to the child it had been a
wonder.

"Did you wrestle with it?" Beatrice asked.

"Aye. It runned away."

Both Beatrice and Owen turned their head toward
the door as if following the departure of the imaginary
beast. "I'm glad to hear it," she said. "Bears aren't
allowed in the inn. Mayhap you'd like some porridge
after such a fierce battle."

Owen stuck his feet up in the air against the rim
of the barrel and somersaulted backward, landing in
Beatrice's lap. "With a sweetcake?" His dark eyes
pleaded with her from his upside down position.

She pulled him upright and hugged him. "Aye,
with a sweetcake, if you finish your porridge. Warriors who want to fight bears need a lot of good
food."

He followed along beside her happily to one of the
long tap room trestle tables. His hair was tangled from
the tussle with the bear and she unconsciously
combed it into place with her fingers. If she could
help it, Flora's child would never have to face any
more adversity than an imaginary bear.

Out of the corner of her eye, she watched her father
lift himself from his bench, trying to disguise what an
effort it cost him.

They sat around the table and Owen lisped the
quick prayer she had taught him, "God bless Mama
Flora." It came out as one word, "Gobblesmaflor."

Undoubtedly it meant little to the child, but Beatrice found the ritual comforting.

Phillip reached across the table and put his hand on his daughter's. "I've not a doubt that our blessed Flora has found peace in another world, daughter. Would that her sister could find a measure of it in this one."

Beatrice pulled her hand gently away from her father's grasp and began ladling the bowls of porridge.

The rumor mill had it that a century before in Normandy, the Hawses had been mere peasants who had made their way up into the ranks of first a knight's army and then a duke's by their strength in combat. In any event, it was certain that the present Baron Hawse's father had been made baron and granted title to considerable lands after returning from the ill-fated Third Crusade in which King Richard had ended up an ignominious prisoner. The senior Hawse had thrown his fortunes to the king's brother, John, at precisely the correct moment and had then further ingratiated himself with the new king supporting him when most of the nobles of the land rebelled.

Gilbert, the present Baron Hawse, did not suffer close inquiries into the Hawse lineage. His power in the shire was nearly absolute. The Hendry lands and the small village of Hendry, which his estate encircled, were the only interruptions in his dominion. Now that wrinkle had been solved with his acquisition of the lands through Arthur Hendry's deathbed grant, though he'd carefully refrained from pressing the claim while Constance Hendry was still in mourning. Sooner or later he intended to have Hendry's wife, as

well as his lands, but the baron was exercising uncharacteristic patience where Constance Hendry was
concerned.

Nicholas had visited Hawse Castle a number of
times in his youth, but the sight of it never failed to
impress him. Built like a fortress, though the days of
Norman-Saxon conflict were long over, the towering
stone structure was surrounded by a stone wall with
battlements on all sides.

As he and his mother rode through the raised port-
cullis into the bailey, he almost felt as if he should
have come garbed in the chain mail armor that had
become like a second skin during his years on the
Crusades.

The baron, however, was anything but warlike as
he strode across the courtyard to greet them, smiling
broadly.

"Welcome to Hawse, my friends," he called. A
woman trailed behind him, unable to keep up with his
pace. He looked back over his shoulder at her and
barked, "Come along, Winifred."

Winifred was the baron's only child, a slender
young woman who looked to Nicholas as frail as her
father looked robust. He remembered her only
vaguely, but was surprised to see her there. She was
a few years older than Nicholas himself, and by now
he would have thought that she'd be married and off
running a castle of her own somewhere.

"I bid you welcome," she said, her voice so soft
he could scarcely hear the words. Her eyes were on
Constance and only darted nervously to Nicholas for
a moment.

Nicholas had always had a natural affinity for putting even the shyest of women at ease. He took her cold hand and raised it toward his lips. "It's good to see you again, Winifred," he said gently. "You've grown into a beauty in my absence."

Winifred blushed with pleasure and let her eyes meet Nicholas's at last. Baron Hawse beamed at the two younger people and took Constance's arm. "Let's be out of this wind," he said. "The table is ready with Hawse Castle's finest fare for our honored guests. Winifred has seen to it."

"'Twas kind of you," Nicholas murmured. He gazed down at her with the seductive smile he had always reserved for females of a proper age to be bedded, and he received the usual response. Her eyes softened, her lips fell open slightly.

Nicholas shook himself. His actions came as natural to him as breathing, but he'd best be wary. Winifred Hawse was not a barmaid, and he had no intention of bedding her. Indeed, if he was to become the reformed man he'd sworn to become on the field of battle, he'd do well to save his smiles for grandmothers and holy sisters.

His concern at the moment was resolving the tangle over the Hendry estates. He'd banish all thoughts of women from his mind until the matter was settled. Unbidden, he had a sudden vision of Beatrice Thibault, as she'd looked just inches away from him at the cemetery.

"I may still call you that?"

Nicholas looked down, startled by Winifred's soft voice.

"I beg your pardon," he said.

"I may still call you Nick, as I did when we were young?" she repeated.

He had no recollection of Winifred Hawse calling him anything at all, but he smiled at her and said, "I'd be injured if you didn't."

He offered his arm to her as they turned to follow his mother and her father across the yard and into the castle keep.

"I'm only saying that you should consider the baron's suggestion," Constance told her son gently. Nicholas sprawled at the foot of his mother's pallet, as had been his custom when he was young. She sat up against the cushions, a shawl wrapped around her against the morning cold. "Winifred is a lovely girl."

Nicholas sighed. "Aye, Mother. But I'm not interested in taking a wife. I've barely returned home. I just want to settle this matter and take my rightful place as master of Hendry." He sat up to throw another blanket over his mother, who had begun to shiver. "We need to build fireplaces in these chambers."

Constance smiled. "You've inherited that trait from your father, at least. He was always wanting to make some change or other to this place."

"Little good it will do me to inherit his character traits if I'm not to inherit his estate," Nicholas grumbled.

"It's more than generous of Baron Hawse to make this offer, Nicholas. You will not find a better match than Winifred in all England. Some day you could inherit all the Hawse lands."

"The baron is still virile enough to remarry and

father a son,'' Nicholas observed, watching his mother carefully.

His remark elicited no reaction. ''Aye,'' she replied evenly. ''But he has remained unwed these many years since his wife's death. Another heir does not seem to be a matter of high importance to him.''

Nicholas could not say why the idea of taking Winifred Hawse to wife seemed so wrong. She was not unpleasant to look upon. Her demeanor was graceful and ladylike. She was, as his mother pointed out, heiress to a considerable fortune. But somehow the idea of marrying her seemed impossible. For one thing, she was so fragile, he couldn't imagine sharing with her the lusty games he'd played with his former partners such as the curvaceous Mollie.

''I'm not ready to marry, Mother. And I shouldn't have to marry in order to inherit what is rightfully mine.''

Constance swung her feet to the stone floor. ''Take some time to think about it, my son. You've just arrived home and all of this has come at you too quickly. We'll invite the baron and his daughter to a dinner here next sennight and see how you're feeling then. Now run along and send my maid to help me dress.''

She stood and crossed the room toward the private garderobe, another of his father's improvements. Nicholas uncurled himself from the bed and left the room to go find her handmaid.

The red-haired servant was in the scullery with two other young girls of the manor. They stopped their chatter when Nicholas entered the room, but all three looked him over from head to toe, their blushing faces glowing with eager smiles. Nicholas had a moment of longing for his earlier, heedless days when he would have taken full advantage of the girls' shameless admiration.

"Good morrow, ladies," he said with a slight bow. "I'd thought the sun was the brightest thing about this morn until I saw your smiles."

They giggled and one of the girls, whose name he didn't know, ventured a sally in reply. Then he told his mother's maid that her service was needed and bid them good day.

Their laughter floated with him as he made his way out to the courtyard, but it did not make him want to turn back and choose one on which to work his wiles. To his surprise, he realized that all his protestations that he was a changed man were very much the truth. He *was* changed. He wanted something more in life than a quick romp in the hayrack with one of the scullery maids.

He wasn't sure exactly what that something was. But, by the rood, he was certain that it was *not* marriage to Baron Hawse's only daughter.

Chapter Four

At the risk of encountering former lovers who might not be as forgiving of past transgressions as Mollie, Nicholas vowed to spend the next few days getting reacquainted with both the Hendry lands and the people he still thought of as *his* tenants. He put Baron Hawse's offer of marriage to Winifred out of his mind and asked his mother not to bring the matter up again until the Hawse's scheduled dinner the following week.

Spring was blossoming in earnest, and riding in the rolling countryside around Hendry Hall lifted Nicholas's spirits. His big destrier, glad to be roaming free after the difficult journey, pranced along like a frisky colt. He'd purchased the bay stallion in the Holy Lands when his own had been killed by an Arab's lance.

Nicholas laughed out loud and bent over the animal's neck. "Aye, Scarab, 'tis easier without three stone's weight of armor and bloody heathens running at you like crazed devils, is it not?"

As if in reply, the horse settled into a long, smooth

gallop. Nicholas threw back his head. The sun on his face and the wind in his hair made him feel truly at ease for the first time since he'd returned to England.

He pulled Scarab up as he reached the top of the hill that looked down upon Hendry. The Gilded Boar Inn stood slightly apart from the village, out on the main highway that led back to Durleigh. Nicholas's good humor faded as he surveyed the modest inn. With a sigh he reined his mount to the north to skirt around it. Much as he'd like to see Phillip Thibault, Flora's sister had asked him to honor their grief and stay away. He felt duty-bound to comply with her wishes, at least for the time being.

Eventually, when he'd reestablished himself at Hendry and the ownership of the estate was no longer in dispute, he'd seek Phillip out in private. He'd always liked the old man, and he felt the need to assure him that, in spite of Beatrice's bitter accusations, he had never meant to do Flora any harm.

He steered a path straight into the village itself, heading for the third in the row of humble wooden homes. Here, at least, he would be assured of a welcome. Growing up he'd spent as much time in the Fletchers' humble cottage as he had at Hendry Hall. More than once a manservant from the hall had to be sent to fetch him when he'd stayed on too many hours and his mother had grown worried.

The Fletcher household had always seemed much happier than his own. Ranulf the Fletcher and his wife, Enid, had raised a brood of seven children. Harold, the middle boy, had been exactly Nicholas's age, and the two had been as close as brothers. When Ranulf had died the year Harold and Nicholas turned sixteen, Harold had taken over his father's trade. By then Nicholas had been sent to squire at Durleigh Castle, and the difference in station had begun to put distance between the two friends, but the bond had never been entirely broken.

Harold had a workshop at one side of the cottage, and if the gray smoke billowing out from the three-sided structure was any indication, he was hard at his task.

Nicholas walked his horse around to the open side of the workshop. Harold was bent over a workbench with feathers scattered everywhere. Nicholas pulled Scarab to a halt and sat watching his old friend. Harold looked much the same as when the two lads had first begun to vie over which village lass they would next woo. But Nicholas's mother had told him that Harold now had a wife and son of his own. It was hard to credit.

As if aware that he was being studied, Harold looked up suddenly. He squinted out into the sunlight, then let the arrow in his hand clatter to the ground, swung his leg over the bench and started toward Nicholas.

"I'd heard ye was back, Nicky!" he called. "Back from the dead, they say, but I told them all along that no bloody heathen arrow was going to put an end to Nicholas Hendry."

Nicholas slid off his horse and met Harold halfway. With a slight moment of hesitation, Harold stopped in front of him and extended his hand. Nicholas ignored the gesture and, instead, engulfed his friend in a great bear hug, which Harold willingly returned.

"Aye, but 'tis good to see you, Harry," Nicholas said with a broad smile.

Harold leaned back and gave his friend a critical look from head to toe. "They've left you none the worse, I trow." He knocked his fist into Nicholas's upper arm. "Ye've grown more solid, if anything. Might even be able to take me in a fall or two."

"I've always been able to take you in a fall or two, you scrawny lout."

The two old friends grinned at each other, for a moment lost back in their youth, ignoring the different paths their lives had taken.

Harold playfully gave a sideways kick to Nicholas's leg in an old wrestling move, but dropped his grin when Nicholas's bad leg buckled beneath him. "Forgive me—" he began.

Nicholas shook his head and tried to keep from wincing. "Nay, 'tis nothing. They whittled at me a bit," he added, rubbing his thigh.

Harold frowned. "Arrow?"

Nicholas shook his head. "Lance."

Harold gave a low whistle. "Then 'tis somewhat of a miracle after all that ye came back to us. Mayhap me mum was right to say prayers for ye."

"Enid? How is she?"

"Salty and ornery and fit as a woman half her age."

Nicholas laughed. "I'm glad to hear it. And what's this about a new young fletcher in the village? Taking your trade yet, is he?"

To Nicholas's amazement, his friend's face flushed with pride. "My boy, Nick. Ah, he's a scrappy youngster, he is. Who'd have thought 'twould be such a marvelous thing to have a son?''

"What do you call him?"

Harold hesitated a moment, then answered, "He's named after my best friend, who I thought never to see again this side of heaven or hell.''

Nicholas swallowed and, for the second time in a week, felt tears sting the back of his eyes. For a long moment, he made no reply, then he clapped Harold on the back and said, "Well, then, take me to see the boy. He must be a scrappy lad indeed with such a name.''

"Mayhap they'll not come into the cottage," Jannet Fletcher said, giving Beatrice a little pat of reassurance.

The two women had heard a rider approaching and, spying through the cracks in the shutters, had seen the greeting between the two men. "I warrant they will," Beatrice argued. "Harold will want to show off his household."

Jannet stepped back from the window and took a quick look around the simple cottage, suddenly aware that her housekeeping was about to be under examination. She retrieved a pair of leggings that had been left by the fireplace to dry. "Well, the boys are off with Enid, so you don't have to worry about him seeing Owen."

Beatrice turned away from the window as well, her arms folded and her forehead creased with worry. "Your mother-in-law could come back at any moment with both boys in tow."

Jannet straightened up from her cleaning and

looked directly at her friend. "Beatrice, you can't expect to keep Owen hidden from him forever. He's a bright active boy and soon he'll want to have the run of the village just like all the other children."

Beatrice grabbed her arms, trying to keep from shaking. What incredibly bad luck that she should be visiting the Fletchers just at the moment that Nicholas Hendry chose to make an appearance. "He can't see him, Jannet. Not yet. He's just learned about Flora's death, and if he sees the child, it might set him thinking."

Jannet picked up a broom from the side of the fireplace and swept some cinders back on to the hearth. "No one knows that Owen is Nicholas Hendry's son, am I right?"

"My father knows. But you're the only other person we've told."

"And you made me swear not to tell a living soul. I've kept my vow. I've not even told Harold."

Beatrice crossed the room and grabbed her friend's hands as they clung to the broom. "You must especially not tell Harold, Jannet. He's Nicholas's friend. You promise me?"

"I've promised, Beatrice. I'll not betray your trust. But I think you might want to reconsider your decision to keep this a secret. Nicholas could do good things for Owen. Even baseborn, he could still become a squire and then a knight—"

"A knight? So he could go off to fight in faraway lands and return to us maimed or not at all? 'Tis not a life I would choose for him."

Jannet shook her head, but her answer was interrupted by the creak of the door. Sunlight filled the room, then was blotted out as the doorframe was filled by the tall figure of Nicholas Hendry.

Harold stood just behind him, his hand on his friend's shoulder. "Jannet, 'tis Nicholas, home from the wars." He peered over Nicholas's shoulder, squinted into the darkness and added, "Ah, Beatrice, I'd forgotten you came to visit with—"

Beatrice stepped forward and grabbed her shawl from the table. "I was just leaving, Harold," she said, interrupting him.

The two men moved into the room and Harold looked around, puzzled. "Where are the boys?"

"With Enid out in the meadow," Jannet said quickly. She walked around Beatrice and gave a little curtsy in front of Nicholas, whose eyes were on Beatrice. "How d'ye do, Sir Nicholas? I've heard much of you from my good husband."

Nicholas turned his head toward her and made a little bow in reply. "I've not yet had the opportunity to hear the same about you, mistress, but I already know you to be a canny young woman for choosing a husband like Harold."

"For shame, Nick," Harold protested. "'Twas I who chose her, not the other way round."

Nicholas grinned. "'Tis always the woman does the choosing, Harold. Did you not learn any of the lessons I taught you?"

Beatrice paid little attention to the banter. She was determined to escape from the cottage and out toward the meadow to intercept Enid before the old woman could return with the two boys. "Good day to you Harold, Master Hendry," she said, nodding to each man in turn. "If you'll excuse me, I'll take my leave."

It was his fourth encounter with Beatrice Thibault, Nicholas mused, as he stepped to one side to allow her to pass, and the ice in her voice had not thawed a bit. He supposed he should be grateful that at least she had not spat at him in front of his friend.

She brushed against him and went quickly out the door. On impulse, he said to Harold, "I'll be back directly," and followed her outside. "Hold a moment, Mistress Thibault," he called to her as she walked quickly toward the road.

She turned back to him, her face set with annoyance. He took a few loping steps to catch up to her. "What is it?" she snapped.

He took a deep breath. "Is there nothing I can say to make you stop hating me?" he asked.

She blinked, obviously taken aback by the question. "I...I don't know."

Nicholas took her confusion as encouragement. "We may meet again, you know, here in the village or at church or at your sister's grave. By my reckoning, 'tis pointless to carry on as if there were some kind of feud between us. Flora would be the last person to want that, you know. She was too sweet a soul to tolerate enmity of any kind."

Beatrice stiffened. "I don't need you to tell me what kind of person my sister was, Master Hendry," she said. But her voice was less harsh than it had been moments ago.

"I'd never presume to do so," he said softly. "They say the bond between sisters is a very special one."

His gentleness seemed to have some effect. Her eyes misted as she answered, ''Aye. Though raised apart we were no less close.''

For the first time her expression held more sadness than anger. It made her look softer. Nicholas felt a sudden urge to put his arms around her in comfort. Instead he said, ''She often spoke of you, mistress, in the short time we had together.''

Beatrice blinked back the threatening tears and looked as if she was about to make some reply when suddenly there were childish shouts in the distance. Her face blanched. ''I must leave,'' she said. Before Nicholas could protest, she'd whirled around and began running down the road.

He watched her for a few moments, sorry that the sudden swell of emotion had made her flee just when it looked as if they might be able to heal some of the hard feeling between them. He'd made a start, he thought, uncertain as to why the idea gave him such satisfaction.

Belatedly remembering his manners and the purpose of his visit, he turned back to the Fletchers' cottage. Harold and Jannet were waiting for him, looking concerned.

''It appears that ye've already made the acquaintance of Beatrice,'' Harold said when Nicholas ducked his head under the lintel.

''She's less than fond of me, I fear. If you remember, Harold, I kept company with her sister, Flora, yjust before I left for the Crusades,'' he explained. ''I could scarce believe it when they told me of her death.''

''It hit Beatrice hard,'' Jannet said. Then her voice

lightened as she added, "Well, now, here comes my baby boy."

She moved past Nicholas and held out her arms as a little bundle of arms and legs burst through the door and jumped into them.

Harold laughed and said to Nicholas, "There he is, the little hedgehog."

Nicholas smiled at his friend's obvious pride. "A fine boy," he said, though in truth he could scarcely judge the squirming toddler who had nearly knocked his mother to the floor with his robust embrace.

It was hard to believe that it was Harold's son he was seeing, hard to countenance that the youth he'd played and fought and wooed with was now a serious man with a family.

"Aye, and when does an old lady get the proper respects due from a rapscallion like yourself, Master Nicholas?" Enid's voice sounded the same as the day he'd left. He turned to her with a grin.

"If I see an old lady, I'll consider it," he shot back. "In the meantime, I intend to collect a hug from my Mama Enid." He proceeded to do so, lifting her off the ground.

"Put me down, Nicky. Ye'll have this old back in pieces, ye will," she protested with a pleased laugh.

Nicholas's plans to meet a number of the villagers that afternoon were curtailed as the Fletchers insisted that he stay for supper and get to know his namesake. Little Nick's shyness with the big stranger lasted only for minutes. Soon he was climbing over Nicholas as readily as he did his own father. The two men took turns keeping the lively youngster entertained until the lad curled up next to the fire and went instantly to sleep.

"You've worn him out, Harry," Jannet remonstrated, but her voice was rich with affection. Harold reached for his wife's hand and gave it a quick squeeze. She rewarded him with a smile that had a hint of seduction at its depths. Nicholas imagined that when their child and Enid were sleeping up in the loft, Harold and Jannet made lusty use of the large pallet in the corner of the room. He felt a pang of envy.

Growing up, the two boys had taken it for granted that Nicholas was the lucky one. He had the fine home, the opportunity to become a valiant knight, the chance to ride off and see the world. But at the moment, Nicholas thought to himself watching the satisfied look on his old friend's face as he helped his wife lift a kettle off the fire, he'd willingly trade his knighthood and all his adventures abroad for the riches Harold had found.

Nicholas knew from the pains his mother had taken preparing for the upcoming dinner that she was hoping that he would agree to Baron Hawse's proposal and marry Winifred. After his visit to the Fletchers, there were moments when Nicholas found himself wondering if the idea had some merit.

It would mean getting the Hendry estate back without a fight, and Winifred would probably give him little trouble as a wife. If she was too frail for the baser pleasures of matrimonial life, he knew he'd have no problem finding lustier partners in the vicinity. Though some of his former lovers were now, like

Mollie, wives themselves, he'd already seen two girls in the village who had let him know that a resumption of their frolics would not be unwelcome.

He sighed as he gave Scarab over to the stable lad and headed for the house. In truth, he'd been dreading this meal all week, and now that it was here he was still not ready to give the baron the answer he sought.

His uncertainty had made him extend his afternoon ride beyond usual, and now he was late. Hawse and his daughter had arrived before him. Nicholas knew that the breach of etiquette had annoyed his mother, but there was no evidence of her disapproval in her smile of greeting. "Our guests are here, Nicholas," she said calmly.

The baron, Winifred and Constance were already seated at the table. Once again, Baron Hawse had taken the chair of the master of the household. Nicholas felt the anger he had kept in check for the past week rise to the surface again. He struggled to keep it hidden as he turned to Winifred and bent over her proffered hand.

"Welcome to Hendry Hall, milady," he said.

Winifred's eyes darted away from him. Her thin fingers were icy. He grasped her hand more firmly and rubbed it between both of his. "You're freezing," he said, frowning. He looked to the end of the room at the larger of the two fireplaces, then at his mother. "We need to get the servants to build up the fires."

The baron, who had not stood at Nicholas's entry, said smoothly, "Sit down, lad. I've already ordered it. They're bringing in more wood now."

Indeed, as he finished speaking, the big doors

across the hall opened and four men entered, each carrying an armful of wood.

"You can't keep your dining hall like an ice house when there are delicate ladies present," the baron said to Nicholas. "I've given orders that the fires are to be kept well stoked from now on."

Nicholas looked at his mother, who merely shrugged. Steaming, he took the seat next to Winifred, who blushed and shyly offered to share the trencher that had been placed in front of her.

Nicholas scarcely tasted the food his mother had spent so much time planning. He was sitting in *his* home, at *his* table and yet he'd been made to feel as if he were some kind of schoolboy who was only playing host when the real master was gone. And not doing a very good job of it. Is this how things would be if he accepted the baron's offer and became his son-in-law?

Realizing that it was unfair to take his irritation out on poor Winifred, he made several attempts to engage her in conversation, but as before, she replied in a voice so soft that often he could not hear her, and she refused to meet his eyes.

"Don't they make a handsome couple?" the baron asked Constance in a loud voice, looking down the table at his daughter and Nicholas.

"Aye, milord," his mother answered dutifully.

To Nicholas's surprise, Winifred bit her lip and her brown eyes filled with tears. He leaned close to her and said in an undertone, "Pay him no mind. Neither you nor I are puppets to dance to your father's strings."

She lifted her gaze to his face for a moment, and her eyes held unmistakable gratitude.

That put a new perspective on things, he thought with some amusement. It appeared the baron's daughter was no more eager for the proposed marriage than Nicholas. He held back a chuckle of irony. When he'd left England he'd had women fighting over who would win him. Since his return, he'd met one who had spit in his face and another who looked terrified at the very thought of sharing a life with him.

He leaned over to the girl again. "But I'm not as bad as all that," he told her with a grin.

Winifred made no reply and continued staring at her soup.

The meal seemed to last forever.

His anger did not boil over until the moment when the baron and Winifred were leaving. Winifred had already offered thanks to Constance and had touched Nicholas's hand with fingers that were not any warmer than when she had first arrived, in spite of the built-up fire and the hot food. She then descended into the yard to allow her manservant to help her into the small covered cart in which she had traveled. It was hard to picture fragile Winifred mounted on a horse, Nicholas realized.

A stableboy brought up the baron's horse, but Hawse lingered a moment to speak with Nicholas. "I've made you a fair proposition, boy. One that any knight in the land would jump at in a frog's croak, hey? I know you've just returned and are still getting your land legs, but if you let this thing go on much longer without an answer, I'll have to start considering it an insult.'' His eyes narrowed. ''And I'll warn you, I don't suffer insults lightly.''

Nicholas had had enough of listening to Baron Hawse stand in the Hendry family home and tell Nicholas what he had to do. ''If 'tis to be settled at once, Baron,'' he said, ''then I'll have to turn you down. You are correct. Any daughter of yours must surely be considered a prize, but I'm not ready to take a wife. Nor am I sure that Winifred is entirely in favor of the proposition.''

The veins on the baron's face seemed to bulge. ''Winifred will favor what I tell her to favor. And you'd be wise to do the same. Otherwise, you'll be left with nothing.''

Nicholas said calmly, ''I'll take your advice under consideration. For the time being, I'll continue to enjoy my single state.''

''Your father was right,'' the baron spat. ''He'd have been better off to have bred no son at all.'' He whirled around, let his manservant boost him up on his horse, and rode off at a gallop, leaving his daughter's cart in the dust behind him.

His parting words seemed to hang in the cold evening air. They could have been merely the product of the baron's venom, but in his heart he knew that his father had probably uttered that exact sentiment.

Winifred's cart lurched and headed off down the road after her father. For a long time after the dust from their departure had settled, Nicholas stood without moving in the chilly stableyard, staring at the black night sky.

Chapter Five

Constance pulled her cloak more tightly around her against the raw spring wind and made her way across the stableyard. Nicholas had left the house before dawn and had not returned all day. It was past the dinner hour. A furrow of worry creasing her smooth forehead, she looked off to the darkening western sky.

Her concern was no less than it had been when Nicholas had been a boy and had disappeared regularly to seek out friends and activity in the village. It had been one more stone to the constant weight she bore over the fact that she'd not been able to provide him with brothers and sisters for companionship and support.

She peered into the dark stable. The light of a single lantern filtered from somewhere in the back. "Nicholas?" she called.

"Aye. I'm back here."

Picking carefully through the straw, she walked between the stalls toward the light. Nicholas was seated on a bench, his armor spread around him. He was rubbing some kind of cream into a breastplate that gleamed in spite of the dimness. "I'd grown concerned," she said without chiding. "You've not eaten this day."

Nicholas looked up. "Forgive me, mother. I'm not hungry."

"'Tis past sundown."

"I'd lost track of the time."

His black eyes were uncharacteristically dull. "You're not ill?" she asked.

"Nay." He looked down at the metal in his hands and continued polishing.

"Then what's amiss?"

He looked up again. This time there was a spark of anger. "I've traveled to the ends of the world and back all by myself, Mother. I've no need of a nursemaid."

Constance gave her foot a little stamp of frustration. "I'm not your nursemaid, I'm your mother. And that I'll be until you travel to your grave and beyond. Whether it pleases you or not."

Nicholas gave a reluctant smile. "Forgive me, Mother. In truth, I know not what ails me. I only know that nothing is as it should be any more. I'd thought to return to Hendry a changed man. Instead, I find 'tis this place has changed, while I remain the same."

Constance frowned. "Life changes things, Nicholas. Your father could not help his dying."

"Nay, nor could he help the fact that he never was able to love his only son." There was no longer any anger in his voice. He set the breastplate next to him on the bench and reached for a gauntlet which he began to polish with the same mechanical precision.

His mother studied him, her eyes full of pain. "You are wrong, Nicholas. Your father loved you as much as he was capable of loving."

"According to Baron Hawse, he loved me so much that he wished that I had not been born." His hand continued its monotonous circles on the metal.

Constance gasped. "I can't believe the baron would have said anything so cruel. And so false."

"Deny it if you will, Mother, but the tale has the ring of truth."

Neither spoke for a moment. Finally, Constance sighed. "I wish your father was still here, Nicholas."

"Aye. So that he could sign away my birthright before my very eyes?"

"I've told you, his actions were to protect me and the people of Hendry." A single tear dribbled from her eye and slid down her cheek.

Nicholas looked up, saw it and stopped his work. "Now I've made you cry. You see, mayhap Father was right. In any event, I'll trouble you no more."

"What are you talking about?" There was alarm in her voice.

"I'm a soldier now, Mother, and 'twould seem to be the best life for me. I was good at it, you know, in spite of what Father might have predicted for me. I'd thought to leave that life and find a new one here, but it appears that fate has other plans for me."

"The Crusade is over. Your place is here."

"The Crusade is over, but the continent is full of land barons who pay goodly sums for the services of a battle-seasoned warrior."

Constance shook her head and reached to pull the iron gauntlet out of his hand. "'Tis said there's a mind sickness comes upon those who've followed the cross, my son. You must give this thing time. Come into the house and have some good beef stock. Tomorrow will dawn a brighter day. And the next still brighter.''

Nicholas stood and gave her a kiss on the cheek. ''Your beef stock can make the dead walk once more among the living, Mother, but I fear it will not cure my ills. But, I'll come with you, just the same. And I'm sorry for making you grieve. Soon you won't have to trouble yourself over me.''

''I've not seen you brooding this way since your sister passed over,'' Phillip told his daughter. ''You must get Nicholas Hendry out of your head.''

Beatrice knew that her father's advice was sensible, but how could she put the newly returned knight out of her mind when she saw his reflection every time she looked at his child? With every tender moment she spent with little Owen, she wondered if Nicholas Hendry's return meant that she might lose the right to raise him?

She sat with her father at one of the trestle tables in the taproom. It was late. Gertie had long since left, and the inn was empty of customers. ''What if he had seen Owen at the Fletcher's?''

''Aye, what if?'' Phillip reached across the table and put his big hand on top of his daughter's. ''Daughter, he *will* see the boy some day. You must face up to it.''

Beatrice pulled her hand away and averted her eyes. ''Mayhap as he grows he'll lose the resemblance.''

Phillip shook his head in exasperation. "Aye, and mayhap the ground will open and swallow Nicholas Hendry up, but 'tis not *likely.*"

Beatrice looked directly across at her father. "I've decided to take him away."

Phillip pushed back his bench, startled. "Away?"

"I'll go back to live with Aunt Mildred." At her father's pained expression, she amended. "We'll all go."

"And leave the inn?" Phillip gestured to the empty room.

Beatrice knew that her father had worked hard to make his way from brewmaster to proprietor of the Gilded Boar. "You could sell this place and start a new one in York."

Phillip merely shook his head. "Owen belongs here, Beatrice. 'Tis where his mother and grandmother are buried. This is our home." He stood. "Come, let's go to bed. You'll feel better on the morrow."

Beatrice turned her head and stared at the fire, making no move to rise. She'd been happy living in Hendry, and she knew that Owen loved his grandfather very much. If she took the boy away, her father would grieve. But if Nicholas Hendry found out about his son, both she *and* her father might lose him. She saw no other solution. She had to make plans to get away.

Nicholas awoke with a start and sat up on his pallet. He could see nothing in the darkness, and it took him a moment to remember that he was back in England in his own bedchamber at Hendry Hall. In his dreams he'd been back in Galilee, wet and cold in a miserable winter rain.

Nicholas lay back on his cot and shuddered, as if he could still feel the bone-chilling drizzle of that long winter. He'd almost died. If it hadn't been for Gervase's healing powers and Bernard's devoted, if untrained, nursing, his leg wound would have finished him.

Perhaps that would have been for the best, he thought with a wave of self-pity. His mother would have shed a tear, but then she would no longer be troubled by worry over him.

Well, that much he could still give her. Once he left Hendry, she could move on with her life without concern for his feelings. It would be best for everyone. He no longer had a place here. No one would mourn his departure. Harold was busy with his new young family. The maidens he'd courted had found new lovers. Flora's sister and father would no doubt be pleased to have him out of the territory.

He winced in the darkness as he remembered Beatrice's unremitting hostility. She'd appeared to be relenting slightly as they talked in front of the Fletchers' cottage, but when she'd run off so suddenly, he decided that he might have been mistaken. As he stared into the darkness of his bedchamber, he could still see her stormy, accusing eyes.

It was the one piece of business he hated to leave unfinished. He wished he could have convinced her that he would never have hurt Flora. Mayhap 'twas not too late. He'd like Phillip to know, too. For the first time since he'd heard Baron Hawse's departing words, Nicholas felt a sense of purpose.

There was time before he left England to put this thing right. Tomorrow he'd pay a visit to the Gilded Boar. Whether or not the Thibaults wanted to hear his explanation, he'd at least have the satisfaction of giving it before he left home, this time for good.

When Nicholas had been wooing Flora, Phillip was the town brewer, but had not yet built the Gilded Boar. He and his daughter had lived in a modest house on a hill just beyond the village, far enough away to keep the yeasty smell of the brewery from wafting out over the town.

He remembered that Flora had often spoken of her sister, who had been sent as a child to be raised in York where the girls' aunt was abbess at the convent of St. Cecilia.

"Beatrice was always the smart one," Flora had told him. "In York she studies with the holy brothers. Speaks Latin, she does, and reads." There'd been no envy in Flora's voice. It was not in her nature to begrudge the unusual opportunities her sister had been given.

But, Nicholas thought as he walked up the road toward the Boar, nothing about Beatrice Thibault's appearance gave the impression that she had been raised by nuns. Oddly enough, in spite of her continued animosity, he found himself wanting to see her again. He'd decided that morning to leave Scarab at Hendry Hall and go to the inn on foot, as if walking the distance would serve as some sort of pilgrim's penance.

As he turned in at the inn footpath, he briefly recalled the last time he'd stood there, wiping Beatrice's spit from his face. The woman did not *act* as if she'd grown up among nuns, either, he decided ruefully.

The day was mild, and the inn door was wide open. Cautiously, he poked his head inside. The taproom appeared to be empty, which was not surprising for the early morning hour. Taking in a deep breath, he stepped over the threshold and entered.

At the sound of his footsteps on the wooden floor, Phillip appeared from a back doorway. He looked much the same as Nicholas remembered him, though perhaps the lines around his eyes were ground a bit more deeply. He looked startled when he realized the identity of his visitor.

Nicholas hurried to speak. "Master Thibault, though you may not be pleased to see me, I would beg an audience with you for a few moments. There is something I need to put right between us. And with your daughter," he added, looking around the room.

Phillip walked toward Nicholas, his expression sober. "Beatrice is not here, lad. Else I might have to ask you to leave. Your presence would cause her much distress."

"I don't want to cause anyone distress," Nicholas assured him. "But I believe she has a false idea of me. I'd like a chance to explain—"

Phillip held up a hand to interrupt him. "Flora is dead, Master Nicholas. Naught will change that. The best you can do for Beatrice is to leave her be. Which means staying away from here."

Nicholas shook his head. "I'd speak with her…and with you, sir."

Phillip gave a sad smile. "I remember that you were ever a stubborn lad. Beatrice will not talk to you.

Put it out of your mind. But I'll hear you out, if you seek to ease your conscience.''

He gestured toward one of the benches and waited while Nicholas took a seat, frowning. "I did not come for my own benefit," he said.

Phillip moved to the end of the bench and sat straddling it, stretching out one long leg on each side. "Then why did you come?" he asked softly.

"Your daughter, Mistress Beatrice, has—" he paused, choosing his words carefully before he continued, "—has accused me of having some part in Flora's death."

Phillip sighed. "Beatrice grieves her sister fiercely, mayhap too fiercely. 'Tis partly my fault for keeping the sisters apart when they were young. She grieves for both the lost future and the lost past. But I was alone and not sure I could handle two babies."

"She's wrong about Flora and me. I'd never have done anything to hurt Flora. We gave our hearts to each other for a brief span, but both understood that 'twould be a fleeting thing, that I'd be setting off for the wars at any moment."

Phillip's eyes were kind. He put his hands on the bench in front of him and leaned toward Nicholas. "I believe she loved you more than you knew, son. Maids tend to give their hearts more strongly than a man. But if 'tis a comfort to you, I place no blame on you for her death. And I know that you made some of her last days happy, for she herself told me so."

Nicholas felt an unaccustomed lump in his throat. He swallowed with difficulty. "I thank you for that, Master Thibault. It means a lot to me. I'd not leave this place having you think me a knave. And I only wish that you could convince your daughter as well.''

"She'll come around to it some day." He swung his leg over the bench to stand, and Nicholas noted that his body trembled with the effort. He rose to his feet as well.

"You don't think I should see her, then?" he asked the older man.

Phillip shook his head. "'Twould do no good. In fact, I'm going to ask you to leave now, son, because I expect her back any minute, and I'd not have you here when she returns.''

Nicholas was surprised at the degree of his disappointment. However, he couldn't refuse to honor the innkeeper's request. "Then I shall take my leave, but I'd appreciate it if you would give her my respects.''

Phillip's eyes twinkled. "Only if I can catch her in such a good humor that she won't throw something at me when I say your name.''

Nicholas smiled. "She has a lively temper. I've witnessed it myself.''

"But a good heart.''

"That I've not had the pleasure of witnessing, but I'll grant it must be so if she's a true daughter of yours.''

He extended his hand and Phillip grasped it warmly. Then Nicholas turned to leave. As he started toward the door, he heard a child talking just outside, and then a woman answering. His heart picked up its beat as he recognized Beatrice's voice.

Phillip had gone suddenly still. Nicholas glanced over at him, puzzled, then directed his gaze back to the door in time to see a small boy skip across the threshold. "Gampa!" the child cried. "We saw the horsies."

Nicholas looked from the boy to Phillip, surprised. "Grandpa?" he asked. "The child is your grandson?"

The question answered itself as the toddler skipped across the room and threw himself into his grandfather's arms. Phillip lifted him and turned toward Nicholas. "Yes," he said calmly. "This is my grandson. He's called Owen."

Beatrice had stopped in the doorway. She appeared to be supporting herself with one hand on the doorframe, and her face had gone white.

"Is this your son, then, mistress?" he asked her. He didn't know why the idea was so strange. He had heard nothing of a husband for Beatrice Thibault, but she was definitely of an age to be married, and even widowed. Perhaps her husband was no longer living.

Beatrice slid her hand down the doorframe and stood erect. She took a long time answering, but finally said, "Nay, Owen is not mine."

Nicholas looked back at Phillip, who said gravely, "Owen is Flora's child." He gave the squirming infant a hug, then set him on the floor and told him, "Run upstairs, laddie, and play in your room for a spell."

The boy evidently could sense, even at his young age, that something important was occurring and that his grandfather was somehow altered by whatever it was. "Gampa come, too," he said, tugging on the old man's hand.

Phillip shook his head. "Nay, Owen. Your aunt

and I must speak with Master Hendry, here. We'll be but a few minutes. Now you run along.''

He gave a gentle push to Owen's back. The boy started walking slowly toward the stairs, but turned his head toward Nicholas. "Be you Masta Henny?" he asked.

The words had a childish inflection, but the boy's dark eyes held a bright intelligence that belied his years. Nicholas felt the gaze like a jolt to his midsection. For a moment, he was speechless. Then, as the child continued to stare at him, he managed to say, "Aye, lad. I'm Nicholas Hendry."

"Gampa's friend?" the boy asked.

Nicholas looked at Phillip. "It's his name for me— Gampa," he explained.

"Aye. I'm Gampa's friend. And I knew your mother."

As he said the words, he was struck at once with a thought so amazing and so incredible that it almost made his knees buckle underneath him. Was it *possible?* If this boy with the sweet, lisping voice and the wise, dark eyes was Flora's son, could he also be *his?*

His eyes went to Beatrice, who still stood in the doorway looking as if a piece of sky had just fallen and clunked her on the head. "Run upstairs, Owen." She repeated her father's instructions.

But Owen was still looking over the stranger with childish curiosity. "Owen friend, too?" he asked.

Nicholas managed to smile at the youngster, though his heart was beating erratically and he felt short of breath. "I'd like to be your friend, Owen."

Satisfied, the boy gave a quick nod, then turned and

raced up the stairs. The room seemed deadly quiet. "Is he mine?" Nicholas said tersely.

Beatrice, looking more composed, shook out her skirts, then stepped into the room. Her expression was the icy one Nicholas remembered from the first time he had seen her. "Yours? Of course not."

Nicholas looked from her to Phillip, who turned his gaze to the floor. "The lad has black hair and dark eyes. Flora was fair."

"Surely you did not think that a pretty girl like Flora would lack for suitors once you were gone? You men are all alike—you each one think that you are the only he-wolf in the pack."

If he hadn't been so shaken by the thought that he might have just been face to face with his own son, Nicholas would have tried to ease her bitterness with a smooth rejoinder. Under the circumstances, he turned once again to Phillip. "Tell me true, my old friend. Was Flora bearing my child when I left here four years ago?"

Phillip raised his eyes to him, then glanced over at Beatrice before he answered, "Flora died unwed and without revealing the father's name."

"Then the boy could be mine." Nicholas felt shaky inside. His palms had begun to sweat.

Once again, Beatrice spoke with scorn. "Nay, he could not. Owen was born full a year after you left."

Nicholas looked at her, trying to determine if she would lie over so important a matter. She met his gaze without wavering.

"Is it certain—" he began.

She interrupted him. "And if you recall, Master

Hendry, I'd asked you not to come to our home. Now I'll be asking you to leave it.''

There was a shout from up the stairs. "Art coming, Gampa?"

Phillip pushed himself up and nodded to Nicholas. "'Twould be for the best if you were on your way, lad," he said.

Beatrice stood watching him, her finely chiseled face as stiff as a statue. Nicholas let out a puff of air. "I have no desire to cause you distress, either one of you," he added with a nod at Beatrice. "I'll bid you good day."

Since Beatrice didn't move, he walked around her to the door. She stood there with her back to him as he gave a final wave and left the inn.

Chapter Six

The baron had postponed a tour of his northern lands and hurried to Hendry immediately in response to Constance's summons. She received him in the small solar at the back of the great hall. However, once he heard the reason for Lady Hendry's alarm, Baron Hawse relaxed.

"'Tis a known fact, Constance. Many men who go off to the Crusades are changed irrevocably. They become accustomed to the warrior's way of life and find they can't settle down to any other."

"I just don't see that with Nicholas," Constance told him. She'd motioned the baron to a seat, but was too agitated to remain still herself and paced back and forth as she talked. "He was always such a gentle lad, more interested in laughing than in fighting."

"You remember him as a boy, Constance. He's now a man. And if he says the life of a mercenary is for him, then you must accept it."

"He's polished up all that wicked looking armor and says he's going to leave on the morrow." Constance turned to the baron, her eyes pleading. "Can you not talk to him?"

There was a momentary gleam of malice in the baron's gray eyes, but he kept his expression properly somber. "I have talked to him. I'd hoped to convince him to form a union with Winifred, but if he's too—pardon me, my dear—too muleheaded to see a brilliant offer when it's handed to him on a platter, then he deserves the life he gets."

Constance raised her eyes to the room's high ceiling where painted angels looked down in frozen witness. She took a deep breath, then spoke in a rush. "Gilbert, I can't help but think that if Hendry Hall were still his, he'd not be leaving."

The baron's expression grew guarded. "The remedy was simple enough. All he had to do was marry Winifred and the lands would have been his as my wedding gift."

"Aye, but..." She walked over to where the baron was seated, sank to her knees on the stone pavement in front of him and put her hands on top of his. "Gilbert, I'm pleading with you. He's all I have left. I'll be all alone."

Baron Hawse did not show any emotion. He moved his hands so that they were grasping hers, then stood and raised her to her feet. "My dear, you're talking nonsense. You'll never be alone while you have me." His voice dropped. "Constance, you know I've wanted you since before you became Arthur's wife. And I've waited for you longer than I've ever waited for anything in my life."

He bent forward and kissed her full on the lips, leaving her stunned.

''Now, I'll hear no more talk of being left alone. As soon as your mourning is past, you'll come to live at Hawse with me. As for Nicholas, he's chosen his own fate. You must let him go.''

The baron decided to take a detour through Hendry on his way back to Hawse. The tidy little village was a nice addition to his already immense estate. Hendry Hall itself he could spare. It would make a handy gift to a worthy steward one of these days, as soon as he could convince Constance to leave it and come to live with him at the castle. His blood quickened at the thought of Constance in his bed.

She was older now, but he still desired her as strongly as ever. He'd first met her when she'd been the daughter of a middling knight who'd had a small estate to the north. She'd been the loveliest maid in all of northern England, and Gilbert Hawse had wanted her with a desperation that defied logic.

When she'd chosen instead to wed with Arthur Hendry, he'd raged for months. It had been the first time in his life that Gilbert had not gotten what he wanted, and he'd vowed that it would be the last.

The village of Hendry was prosperous. The tenants paid their rents promptly and had made little fuss at the extra taxes he'd tacked on the previous year to cover a king's duty he owed. He'd let his stewards deal with the town and knew only few of the people.

He reached the end of the street and turned his horse to cut in front of the Gilded Boar Inn. A woman and child were coming down the hill just behind it— Beatrice, the innkeeper's daughter. She was one tenant he knew by sight. He made it a practice to keep track of the attractive females who were under his authority.

He stopped his horse a moment to watch her. She walked with long strides, not mincing her steps like the women in the more noble circles he frequented. The swing of her arms and the tilt of her head gave the impression that she was savoring the fine morning and the spring air.

The baron felt a stirring at the base of his loins. She'd be a lusty one, he thought to himself. And he was past due.

His eyes went to the boy scampering along beside her. Was she married? he wondered with a frown. Husbands always complicated his liaisons.

He continued to watch until the woman and child reached the doorway of the inn. When he returned to Hawse he'd make inquiries. One of his stewards, Leon of Ryminster, was the man he usually trusted to handle his more delicate requests.

The woman paused in the doorway for several moments. The baron licked his lips as he studied the long, graceful line of her back, the gentle swell of her hips. Then he turned his horse toward home. He'd send for Leon on his arrival and set him to find out everything there was to know about Mistress Beatrice of the Gilded Boar.

The midsummer sun was low in the sky when Nicholas returned to the village that evening. He'd been riding all day with no destination. His mind was a jumble. For the first hour he'd convinced himself that his suspicions had been unfounded. That the intense feeling he'd had when he first looked upon the young boy had been nothing more than normal interest in a pretty child. But then he'd remember how white Beatrice had looked when she'd first seen him in the room. There'd been fear in her eyes, and he'd remembered her words to him when she'd come to Hendry Hall. *You killed her,* she'd said. Was it not a broken heart that had killed Flora, but rather her delicate body, broken by the birth of the robust young lad he'd just met?

He tossed the question around in his head for hours as he let Scarab wander where he willed. Finally his meanderings took him back to the village and up the familiar path to Harold Fletcher's door. As he approached, the cottage door opened and the arrowsmith emerged.

"Forgive me, Nicholas," he said. "'Tis late and my good wife has gone to bed with little Nick. He's been on the fussy side today."

Nicholas slid from his horse, his leg cramped from the hours in the saddle. "'Tis I who should ask forgiveness, Harry, for arriving at such an hour."

Harold peered at his friend's face in the gathering dusk. "What ails you, Nick? You look as if you've been riding with a goblin on your tail."

Nicholas gave his head a dazed shake. "I've been riding since morning."

"Where?"

"Nowhere. Just riding in the hills."

Harold looked concerned. "Have you eaten?"

Nicholas shook his head.

Harold took Scarab's reins and tied him to a nearby bush. Then he gave Nicholas a shove toward his workshop. "Go sit on the bench before you pass out from hunger. I'll be back directly."

Nicholas ducked under the low hanging roof of the little shed and dropped wearily on Harold's workbench. In a few moments, Harold returned with a bowl of food and a small lantern. He set the dish on the bench in front of Nicholas, lifted the spoon from it and said, "Eat."

"I shouldn't be bothering you—"

"Eat," Harold repeated. "Then you can talk."

After the first bite, Nicholas realized that he was famished. Both men were silent as he finished every last drop of the lukewarm stew.

"Thank you, Harry," he said as he scraped out the last spoonful.

Harold sat facing him on the narrow bench. "Now you can tell me what's eatin' at you, Nicky," he said.

"I went to the Gilded Boar today and saw Flora's son."

"Ah, he's a bright young boy, ain't he? Almost as bright as my Nick," he added with a laugh.

"Who is the boy's father?" Nick found himself holding in a breath as he asked the question, but Harold merely looked puzzled.

"Why, no one seems to know. We took it to be an itinerant of some sort, since no one ever came around to claim the title, not even when poor Flora..." His voice drifted off.

Nicholas rubbed a hand over his eyes. "Harry, Flora and I were lovers before I left for the continent."

Harold's jaw hung slack with amazement. "I never knew."

"Nay, your father had died and you'd become a respectable working man all at once. We saw little of each other, as I recall."

Harold nodded, was quiet a long moment, then asked, "Are you saying, Nicky, that Owen is *your* son?"

"I don't know. Her sister swears it's not so."

Harold tipped his head, considering. "'Tis not customary for Beatrice to tell falsehoods."

"This is not a customary situation."

The two men regarded each other soberly. "Nay, 'tis not."

"Owen and your little Nick are friends?"

"Aye. Owen's a little older than Nick—"

"How much older?"

Harold paused, as if counting, then answered slowly, "Six months. Owen was born a little over three years ago, early in the spring."

"Nine months after our departure," Nicholas said, growing more certain by the minute that the energetic youngster he'd seen that morning was his own flesh and blood.

"Aye, 'twould be thereabouts."

"You're certain about the date, Harry?"

"Deadly certain. I'd not forget such a thing. We'd just discovered that Jannet was with child when poor Flora died giving birth to Owen. The mere thought of it kept me awake nearly every night until Jannet came safely through her time."

"So 'twas the birth that killed her."

"Flora? Aye." Harold put his hand on his friend's shoulder. "I'm sorry, Nicky."

Slowly Nicholas stood up from the bench. "Thank you for telling me. And for the supper."

Harold stood as well. "What are you going to do?"

"Right now, I'm going to ride back to Hendry Hall. I'd thought to be riding *away* from it tomorrow for good, but things have changed. Hendry Hall is *my* home and one day shall be my son's."

"Of course 'tis your home, Nicholas." Nicholas had still told no one about his father's deathbed decisions. "But I was talking about the boy. What are you planning to do about him?" Harold's face was worried. "Beatrice loves the child as dearly as any mother, Nicholas."

"I can see that. But he's my son, Harry, and I intend to be a father to him."

Harold picked up the empty dish from his bench and the two men moved out into the yard. It had grown dark, the only illumination a bright half moon just rising in the eastern sky.

Harold made an attempt to lighten the mood. "So you've bested me once again, Nicky," he said giving his friend a cuff on his arm. "I'd thought to be the first of us to see a crop come to harvest, but now it turns out you've a son, older than mine."

"I can hardly believe it myself, Harold. I'll confess that the whole notion has me dazed."

Harold grinned. "You'll get used to it, Nicky. And don't fret yourself, you'll make a brave father."

Nicholas untied Scarab, suddenly struck with remorse that he'd kept his poor mount wandering all day. In the war, the animal had been tireless, going hours without stopping, but he'd planned to reward him with a more leisurely life in England.

"I'm not sure I feel brave about much of anything, Harry, much less fatherhood. But the lad's mine, and I intend to claim him."

He swung up on his horse, his face set and grim. Harold reached up and put a hand on the saddle to hold him. "I'd not do anything rash, Nicky. The boy has a happy home, the only home he's ever known. If you make enemies of the people Owen loves, you'll only make the boy and everyone connected with him, including yourself, miserable."

Nicholas looked down at his friend. He was bone weary, but Harold's wise words penetrated through his exhaustion. A few moments ago in the workshop, when he'd learned for certain that Owen was his son, he'd had the impulse to ride that moment to the Gilded Boar and seize the child. But Harold was right. Owen had a home, and he had an aunt and a grandfather to love. Nicholas would curb his impatience. He wasn't fighting the heathens any longer. This battle was not to the strong, but to the wise. And he'd take all the time necessary to wage it.

Constance stood in the door of his bedchamber, her hands on her hips. "If 'tis your intention to make me glad that you're leaving me once again, then you're doing a good job of it."

Nicholas blinked the sleep from his eyes and pulled the blanket up to ensure that his naked body was decently covered. From the sun slanting into the room, he could see that it was already midmorning, but even so it had been only a few short hours since he'd arrived at the hall and stumbled into bed.

"I'm sorry, Mother," he mumbled. There was a

sour taste in his mouth that echoed the leek stew he'd gulped at Harold's in the middle of the night.

"You ever were a one for running off, Nicholas. I used to despair of it, but I'll not any longer. Hie yourself off to the ends of the earth, if you like, and just see if I bother to even notice you're gone."

Nicholas smiled. He'd faced the storm of his mother's anger often enough to know that it blew over quickly and left little lasting damage. He sat up, unconsciously rubbing his bad leg, which was nagging after all the riding the previous day. "Then I'll be disappointing you once again, Mother, for I'm not leaving."

She blinked at that. "Not leaving?"

"I've changed my mind. I intend to stay at Hendry Hall."

"When did you decide this? And where *were* you yesterday from dawn till who knows what hour of the night?"

This time Nicholas actually chuckled. Somehow having his mother scolding him for sneaking home in the middle of the night made it seem like he had at last returned to the home of his youth. He was once again the young swain who had stayed out too late plying his charm on a willing young village girl. It was as if nothing had changed.

But, of course, the feeling was an illusion. His father was gone. His mother was older, sadder. And he was more realistic.

Sobering, he said. "Forgive me, Mother. I had some thinking to do, and, as you know, I do it best when I'm by myself. It was irresponsible of me not to send you word, and I beg your pardon."

Constance took a step into the room and peered at her son. "Are you speaking truly, son? You're not going to leave after all?"

He nodded. "I've realized that I've things to hold me here. For one thing, my mother's here to scold me when I act like a lout," he added with an affectionate smile. He made no mention of the other matter that had changed his mind about leaving. As much as he wanted to recognize Owen as his son and begin to raise him under his own roof, he'd decided that he would reveal nothing until he could work things out with the Thibaults.

Constance walked over to him and placed a hand along his cheek. "The saints be praised, Nicky. I know this homecoming has been hard for you, but I know things can work out for the best. If you will just work with Baron Hawse—"

Nicholas's smile faded as he interrupted her. "I'm staying here, but I'm not marrying the baron's daughter."

Constance bit her lip. "She's a kind little thing," she said, her voice wistful.

"Aye. 'Tis nothing against the girl. I have no desire to marry."

"We'll talk to Gilbert. I'm certain he'll come up with another solution."

Nicholas winced at his mother's use of the baron's Christian name. He did not have his mother's faith in the baron's solutions. "I know you hold the baron in some esteem, Mother, but you may as well know that I intend to fight him for my lands."

He could see that she was near tears. "I'd see you at peace, son."

He reached for her hand and gave it a squeeze. "Don't worry, Mother. I'll deal with the baron. As soon as I get this matter settled, you won't have to have anything more to do with him."

Constance looked away, avoiding her son's dark eyes. "It may be a bit more complicated than that," she said softly.

"Complicated in what way?"

She turned her head back to him and met his gaze directly. "I may be in love with him," she said.

Nicholas felt his stomach roll uneasily as he turned Scarab toward the Gilded Boar. He'd faced thousands of screaming Arabs on the field of battle with more calm than he could muster at the present moment. Now that he knew Owen was, indeed, his son, he was utterly nervous at seeing the boy again. What if the child took a dislike to him? Which wouldn't be too unlikely, given the attitude of the boy's aunt.

He'd thought of bringing a gift, but had decided that it was too blatant a tactic for this visit. He did not want to appear to be trying to buy the lad. But at the last minute, he'd tucked a sweetcake into his pouch.

It was cooler than the previous day and the door to the inn was closed. He wondered if he should knock, but, deciding that it was, after all, a public establishment, he opened the door and went in.

Once again the taproom was empty of customers, but his eyes went immediately to the corner of the room where Owen was seated cross-legged on the floor, stacking tankards, one on top of the other. There was no sign of Beatrice or Phillip.

"Good day," he said to the boy.

Owen looked up and pointed at Nicholas. "Masta Henny," he lisped.

Nicholas felt a surge of pride at the boy's good memory. "Aye, Owen," he said, "I'm Master Hendry. But you may call me Nick. 'Tis an easier mouthful." He walked over to the child, suddenly realizing that he'd had a stroke of luck finding him alone. Squatting down, he gestured to the tankards. "What are you building?" he asked.

But Owen was frowning, his thoughts on Nicholas's earlier words. "Nick my friend," he said.

"Aye, I'd like to be your friend."

The boy shook his head. "Nick." His little voice was insistent. "My friend."

All at once, Nicholas saw the problem. "Ah, *little* Nick is your friend, is he not?"

Owen nodded and turned to place the mug he was holding on the top of three others. The pile wobbled precariously. Nicholas reached out and straightened them up so they wouldn't fall. "Are you making a tower?"

Owen reached for another tankard. "A castle," he said. He eyed the pile of four tankards and evidently decided that he'd not risk it. "With *two* towers," he added, plunking the fifth tankard on the floor next to the pile.

Nicholas laughed. The boy was not only intelligent, he was clever as well. Nicholas felt a rush of warmth centering at his heart.

"'Tis hard work to build a castle with two towers. Mayhap the builder should take some nourishment as he works."

He produced the sweetcake from his pouch and was rewarded by Owen's brightened expression. Before he reached for the cake, Owen asked politely, "'Tis for me, truly?"

"Aye, lad. I know of no other castle builders in the vicinity."

Owen plucked the cake from Nicholas's fingers and took a big bite, beaming. As he chewed, he looked down at the remaining cake, crumbling in his fingers, and broke it in two pieces. He held one out to Nicholas. "Masta Henny castle builder, too," he said.

"Thank you, Owen. 'Tis a noble thing to share." Solemnly he took the mangled pastry and popped it into his mouth. He thought it the sweetest thing he had ever tasted.

"What's going on?" Beatrice's voice was icy. Suddenly the room felt as if the door had opened to let in a winter wind.

He turned his head to see her coming down the stairs with an outraged expression on her face.

"Owen and I are building a tower," he said, keeping his tone calm.

"A *castle*," Owen corrected with some impatience.

"Aye, a castle. With two towers." Nicholas jumped to his feet as nimbly as he could with his bad leg.

Beatrice descended the final two steps. "You've no right to come here," she said. There was a slight shaking to her voice.

Nicholas took a step toward her and met her gaze. "I think I do, mistress," he said. "I think I have a very important right to build a castle with my—" he made a significant pause before finishing "—with Owen."

She closed her eyes briefly, then opened them and looked over at Owen. "Sweetling, you need to go outside and play in the yard for awhile."

Owen's disappointment was obvious. He feebly protested, "But...I'm building a castle..." yet he obediently got to his feet.

"Let the boy finish his play, mistress," Nicholas urged. He moved closer to her and continued in a low voice, "This is not the place to discuss what is between us. Not with the boy within earshot."

Owen was watching the two adults, his eyes hopeful. Bits of cake clung to his mouth.

"We have nothing to discuss," Beatrice ventured.

"Nay, you'll not put me off again. Now may not be the right moment, but we will discuss this matter. Either that, or I can take actions on my own."

The anger in her eyes changed to something akin to fear.

"Very well. We can talk," she said.

Nicholas turned his head to Owen and smiled. "Your aunt says you may continue building, lad."

Owen grinned and dropped once again to the floor.

"Only until the noon hour, Owen," Beatrice cautioned. "Then Gertie will come and will need the tankards."

The boy nodded happily.

"Gertie is the barmaid who served us that first day?" he asked.

"Aye. She helps in the afternoons." Her face flushed and he wondered if she was now embarrassed at the way she had greeted him on that occasion.

Though her demeanor toward him had not softened substantially, he had the feeling that some of her hostility had dissipated. Perhaps there was a chance for the two of them to work peaceably together for Owen's welfare.

"Will you come to Hendry Hall for our discussion?" he asked her.

She was still watching Owen at play, and he was surprised to see her eyes suddenly brim with tears.

"We could talk there in private," he said gently. "No one need hear our conversation."

She was silent for a long time, then finally she turned her gaze to him. "Flora left her child in my care," she said stiffly. "I intend to raise him the way she would have wanted."

"You've done her proud, mistress. He's a fine lad in every way. I have no intention of interfering with that. But we do need to talk," he said again. "Will you come to Hendry Hall this afternoon?"

She nodded, blinking back the tears.

He started to leave, then on an impulse, turned back to her. "Will you come to sup with us?"

The question surprised them both. It was not unusual for one of the male tenants to dine with the liege lord if the man were important enough, a guild leader or the like. But it was unheard-of for a female villager to sup at the master's table. Nicholas had never before issued such an invitation, and even now he wondered what his mother would make of it.

"You're asking me to come for dinner?" Beatrice asked, the startling request had banished the threatening tears.

Nicholas gave a little shrug. "Aye."

Beatrice glanced over at Owen, who was still happily stacking his mugs. "'Tis not custom," she said. "Why would you make such a gesture?"

Nicholas ventured a smile. "Mayhap 'tis a strategy of battle. On the Crusades we used to say that if a man broke bread with you, he could not be your enemy."

She appeared to be lost in thought for a long moment, then finally she said, "I do not intend to do battle with you, Master Hendry, for I have the right of this matter. But, aye, I'll dine with you this night."

Chapter Seven

"Lord luv ye, mistress, but he's an 'andsome one." Gertie's eyes sparkled as she spoke of the black-haired knight who'd smiled at her and called her "sweetheart."

Beatrice gave a disdainful sniff and finished wiping out the tankards the barmaid had brought into the pantry. The inn had had a busy afternoon, which for the Gilded Boar meant anything over half a dozen customers.

"Handsome of face, mayhap, not of manner."

Gertie shook her head. "Nay, of manner as well. He was ever so polite that first day. His companion, as well. We don't see fine gents like that in Hendry."

"Well, you'll see him now. He's come back to live."

"Aye, and invited ye to his table. Just imagine, mistress. Mayhap he's taken a fancy to ye."

Beatrice clunked the last hard tankard on the counter. "I have some business with Master Hendry, Gertie. That's all. You should stop filling your head with romantic notions."

Gertie was only fourteen, but she was a pleasing, generous girl, and Beatrice suspected that she'd already had ample opportunity to experience romance firsthand among the village lads.

She giggled and said, "'Twould not be a hard notion to conjure, mistress, with such a one as Nicholas 'endry.''

"That depends on who's doing the conjuring. For me it's impossible." Then she wiped her hands on the towel and turned to leave.

"Pity," Gertie said with a sigh as Beatrice headed up the steep stairs to her bedchamber.

Beatrice's head ached. She could not imagine why she had agreed to Nicholas Hendry's absurd suggestion that she dine at his home. She should have called her father to take Owen away and had it out with the knight then and there. It had been obvious from the certainty in his voice that he knew the truth. Perhaps it had been inevitable that he would discover that Owen was his son. But the battle, as he'd called it, was not lost. Owen was her child as surely as if he'd sprung from her own loins.

So what had possessed her to accept an invitation to the enemy camp? No doubt Nicholas's mother would be scandalized by her appearance there. Unless, Beatrice surmised, she was used to her son bringing home women from all stations. If Nicholas's reputation was justified, he'd had ample candidates. Perhaps they *all* had dined at Hendry Hall.

With a sigh she pulled the big chest from underneath her pallet and opened it. The clothes were musty, she told herself as she pulled the garments out, one by one. It was not merely female pride that made her want to pick just the right ensemble to wear to Hendry Hall tonight. Her dress clothes simply needed airing.

She made a little face of disgust. Perhaps, she admitted, there was some element of pride. She cared little for what Nicholas thought, but it wouldn't do to have Lady Hendry think that her son had invited a ragamuffin to sup at their table. Constance was highly respected in the neighborhood. She had made herself a favorite among the villagers with her visits to sickbeds and gracious charity when families were in need.

It was for Lady Hendry that she was dressing in the silk surcoat that she'd not worn since she'd arrived from York, she told herself once again. Not for her son. She repeated it over and over as she sat brushing her hair until it shined like a polished chestnut.

Nicholas Hendry had killed her sister. And she'd never stop hating him.

His mother had been surprised at Nicholas's request, but she'd told him that he was welcome to have anyone he chose at their table, and she'd greeted Beatrice as graciously as if the innkeeper's daughter had been the queen herself.

Nicholas himself was feeling less at ease. His comment about not wanting her to be his enemy had been true, but he was no longer sure that inviting her to dinner had been wise.

When he'd made the invitation, he'd had some vague idea that receiving her here in Hendry's great hall would give him some kind of advantage over her. She was an intelligent woman, and certainly she would see that the surroundings he could offer Owen at Hendry Hall far surpassed her father's humble inn.

But as the meal progressed, it seemed as if he was the one at a disadvantage. She comported herself like a noblewoman. She'd been raised in a convent, Harold had said, which might explain why she seemed learned on so many subjects.

Throughout the dinner, she met all his remarks with cool disdain, whereas when Constance pressed her for details about her days in York, she answered warmly and without reservation. By the end of the meal, he was in an ill humor, which was not helped by the fact that his leg was throbbing with an intensity he had not felt since the wound was fresh.

Neither he nor Beatrice had brought up the reason for their meeting, and Nicholas did not intend to discuss the matter in front of his mother. After a final sweet of quinces in honey, he pushed back the master's chair and rose to his feet, rubbing his leg in the process. "We may have our meeting now, mistress, in the solar."

Beatrice stood and turned to Constance. "I thank you heartily for the wonderful meal, Lady Hendry, and your amiable company. In the village they call you the lady of grace, and now I know why you have earned the title."

Constance smiled up at the younger woman. "My dear, you are welcome at our table any time."

Nicholas felt something akin to jealousy at the warmth of the smile Beatrice bestowed on his mother. Controlled neutrality was the best he'd ever had from her, and her more usual expression toward him was hostility. Still, she was his son's aunt, and he was determined to change her opinion of him.

They made their way into the solar. Though it was evening, the last rays of the sun still filtered in through the high window, giving the stone walls of the room a reddish cast. The painted angels peered at them from above.

Beatrice sat on a small wooden-backed bench, and he pulled up another beside her. This was not a discussion that could be held politely from two sides of a room.

He took a deep breath and began. "Owen is my son."

Beatrice looked away from him. "I told you he is not."

"Forgive me, mistress, but you lied. He was born nine months after I left for the Crusades. And even you would not try to convince me that Flora would have sought another suitor so soon after my departure."

She waited such a long time that he thought she was going to refuse to talk with him at all, but finally she turned her eyes back to him and said resignedly, "Not soon nor ever. Flora was deeply in love with you."

Nicholas felt a flush of triumph. In his heart, he'd been certain that Owen was his son, but the confirmation was sweet. "Then you admit it. Owen's mine."

The blue eyes flashed. "He's your *son,* but he's not *yours.* My father and I have raised him. We're the only family he knows."

"Aye. I'm grateful that the boy had a loving aunt

and grandfather to care for him. But if I'd been here, I would have claimed him as my own.''

''Indeed?'' She sat regal and proud in her stiff-backed seat. ''Would you then have married my sister?''

The question hung in the chilling air between them. Both knew that it would have been highly unlikely for the son of the liege lord to marry one of the tenants, no matter how respected the Thibault family was among the villagers.

Beatrice gave a bitter smile. ''I thought not. So her heart would have been broken in any event. Mayhap 'twas a blessing she was taken.''

The notion of marrying Flora had never occurred to Nicholas. He'd given little thought to such matters as marriage in those carefree days. Nor had he thought much about the feelings of the girls with whom he'd shared his youthful passions. Would he have broken Flora's heart, as her sister accused? Most likely.

''None of us can go back and change the past, mistress,'' he said slowly. ''But we can see to it that past mistakes don't continue on into the future. I was not a good suitor for your sister, but I want to be a good father for our son.''

The conversation was proving to be as difficult as he had feared. He turned on his low seat, trying to find a comfortable position for his leg. The throbbing had turned into a burning sensation. He moved once more, then let out an involuntary sound as a stab of pain shot clear up his thigh.

Beatrice looked at him, puzzled. ''Are you in pain?''

He nodded, biting his lip to keep from crying out again as there was a third stab, then a fourth. Finally the spasm subsided and he let out a long breath. "Forgive me," he said. "The remnants of battle."

"You were wounded?"

"Aye. A lance wound."

Beatrice studied his upper leg, watching his hand rub back and forth to relieve the ache, then after a moment her cheeks reddened as she realized that she'd been staring for an unseemly amount of time at what could be considered a delicate part of his body.

Growing up in York, she'd learned nursing from the holy sisters. She had, in fact, been known to have a gift for it. At the convent, those who were ill or in pain had often come to seek her out. It had been one of life's ironies and her greatest grief that all her skills had been unable to save her sister.

She recognized the signs of pain in Nicholas's strained face, and her instincts told her that she could help him. But, though she'd always considered her skills as a holy charge, she simply could not bring herself to offer them to this man. She knew the intimacies involved with relieving someone of pain. She'd not put herself on those terms with Nicholas Hendry.

Still, seeing his misery, she couldn't help experiencing that special feeling she always had for those who were suffering pain. It made it hard to keep her voice cold. "At least your wound has healed, Sir Nicholas. My sister's never shall."

The burning in his thigh along with Beatrice's continued implacable animosity finally unraveled the edges of Nicholas's temper. "I'll tell you one more time that I grieve for Flora. If I could move the earth to bring her back, I would. However, that is beyond my power, beyond yours. What I can do is to be sure that her son—*our* son—grows up noble and strong as she would have wished. Is not that what you want for him as well? 'Twould seem to me, mistress, that our goals are the same.''

Beatrice did not know whether it was his sudden flare of anger or the pain that was still obvious in his face, but all at once she felt herself paying some heed to his words. For years she'd held the idea of him in her mind as a heartless philanderer, but that image was getting harder and harder to summon.

She was finally realizing that the fact that Nicholas wanted to help in raising his son meant that he was not entirely without a sense of responsibility. It was, in fact, true that their goals were similar. They both wanted what was best for Owen.

She had a sudden memory of Flora on her death-bed. ''Do not hate Nicholas, please,'' she'd whispered to her sister. ''His heart is good.'' Beatrice had paid little attention. She'd had months of listening to her sister extol the virtues of the knight who had loved and left her. She'd thought her poor sister deluded.

She looked up at him. The anger had left his black eyes. In the reddish light his dark features looked strikingly handsome. If Flora had been deluded, it was easy to see why. She formed her words carefully. ''I'll grant you that much, Master Hendry. We both want the boy to grow strong and happy.''

Nicholas seemed to relax in his chair. His hand stopped rubbing at his leg. He gave a slight smile. ''I sense that it cost you dear to attribute any kind of good motive to me."

She answered him with a tentative smile of her own. "Aye, it cost me."

Nicholas leaned toward her. "I told you from the beginning that I am not a monster, mistress."

"I no longer consider you a monster."

Nicholas smiled more broadly. "'Tis a start."

"I still, however, consider you a scoundrel," she clarified, but there was no longer any bitterness in her voice.

"Well now, I must admit that you're not the first to make that particular charge, so mayhap it has a pinch of truth."

His hand had begun to rub at his leg again. "Does it nag you daily?" she asked, before she could stop herself.

He looked surprised at the question. "Nay. I foolishly rode for too many hours yesterday." One black eyebrow lifted. "'Tis an unsettling matter to suddenly discover that one is a father."

"Do you think the riding reinjured your leg?"

Nicholas shrugged. "I suppose so. The wound was seeping this morning. It hasn't done that for a long time."

Beatrice frowned. "Seeping? That's not good."

"I've lived with it for nigh on a year, now. I trust some day it'll heal for good."

After a moment's hesitation, she reached over and put her hand on his thigh. It was rock hard, and for a moment, her cheeks grew red again, but as she felt heat radiating through the thick tunic, her nursing instincts supplanted her embarrassment. "'Tis warm. It should be tended, mayhap lanced."

Nicholas gave a rueful chuckle. "The one lancing was enough, thank you very much. I'll not ride for a couple of days and it'll calm down."

If he had been a young man in the village, she would have been more forceful. She'd pay little attention to his demurral, knowing that men were ever wont to balk at any ministering, especially if it might involve pain. But this was Nicholas Hendry, whom she'd sworn to hate forever and who was now making her change her mind by some mysterious force of will that she had yet to understand.

She hadn't asked how he had determined the date of Owen's birth. There were a number of ways he could have discovered it. And perhaps it wouldn't be such a bad thing. He could visit Owen at the inn and provide a male example to him. He could engage him in some of the manly play that her father was getting too old for.

Suddenly she wanted to leave, to be gone from Hendry Hall and away from the presence of its compelling, virile scoundrel of a master.

"We need to settle our business, Master Hendry. Am I to understand by this audience that you wish to acknowledge Owen as your son?"

"Of course."

Beatrice felt the shakiness inside again. It had been easier to hate Nicholas than it was to try to cooperate with him. "I suggest you get to know him a little first before we tell him."

Nicholas nodded. "I'm agreeable to that. I want to do this thing right."

"When would you like to see him again?"

"Tomorrow morning," he said promptly.

He was eager, it appeared. She was to have no time to think how this event would alter Owen's life…and her own.

She stood and tried to keep the shaking from reaching her knees. "We'll expect you tomorrow then," she said. "Midmorning."

He stood, his dark eyes studying her, carefully banked triumph in his expression. "My thanks," he told her. "You'll have no cause to regret this."

He hesitated a moment, then offered an arm to escort her out to the door as if she had been a noble lady with a litter and footmen waiting at the door. She looked at the extended arm as if it were some kind of weapon. Her evening had been unsettling enough. She had no desire to touch him again. She gave a little shake of her head. "You needn't see me out. I know the way." Then she turned before he could protest and left the room.

Phillip's eyes were sad. "Mayhap I should never have called you from York," he told his daughter. "You might have been a married woman with a child of your own by now if you hadn't come hurrying to your sister's side."

"Ah, Father, how could you think I'd be anywhere else but my sister's side at such a time? And you know I love Owen as if he *were* my own child."

"Aye, but he's not yours. That's the problem."

They were working together in the little kitchen behind the inn, preparing a huge bowl of dough to be shaped into loaves and baked in the big stone oven.

Normally Gertie helped with the task, but the barmaid's mother had just lost her third baby in a row and needed her daughter at home.

Beatrice began to roll up her sleeves in preparation for kneading the mass of dough. "Mayhap 'tis no problem at all. Nicholas Hendry appears to be a more reasonable man than I'd suspected."

Her father shook his head sadly, then gave her a little push away from the table. "I'll mix the bread, lass. You'd best get back to the boy."

Beatrice gave a doubtful glance at her father's hands. Today was a good day. The trembling was hardly noticeable. "Are you sure?" she asked. She knew that, though her father would never admit it, he actually enjoyed cooking.

"Aye. Run along."

She started to leave, then turned back to say, "He just wants to come and visit. 'Tis reasonable for a man to want to get to know his son."

Phillip dug his big hands into the doughy mass. "Aye, 'tis reasonable," he agreed, but his doubt was written on his face.

"And 'tis a good thing for Owen, as well."

"Aye." Phillip picked up the entire glob of dough and smashed it on the table.

"Once he knew our secret, there was really no way to stop him from coming."

This time her father didn't reply. He started a rhythmic massage of the bread. Beatrice sighed. If she admitted the truth, she also was concerned about Nicholas Hendry's visit. She watched her father a moment more to be sure that he did not need help. The sight of him, flour up to his shoulders, made her smile.

She loved him no less dearly for not having been raised under his roof. She understood that he had sacrificed the joy her presence gave him in order to give her the opportunities she'd had in York. Nevertheless, they'd visited as often as possible, and he'd always been concerned for her welfare. She wondered fleetingly if the worry on his dear face this morning was only in part for his grandson. Her father was a sharp observer, and it was likely that he had noted that in anticipation of the knight's visit, his daughter had once again dressed in her finest frock.

"I'll call you when Master Hendry arrives," she told him.

He glanced up with a brief smile. "No need, lass. 'Tis Owen he comes to see."

She'd thought about preparing Owen for the visit, but had changed her mind. It was not *her* task to see that the boy accepted his father. If Nicholas Hendry didn't have the wits to handle the matter, it would only serve to prove her earlier contention that Owen would be better off never knowing about the relationship.

But, of course, she might have known that Master Charm, the man who had, by all accounts, enchanted villager maids and noble ladies alike, would have no trouble captivating a small boy.

His glance went only briefly to her as he stepped into the doorway of the inn, then found Owen. The boy remembered the sweetcake, and was not disappointed when Nicholas pulled another one from his pouch and handed it to him. He held his left hand behind his back, provoking the boy's curiosity enough to make him delay stuffing the sweet into his mouth.

"'Tis a gift for you, lad," he said, which made Owen's eyes go wide.

Beatrice felt as if she were only an incidental bystander to the exchange.

After a few seconds of teasing, Nicholas moved his hand from behind him and produced a stick with a small leather horse's head, complete with bridle, at one end.

Owen shrieked, "Horsey!"

"Aye, Owen. 'Tis *your* horse. 'Twill serve until you're old enough for a real one."

Owen, still holding the cake in one hand, eyed the contraption hesitantly.

Nicholas grinned at him. "Of course, riding and eating all at once is a more advanced skill. Mayhap you should sit down and finish the cake first."

Owen looked over at Beatrice, who nodded. Then he went obediently to the small stool in the corner, which was his usual seat. He started eating the sweetcake, but his eyes were on the hobbyhorse in Nicholas's hand.

"It has real reins, you see," Nicholas told him, lifting the leather straps. "You need to use them to let the horse know where to take you."

Owen nodded soberly. "Can I ride to Gampa?" he asked, looking at Beatrice.

"When you finish your sweet," she said. She looked over at the horse. It was obvious even from across the room that the workmanship on the head was very fine. The two rosettes that held the reins in place appeared to be made of silver. "'Tis too fine for a small child," she said to Nicholas in a low voice.

"Nay, 'tis meant for a child, mistress. In fact, for this child." He pointed to his own chest. "'Twas mine as a lad." In the eagerness of his smile, Beatrice could see traces of the young boy he had been.

Owen crammed the last bit of cake into his mouth, then jumped off the stool like a prisoner set free from a cell. This time there was no hesitation as he reached for the stick horse and put it between his legs. It was the perfect size for him.

He looked up at Nicholas, beaming. The knight smiled back and bent down to help him adjust the head and reins so that he could appear to be riding. When Owen was set, Nicholas ruffled a hand through the boy's black curls.

"Not too fast, now, to start," he warned. "Just a slow trot, then you can try a gallop later on."

Cautiously, Owen gave a couple skips, dragging the stick along behind him. He laughed with delight and looked up at Beatrice. "I'm riding, Aunt Beady," he told her.

"Aye, sweetling. I can see. You make a brave horseman."

He made a turn around the room, shouting, "Gid-dup, horsey!" Then he stopped and said, "Can I ride out to the kitchen to Gampa?"

Beatrice glanced briefly at Nicholas. Then she nodded. "You can ride out to show him, then come straight back. You can't be disturbing Gampa while he's making the bread."

"I not 'sturb Gampa," he said, then he turned his horse's head and galloped out the door.

Nicholas watched him go, his smile broad. "I'm pleased that he likes it. 'Twas my favorite toy."

His grin made him look boyishly handsome. Beatrice felt the now-familiar unsettling in the pit of her stomach, this time combined with a measure of fear. As much as she tried to tell herself that the notion was impossible, she was very much afraid that she was becoming attracted to the man she had once thought of as a monster.

Chapter Eight

Leon of Ryminster was the most diligent and least scrupulous of Baron Hawse's many retainers. Consequently, he was often the one chosen to deal with the most unpleasant matters that arose managing the baron's estate. Leon was also one of the few men aware that the baron's vast holdings had been granted to him by the late King John in exchange for numerous unlawful acts committed in the king's service that had long since been covered up and forgotten.

"You're sure about this?" The baron leaned on the arms of the big, carved chair in his antechamber where he usually conducted his business. He put his face closer to his steward's, who sat on a small stool at his feet. "The boy is not hers?"

"Aye, milord. The child was born to the sister, who died giving it birth. Beatrice is the aunt."

"Who is the boy's father?" Baron Hawse asked.

"Apparently the sister took that secret with her to the grave. But I could make further inquiries and find out for you, if you wish."

Hawse leaned back in his chair and smiled. "Nay.

Who cares about the paternity of a bastard brat. The important thing is that 'tis not the girl's. And no other lovers, you say?''

''Everyone we talked to swears not. She's too waspish and too learned for the men of Hendry, they say.''

''A spirited virgin, then. What a delectable treat.'' The baron licked some oozing saliva from the corner of his mouth.

''Shall we bring her to you?'' Leon moved his long legs, cramped from sitting on the low seat.

''Nay. She'd resist and cause a stir, no doubt. I can't risk something like that right under Constance's nose. I'll find a better way. Let me think on it.''

Leon hesitated a moment, waiting to see if the interview was ended, but Baron Hawse seemed lost in a pleasant daydream. Finally his master turned his head and said, ''Did you not know, Leon, that anticipation is a good part of the pleasure? The longer you wait for something, the richer it tastes at the end?''

Leon nodded, his expression unchanging.

''I wager Mistress Beatrice will taste rich as sweet cream,'' the baron continued, nodding.

''Aye, milord,'' Leon answered, and once more shifted the position of his aching legs.

Nicholas had come each day without fail, just past the hour for morning prayers, though, Beatrice noted, he did not come from the direction of the church. One day he brought a painted wooden top that had Owen dancing in delight. On another he brought a metal hoop, and taught the boy to roll it with a stick. And each day there was a sweetcake or a bit of honey toast from the pouch that hung at his waist. Owen was thoroughly fascinated by the new presence in his life, and from the moment he awoke in the morning he began talking about the prospective visit from "Masta Henny."

Phillip watched the visits with a benevolent, though slightly sad, smile. His trembling was growing worse each day. It simply was no longer possible for him to drop down to the floor to play with the youngster as he had been wont to do. His hands were no longer steady enough to spin a top or steer a hoop. Nevertheless, Owen's shouts of laughter lightened everyone's heart.

Beatrice's feelings were even more mixed than her father's. For the first few days, she tried to keep herself busy with other tasks during Nicholas's visits. But Owen always wanted to show her his new toy or his new skill and, inevitably, she ended up in the middle of the activity—directly between Owen and Nicholas Hendry.

After two weeks of it, she was exhausted. It had grown harder to sleep at night, and she'd been awakening long before dawn, anticipating the knight's visit every bit as strongly as Owen.

"You can't keep bringing him gifts all the time," she snapped one morning after Nicholas had unveiled a game of draughts which was obviously expensive and far beyond anything a boy of Owen's age could comprehend.

Nicholas looked up, surprised at her tone. "I'm not planning to try a game with him as yet. He can move the pieces around the board and pretend. Before long, he'll want to learn the rules."

"By then he'll have lost half the pieces. It's far too dear a set for a young child."

Nicholas shrugged. "If pieces are lost, we'll have new ones made."

They were seated at one of the inn's trestle tables, watching as Owen sprawled on the floor playing with the polished stone pieces of his new game. Beatrice met Nicholas's eyes across the table and said sternly, "'Tis not fitting for a boy of his station."

Immediately she knew she'd made a mistake.

Nicholas lifted his head. His voice was sharp. "And what would that station be, mistress?" he asked. "The first-born son of a landed knight?"

Beatrice lowered her voice. "The bastard son of an unnamed father," she corrected.

Nicholas lowered his tone to match hers. "The father is unnamed only because you asked me to wait to acknowledge him until he got to know me better. Mayhap that time has now come."

A cold fear raised bumps on her arms underneath her thin undergown. "What do you mean by acknowledgement?" she asked. Over the past few days of Nicholas's visits, she had come to realize that he had the power to take Owen from them, if he so chose. In addition to her own feelings on the matter, she worried that to lose Owen after already losing Flora would be a deathblow to her increasingly frail father.

But Nicholas's answer made her relax her stiffened spine. "I'd have it known in the village that the boy's mine," he said.

She replied slowly. "Very well. Would you like me to tell people? Or shall we ask the Fletchers to give out the word?'' She smiled briefly. "'Tis not hard to spread gossip in a town like Hendry.''

Nicholas returned her smile, but said, "'Tis not gossip we're spreading, but truth. We're righting a wrong, if you would have it that way.''

"Aye.'' Though the chain of events since Nicholas had arrived home worried her, she had to admit to herself that Flora would have been thrilled to know that Nicholas was accepting Owen as his own.

Nicholas smacked his open hand on the table in front of him. "Midsummer's Eve,'' he said, his voice excited. "We'll let the truth be known by one and all at the festival.''

She did not entirely follow his idea. "In what manner?''

"We'll go together, you and I and Owen. And Phillip, of course. To all who ask what I'm doing carrying the innkeeper's grandchild, I'll say, the boy I carry is my own son.''

"Midsummer's Eve is two days hence.'' Beatrice wavered.

"Aye, as I said, 'tis time for this truth to be known. Are you agreed?''

Both their heads turned to watch Owen, who was carefully making a trail of draught pieces, first dark, then light, then dark.

"Aye,'' she said, but the word came out as little more than a whisper.

How does one prepare a three-year-old child to meet his father? Beatrice thought as she tucked Owen cozily under his blankets.

"Fair tomorrow?'' he asked sleepily.

"Aye, sweetling. Tomorrow's the fair. Master Hendry is coming to take us."

"Masta Henny Owen's friend."

Beatrice sighed. Owen's lids were drooping. It didn't seem right to bring up such a momentous announcement when the child was half asleep. When Nicholas had wanted to tell him that morning, she'd asked him to let her explain to Owen in her own way. It would be easier alone, she'd thought. Now the day was nearly over and she still hadn't done it.

"Aye, Owen," she said, ruffling the hair that matched his father's color so exactly. "You know Master Hendry was away for many years fighting in the Holy Crusade."

Owen's eyes opened more widely. "Where he got Scab?"

"Aye, where he got Scarab when his other horse was killed." Nicholas had taken his son for a ride on his big destrier. Owen had been so excited he'd almost squirmed right out of the saddle.

"Will we ride Scab to the fair tomorrow?"

"I think we'll walk, sweetling. We won't all fit on Scarab."

"You and Gampa walk, and Masta Henny and I ride Scarab."

The sleepiness had vanished and once again Beatrice berated herself for leaving this task to the last minute. "I don't think Master Hendry will even bring his horse, Owen. Scarab wouldn't be happy at the fair with so many people around. But I'm trying to tell you something about Master Hendry."

Owen pulled down the blanket and sat up, suddenly serious. It was as if he realized that what his aunt was about to tell him was of major importance. "What about Masta Henny?" he asked warily.

Beatrice struggled with the words. Suddenly she wished that she *had* let Nicholas tell the boy himself. How did you explain something to a child who was too young to even understand how babies were made? "Master Hendry is going to be your new papa," she said finally in a rush.

Owen looked at her in disbelief. "Papa? My real papa?"

"Aye. Your real papa."

Owen's shocked expression dissolved into a smile so joyous that Beatrice felt as if someone had squeezed her heart.

"Owen's own papa?" he confirmed one more time.

"Aye."

He reached for his aunt and burrowed his face into her chest as she returned his embrace. She wasn't sure, but she thought he might be crying. She held him a long moment, crooning a bit, then she pulled away and looked down at him. His plump cheeks were damp.

"Does that make you happy, sweetling?" she asked.

She already knew the answer before she saw his happy nod.

"Can I call him papa?"

"Aye."

"Can I tell Nick?"

"Master Hen—your papa wants to tell everyone at the fair tomorrow."

Owen's eyes danced. "That's better than riding Scab," he said, bouncing a little on the bed.

"But you must go to sleep now, so you won't be too tired."

He bounced a couple more times, then obediently slipped back down under the cover. Once within the warmth of the blanket cocoon, he immediately began to grow sleepy again. "I never had a papa," he said, his voice already groggy.

"Well, now you do."

He gave another happy nod, then closed his eyes and drifted off. Beatrice sat watching him for a long time. She was relieved that his excitement could flare so high, then dim like a banked fire. The resilience of youth.

She gave a sigh as she stood and made her way across the room to her own pallet. She herself would not be so fortunate. She, too, would like to rest up for the fair on the morrow, but she had the feeling that it would be long hours before she would find sleep.

The Midsummer's Eve fair at Hendry had grown through the years from a small religious festival to a full-blown regional fair. By now, the event drew an impressive assortment of itinerant jugglers, fire-eaters, bear-baiters, mummers and minstrels, fascinating characters for children who had never traveled beyond the outskirts of their own village.

It was Owen's first fair, and his reaction did not disappoint the adults who accompanied him. He scampered wildly from one attraction to the next and, when he started to grow tired, he let himself be hoisted into Nicholas's arms.

True to his words, Nicholas stopped frequently and

introduced Owen as his son, eliciting more than one look of astonishment from the villagers.

Owen had taken to calling him "Papa" as naturally as if he'd been doing it from the beginning. Nicholas seemed to puff himself up every time the boy used the term. Beatrice couldn't help but be touched by his obvious pride.

Phillip was flagging by the time they reached the end of the row of trade booths. Nicholas was the first to notice the old man's difficulty. "We'll stop here a spell and sample this fine lady's pasties," he said, with a wink at the middle-aged woman who was arranging a tray of the fried meat pies.

The pasty seller giggled and her cheeks flushed. "Lord love ye, sirrah. If 'tis fine ladies ye seek, ye be looking in the wrong place."

"'Tis fine food we seek, mistress," Nicholas told her, bending over the tray and taking a deep sniff. "And I do believe we've found the right place."

"That ye have, master," she said with a laugh. She cast a curious glance at his companions. "How many will it be? For yerself as well as yer goodwife?"

Now it was Beatrice's turn to blush, but Nicholas seemed not to notice. "We need four, I think. Will you try a pasty, too, son?" he asked Owen.

Beatrice looked doubtfully from the pies, which were the size of a big man's fist, to the small child, but Owen chirped, "Aye, Owen wants a pasty, too!"

Nicholas pulled some coins from his pouch and gave them to the woman who handed a pie to Phillip and Beatrice. Then she reached over the tray to pass one down to Owen.

The boy immediately chomped into a corner, releasing a spray of juice all down his front. Realizing the mess he'd made, he looked to Beatrice for help, but before she could react, Nicholas had gone down on one knee beside the child and was wiping him with a kerchief. "First time eating a pasty's a bit of a trick, son," he said, his tone reassuring. "You have to hold it carefully with both hands."

He plucked the pie gently from the boy's hand and turned it so the juice would not run out, then folded Owen's tiny fingers around it. "Just nibble along the edge, bit by bit, like a rabbit nibbling a carrot."

Owen followed his prescription and began a more successful negotiation of the pie. Nicholas straightened up, smiled down at the boy, then reached across to the woman for his own pasty. "I'll be nibbling, too," he said to Owen. "See?"

Beatrice watched the exchange, fascinated. Nicholas may have had little experience at being a father, but it seemed to come as naturally to him as breathing.

After another thank you to the pasty woman, they wandered through the crowd toward a grassy embankment where they could sit to finish their pies. Without asking, Nicholas took a strong hold of Phillip's arm to help him down.

When they were all seated, Owen held his half-eaten pasty out to Nicholas. "Papa finish," he said.

Nicholas laughed. "'Tis a mighty pie for such a small stomach, eh?" He scooped the boy into his lap, took the remainder of his pie and finished it in two big bites.

"Nibble, Papa," Owen scolded.

Nicholas laughed again and rolled backward on the

grass, giving Owen a hug that tickled him and made him forget all about his father's eating habits.

"Nick!" Harold Fletcher's voice rang out from amid a group of people who were gathered around a troupe of acrobats. Nicholas sat up, still holding Owen on his lap, and squinted in the sunlight. Then he raised his hand in greeting as Harold separated himself from the group and started toward them, followed by Jannet and little Nick.

Owen scrambled off Nicholas's knees and ran to greet his friend shouting, "Nicky, I have Papa, too."

Nicholas rose to his feet, wiped the remaining grease from the pies along the sides of his tunic and greeted the approaching couple.

Beatrice stood more slowly, but Phillip remained on the ground.

"We heard the news, Nick," Harold said with a grin. "In faith, the entire village is fair buzzing with it."

Jannet looked anxiously at Beatrice. "I swear, my friend. I never said a word."

Beatrice smiled her reassurance. "Aye, Jannet, I know. 'Twas foolish of me to believe it a secret that could be kept."

Harold clapped Nicholas on the back. "Congratulations, *Papa.* You've a fine boy."

Nicholas looked over at the two boys, who were busy studying a piece of discarded fruit that was collecting flies in the dust. "Aye, he's a fine one. Who'd have thought two rogues like us could produce such worthy offspring, eh, Harry?"

The two men exchanged quips as Beatrice and Jannet looked on with expressions of feminine tolerance for their malefolks' tomfoolery. It was almost as if they were two married couples, enjoying one another's company as they accompanied their children to the fair. Beatrice flushed at the notion and dismissed it as absurd.

Little Nick ran up to Jannet and tugged at her arm. She leaned down to hear his lisped request, then straightened up. "We were just about to head over to the grainery where there's to be a bear dancing, they say. Nicky wants Owen to come with him. Would you all like to go?"

Owen added his own plea to Nicholas, "Bear, Papa!"

Nicholas grinned. "I'd not mind seeing a bear myself." He turned to Beatrice. "Shall we go?"

"Surely—"

She started to speak when Phillip interrupted her. "I fear these old bones have had all the fair they can take for one day. I must return to the inn." He tried to stand, but wobbled, and fell back again, heavily.

"Father!" Beatrice exclaimed. "Are you ill?"

Once again he struggled to stand, and this time Nicholas and Harold each took an arm and boosted him upright. "Nay, I'll be fine. I'm just fashed, is all. You young folk go on and see your bear."

Beatrice shook her head. "Nay, we'll take you home. I'll brew some of your special tea."

"Aye," Nicholas agreed. "The bear will wait."

Owen's face fell.

"Let Owen come with us," Jannet suggested. "We'll guard him well until you can get back to us."

Nicholas and Beatrice exchanged a look. Phillip said, "I don't need any help."

Beatrice decided the matter. "You may go with Nicky to see the bear, Owen. Mind you stay with the Fletchers and don't stray. We'll catch up to you later."

Nicholas crouched down and gave Owen a hug. "Be a good lad, now."

"Aye, Papa," Owen said, and scampered off with little Nick and his parents.

Nicholas stood up. "I'd be honored to lend you my arm, sir, if you feel the need."

Phillip shook his head. "Just stay beside me, lad. If I can't walk a simple path to my own house, then we'll know I'm in a sorry state indeed."

Beatrice bit her lip, but remained silent as her father straightened up and started walking toward the inn.

Phillip had let Beatrice fix his tea and help him into his bed, then he had insisted that she return with Nicholas to the fair. Nicholas offered to bring Owen home himself, but he added, "Owen will be disappointed if his aunt Beady doesn't see the bear."

Finally convinced, she agreed to start back toward the village with him.

"It was too much for Father, today. I shouldn't have allowed him to accompany us," she said as they left the inn.

"Nay, 'tis not a woman's place, or a daughter's, to rob a man of his pride," Nicholas chided gently. "You must let your father do as much as he is still able, else his soul will shrivel more quickly than his body."

"You may be right. My father is a proud man.

Once he feels he can't function, I fear 'twill be the end.'' Beatrice slowed her pace and looked at him with an expression of respect he had not seen on her face. "You hardly know my father, Master Hendry. How is it that you see this more clearly than I?"

Nicholas's gaze became unfocused. "During the Crusades I saw many men let their will to live die. In each case, the body soon followed."

They'd paused at the edge of the village in the long evening shadows of a grove of trees. The sounds of music and revelry from the fair drifted toward them, but it seemed as if they were in their own private place, hidden from view.

"You are not the man I expected you to be," Beatrice said after a long moment.

Nicholas gave a little shudder to shake off the haunting memories, then looked down at her and smiled. "Owen now calls me Papa. Mayhap his aunt should take his example and learn to call me Nicholas. Will you say it for me?"

The flickering shadows of the midsummer twilight lent an air of unreality to the scene. Beatrice's eyes were inscrutable as she paused, then moistened her lips and said, "Nicholas."

The word seemed to stir a wave inside him. He looked down, his gaze taking in the gentle swell of her bodice, the narrowness of her cinched waist. As the wave intensified, he suddenly recognized the familiar sensation. He'd not felt it for a long time, but what was washing through at the moment was unmistakably desire.

With a feeling akin to panic, he tried to tell himself that he was mistaken. He'd sworn that he was a changed man. His former self had seduced Flora and left her with a son who had caused her death. He'd vowed that such a thing would never happen again. Yet as Beatrice swayed ever so slightly closer to him in the shadows, he could not deny the feelings. He wanted Flora's sister.

Chapter Nine

Beatrice felt as if the mead they had drunk at the fair at midday was still swirling inside her head. She'd said his name, as he asked, and the mere saying of it seemed to release something deep within her. It was as if she'd surrendered a part of herself to him, as surely as if he had claimed a kiss.

He was looking at her strangely, his eyes sparkling black in the shadows. His lips were slightly parted, and his gaze was fixed on her own mouth. For a fleeting moment, she thought he *would* kiss her, then she dismissed the idea as impossible.

She laughed nervously. "Why do we stand here?" she asked. "'Tis as if we've been frozen by the wood sprites of Midsummer's Eve."

Nicholas's smile was as forced as her own. "I see only one otherworldly creature in these woods," he answered. "And she's more faerie than sprite. The faerie queen, mayhap, judging by her beauty."

His voice had gone lower, rougher. Beatrice sucked in a breath. This was how he did it, she thought, willing her reason to take hold of her quickening senses.

This was how Nicholas Hendry charmed his women until he had his way with them. This is what he had done to poor Flora.

She took a step back. "In truth, I see neither sprites, nor faeries, nor will we see the bear if we continue to stand here."

He reached out and took hold of her upper arms, preventing her from moving away. "Not a faerie then, a woman, but beautiful, nonetheless."

His gaze held hers for a long moment as she struggled once more to keep her wits. "We must go, milord."

He shook his head. "Nicholas."

"Nicholas." Her tongue caught on the word. "They'll be looking for us."

The sun had finally sunk low in the sky. A sudden breeze ruffled the trees around them and seemed to dim the distant sounds from the fair.

Nicholas bent down and plucked a bright gillyflower that had sprouted at the edge of the trees. Leaning toward her, he pushed the stem of the blossom gently into her thick hair. "I wish that you were a faerie, this night, Beatrice," he said, using her name for the first time. "And I the king of the sprites. For then we'd spend this long midsummer twilight in revels."

"I'd not—" she began.

But before she could say anything more he bent his head and put his lips on hers. It was a light, warm touch, one that might, indeed, have been bestowed by some kind of magical creature, but she felt it all the way through to her toes.

He leaned back and released her arms. "Forgive

me,'' he said at once. He looked unhappy, and she found herself wanting to comfort him.

"Mayhap there is a sprite around after all," he said. His voice still sounded odd. "'Tis said they come to earth to tempt humans into folly."

Beatrice unconsciously lifted her fingers to her lips. She could still feel his touch there. "If 'twas a sprite's folly, the creature reached us both," she said.

He looked surprised at her admission. His expression relaxed and he cocked his head. "He may still be around, the naughty imp," he said with a grin.

Relieved that the odd tension was fading, Beatrice managed a smile of her own. "Then we'd best leave this place," she said firmly.

Nicholas gave a mock sigh. "They do say that Midsummer's Eve can tinge ordinary folk with a touch of madness."

"I believe it," she said, brushing her lips once again. "Owen will be wondering what has become of us."

The mention of the child's name seemed to bring them both back to reality. "Aye," Nicholas said simply, but as they turned to leave, he took a gentle hold of her arm, and didn't let go until they reached the village.

"Aye, Flora, the brewmaster's daughter. I remember her. She was a winsome little thing." Nicholas had joined Constance in the solar where his mother was taking advantage of the bright morning sun to finish some difficult detail work on her sewing.

"You knew she died giving birth to a child?" he asked her.

Constance nodded. "No one wanted to speak of it once she was gone. It seemed cruel to besmirch the reputation of a soul departed, but I believe no lad ever came forward to claim the babe."

"The baby's mine."

Constance let out a cry as the needle pierced deep into her finger. She looked up at her son, aghast. "Yours? But you weren't even here."

"'Twas bred before I left, Mother. The boy's past three years now. His name is Owen."

Constance set her sewing on the bench beside her, then sucked at the finger she'd pricked. Nicholas knew she was weighing her words carefully. "My son, 'tis a noble impulse for you to claim this boy, if it is true that you…knew the mother, but you've been gone a long time. How can you be certain—"

"I'm certain," he interrupted. "Owen's my son."

Constance was silent.

"I'd thought you might be somewhat pleased to know that you have a grandchild, Mother."

She studied the wounded finger, squeezing it to see if the blood had stopped flowing. "'Tis, indeed, momentous news, Nicholas. But the circumstances are not ideal, as you must realize."

"Life is not ideal, Mother. But my son is as near to it as I'd ever thought possible. He's bright and loving. You'll be charmed."

"If I recall correctly, Master Thibault now has an inn."

"Aye, the Gilded Boar."

"'Tis not a likely place to raise a child."

"There's little traffic. Travelers through Hendry are

few and far between. And the boy is cared for there by his aunt.''

Something in his voice made his mother lift her head sharply. ''Of course, Beatrice. The woman you invited to dinner.''

''Aye. She came that night to discuss the matter.''

''I liked her,'' Constance said. The initial shock over Nicholas's news appeared to have passed, and his mother was digesting the matter with her usual calm.

Nicholas had declined a seat. He was anxious to be off to pay his visit to the inn, but after his appearance with Owen at the fair yesterday, he'd decided he'd better talk with his mother before she heard the tale from one of the servants.

''You'll like Owen, as well. Shall I bring him around this morning?''

Constance frowned. ''Nay, not this morning. Baron Hawse will be calling. We wouldn't want to make him suspicious.''

If Baron Hawse was calling, Nicholas would be happy to stay away, but he didn't like the implication of his mother's remark. ''You don't need to make him suspicious, you can tell him directly. Owen's paternity is no longer a secret.''

Now his mother looked concerned. ''Son, you must take some time to think about this. 'Tis a tragic thing about the girl's death, and you'll want to make discreet arrangements to provide for the child, but—''

''Mother, Owen is my son. I intend to raise him. There'll be nothing discreet about it.''

Constance pursed her lips. ''Sit down, Nicholas,''

she said after a moment. "I'm getting a sore neck looking up at you."

Impatiently, Nicholas ignored the stool she indicated and dropped to the stone floor near her knee. He should have realized that this interview might be more difficult than he had anticipated. He'd had time to adjust to the news, but this was still a shock to his mother. He reached out and took her hand. "You'll love the boy, Mother. I promise you."

Her expression was worried. "Son, Baron Hawse is coming this morning at my request. I didn't want to worry you, but he's been pressuring on this issue of the estates."

Nicholas scowled.

"He says he's willing to put his offer back on the table. About you and Winifred. It wouldn't be a good time to have a scandal arise. I'm asking you as a favor to me to keep this thing secret until we decide the best course."

"'Tis late for that. Unless you think the two hundred onlookers at the fair yestereen are likely to hold their tongues."

Constance shut her eyes and said weakly, "Oh."

Nicholas jumped up and said briskly, "Don't worry about it, Mother. I'll deal with the child and with Baron Hawse, as well. In the Holy Lands I swore that if I ever made it home again, I'd get my life in order, and I intend to do just that."

Then, before she could make any further protest, he leaned over to give her a kiss and walked quickly out of the room.

Gilbert Hawse kicked at his kneeling steward with the toe of his boot just hard enough to send him sprawling backward. "Am I to be the last person in all of England to know what goes on under my very nose?" he roared.

"'Tis said that no one knew until yesterday at the fair, milord. The girl told no one before she died." Leon straightened around and resumed his position next to the baron's chair.

"She must have told her sister and her father. Now they've told that young rapscallion, and he, in turn, has told the whole world, it would appear. 'Twas ill luck that Nicholas Hendry didn't die at the end of the heathen's spear as was reported."

Leon gave his master a sly look. "He had no one to help him along to the hereafter the way his father did."

Baron Hawse shoved the steward once more with his foot. "Hold your tongue, you flap-mouthed idiot."

Still unperturbed, Leon picked himself up again and said, "There's no one to hear us."

"I told you never again to speak of Arthur Hendry's death. The deed's done and forgotten."

"Aye, milord. But the son lives yet."

Baron Hawse retrieved a small horn painted with the image of a woman from the table beside him and held it. "Aye, Constance," he said, no longer paying any attention to the steward still crouched at his feet. "Your son lives yet. And his son as well. 'Twill be a bit more complicated than I had expected to have both you and the Hendry lands as well. But in the end this will only make the prize more precious."

He lapsed into silence. Leon waited several moments before asking, ''Would you have me get rid of the child, milord?''

The baron looked surprised to see that the steward was still at his feet. "I don't hold with murder, Leon. I've told you that before." Then, when Leon lifted an eyebrow, he amended, "At least not when there are less objectionable ways to obtain one's desires."

After the interview with his mother, Nicholas was later than usual with his morning visit to the inn. He was surprised to see Owen alone outside, riding his little hobby horse back and forth on the path to the road.

The boy gave a shout when he saw Nicholas. The stick horse clattered to the ground as he ran and threw himself into his father's arms. Nicholas lifted him into a solid hug. "Where were you riding this fine day, Sir Owen?" he asked after setting the boy back on the ground.

"Owen go on the path, not on the road," he replied, his little face looking worried.

"Nay, lad, I'm not scolding you. Did your aunt tell you that you were to stay on the path?"

"From inn to road, no more."

"Well, I shall tell her that you were following her instructions with great care." He could hear nothing of the usual morning activity from inside the inn. "But where is she?"

Once again, Owen looked concerned. "Upstairs. Gampa too sick."

Nicholas looked up at the second floor of the inn. Though it was a warm day, none of the shutters had been opened. Alarmed, he started walking toward the inn door. "I need to go see Aunt Beatrice and your Grandpa," he told the boy.

Owen's face fell. "Papa not play with me?"

"You're to come to play with Nicky this morning, Owen." Jannet Fletcher was coming at a fast pace around the corner of the inn. When she saw Nicholas, she stopped to straighten her wimple and tuck in some errant blond hairs that had escaped from underneath the headpiece. The exertion of her walk had flushed her cheeks, and for the first time Nicholas noticed with surprise that Harold's wife was pretty. His surprise was not that Harold had chosen a handsome bride, but that Nicholas had by now spent some considerable time in her company and had not even thought to notice.

"Good day, Mistress Fletcher," he said with a slight bow.

She bobbed a curtsy. "Good morrow, Sir Nicholas. I've come to collect Owen. I promised Beatrice I'd take him for the day."

Nicholas glanced again at the closed shutters. "Is something wrong?" he asked.

"'Tis Phillip. He's faring poorly."

"Gampa so sick," Owen put in.

Nicholas thought of offering to take Owen back to Hendry Hall. One day soon he intended to make it the boy's permanent home. But, as his mother had said, he did not want to run into Baron Hawse. He nodded to Jannet. "'Tis kind of you to care for him."

"Ah, 'tis no problem, he's such a good child. Less trouble than little Nick, if truth be told."

Nicholas turned to Owen. "You go with Mistress

Fletcher, Owen, and I'll come there to fetch you later in the day.''

"With Scab?"

Nicholas grinned. "Aye, on Scarab, if you like. We'll take a little ride.''

Jannet stretched out her hand for Owen to take, then turned to leave with the boy scampering beside her. Nicholas, his smile fading, walked into the inn. The taproom was empty and the place was completely quiet. After a moment's hesitation, he climbed to the second floor.

The stairway ended at a narrow passageway. On one side were two doors that led to bed chambers with multiple pallets that could be used by travelers. On the other side was one door that led to a larger room. Beatrice was seated inside next to a bed where Phillip was sleeping. When she saw him appear in the doorway, she appeared startled, then put a finger to her mouth to caution him not to speak. Then, with a quick look at her father in the bed, she rose from her seat and motioned to Nicholas to follow her downstairs.

When they reached the taproom, she said, "I'd given up expecting you today. I thought you might be busy after taking the day off for the fair.''

Her words boosted Nicholas's spirits. It sounded as if she'd been waiting for him to appear and had been disappointed when he had not. But he'd explore the meaning of that further after he found out about Phillip. "Owen says your father is sick.''

"The fair was too much for him yesterday, I trow.'' She sounded uncharacteristically weary herself. "The palsy's been worse than ever. He slept little all night.

I gave him a potion this morning, and now he's finally resting.''

"A potion?"

"Of lungwort. I picked it yesterday on Midsummer's Eve, so 'twill be specially strong.''

Nicholas deliberately tried to keep his tone light. "Do you act as apothecary, then, mistress, as well as keeping the inn, brewing the ale and caring for the child?''

He was rewarded by a brief smile from her, but her eyes were shadowed. "I learned the healing arts from the nuns who raised me,'' she explained. "But for all their power, I was not able to heal my sister. And now—'' her voice cracked "—'twould appear that I can do little to save my father, either.''

Tears welled into her eyes, and Nicholas was seized with an overwhelming desire to take her in his arms and kiss them away. Instead, he said gently, "I'm sure you bring your father great comfort, Beatrice, with both your herbs and your presence here with him. In the end, healing is in the hands of the Lord.''

She nodded. "I know. I said prayers as well, but, as Sister Agnes used to say at the convent, if the Lord's tending the garden, it doesn't hurt to help him out by pulling a few weeds now and then.'' She smiled and gave an unladylike sniff to rid herself of the tears.

"Sister Agnes sounds like a wise woman.'' The tip of her nose had grown red and her hair was tousled as though it had not yet seen a comb that morning, but to Nicholas, she looked utterly beguiling.

She took in a long breath. "Aye, she was. She's

gone now, too. Forgive me, Master Hendry, for burdening you with my problems.''

Nicholas reached out and held her chin with his fingers. ''You've hardly burdened me. And I'd thought, as of yesterday, we were on less formal terms, you and I.'' She blushed, obviously thinking of their brief kiss, but he continued, ''You were to call me Nicholas.''

She stepped away from his hand and walked past him over to the fireplace at the far end of the room. The fire was banked, so she began to stir it with a poker. ''Aye, I'll try to remember, though I have to tell you, Nicholas, I never thought to be calling you by your Christian name.''

Nicholas walked up behind her and said with a twist of humor, ''You never thought to be calling me anything less than a varlet, I trow.''

She gave a low laugh, and Nicholas was surprised to realize how good it made him feel that he had been able to lift her spirits and take her thoughts away from her worry, if only for a moment. He reached into the woodbin and picked up a couple of small logs to throw on the nearly dead fire.

''Thank you,'' she said in acknowledgement.

''Do you have enough wood? Would you like me to fetch more?''

She looked around at him in surprise. ''I'd not ask you to be doing menial tasks.''

''Why not? You need the help with your father unwell. Owen's a willing lad, but he's still a mite wee to be of much use.''

''I'd thought of asking Harold Fletcher for some help. Or one of the village lads.''

Nicholas shook his head, picked up the woodbin and emptied the remaining logs on the fire. "Nay, put me to work. Mayhap I'll convince you that far from being a varlet, I'm actually a useful fellow at times."

She hesitated, her expression skeptical. "You'd not do this kind of menial work in your own home."

"Perhaps not, but I can assure you, I did far worse than this on the road to Damietta, and I believe I'm none the worse for it."

Their faces were only inches apart. The heat from the new logs' initial flare wafted up between their bodies.

"If you're serious…" Beatrice began.

"I've never been more so," Nicholas replied firmly.

"Then I accept your offer of help."

Nicholas grinned. "Good. What should I do?"

Beatrice still looked doubtful as she asked slowly, "Have you ever brewed a batch of ale?"

Chapter Ten

By midafternoon, Nicholas's back ached from picking barley off the malting floor, his tunic reeked of fermented grain, his eyes stung from the pungent steam of the boiling mash and the palms of his hands burned from handling the hot kettles as he added in the hops.

"I may never drink another jug of ale in my life," he told Beatrice with a smile as she came to check on his progress. She'd been back and forth between the inn and the brewing shed. Phillip was up and feeling better, but she hadn't allowed him to try to descend the steep inn stairs.

"I've watched my father brew ale my entire life," she said. "Yet I never realized how much work it is until lately when he's been unable to keep up with the job. He used to take half a dozen barrels to Ryminster every month, since there's no brewer there, but this past year we've only been able to produce enough for Hendry."

Her tone was matter-of-fact. She didn't appear to be looking for sympathy, but nevertheless Nicholas felt an odd kind of protectiveness. Growing up as an only child, he'd never really had to consider the needs of anyone other than himself. But since arriving home, he'd had his mother's welfare to think of, then his son's. It was an odd sensation, but not entirely unpleasant.

"Can your barmaid be of help?"

"Aye, when she's not needed by her own family."

"Is there no man from the village you could hire to help your father?"

Beatrice hesitated a long moment. The relaxed manner she had adopted with him during the afternoon disappeared as she said stiffly, "When Father decided to open an inn, your father's steward doubled our rent taxes. But of course, we don't have enough paying visitors at the inn to cover the amount. Nor did the inn double the sales of father's brew, though the ale license was doubled as well. In the end, the inn has cost him dear, but he loves it."

Nicholas frowned and rubbed his leg, which had gone stiff from the crouching and bending of the brewing process. "Did your father not appeal the raised rent?"

"Aye. 'Twas of no avail. And then Flora died and my father was busy trying to keep his business running while dealing with his own grief and mine and serving as father to a fatherless grandson. All this while his palsy grows worse each day."

"He's not had an easy time of it. Yet he is the same positive spirit I remember from before I left. 'Tis the same spirit I found so appealing in Flora. She was ever sunny, no matter the clouds in her life."

Beatrice gave a sad smile at the memory. "Aye.

She and I were different that way. Flora could never see the bad in anything nor anyone. While I have oft been accused of going out of my way to look for trouble with my infernal temper.''

''That same temper that causes you to greet strangers by spitting in their faces?'' he asked ruefully.

Beatrice scuffed the toe of her slipper in the dirt floor of the shed. ''Aye. The very same.''

She lifted her eyes to his. Even in the shadows, the blue was bright as an autumn sky. Nicholas's palm grew sweaty where it rubbed the rough fabric of his tunic. He pulled his hand away and, before he realized what he was doing, raised it to her cheek. ''You thought me a monster, as you yourself termed it. I hold you to no blame.''

''Thank you,'' she said, her voice growing husky.

Her cheek was smooth as alabaster under his rough fingers. He let his hand stroke upward into the thick waves of her hair. It was surprisingly warm and soft. She appeared to be holding her breath.

''Mayhap in return, you'll not blame me for this.'' He lowered his head and took her mouth with his own. This was not a brief kiss like they had shared the other day on the way to the fair. This time his lips opened hers and sought something deeper within, liquid and magic. He willed her to feel as he was feeling, melted and needy.

On Crusade, he'd occasionally tended to the baser instincts of his body with women of the trade. But this sweeping away of the senses was something different. This he had not felt for years, perhaps never.

The sour odor of mash and yeast that permeated the shed seemed to fade as he suddenly tasted and smelled only her, the sweetness of her lips, the lavender scent of her hair. He pulled his lips free long enough to groan, "Ah, Beatrice," then joined their mouths again as her arms crept around him, tentative at first, then firm.

He pressed his own arms against the back of her waist, moving her against his body, which had hardened the instant their lips met. He lifted her slightly off the ground as her softness nestled against him.

He moved his mouth from her lips to her delicate chin, and then to the side of her neck, just below her ear. A murmur from the back of her throat told him that he had found a sensitive spot, so he teased it a little with his tongue. This was familiar territory to him—a warm and willing woman, soft and pliable in his arms. Distantly, like a faraway call, his conscience was calling him to slow down, to pull away, but he refused to answer. He could feel his body preparing to continue the tender assault.

It was she who pulled away finally. Her head had fallen back and his mouth had sought the tender skin at the base of her throat, when suddenly she clenched at his arms and said, "No!"

He released her at once and stepped back, the wanting still thrumming through his midsection. "Forgive me," he said.

She crossed her arms and held them tightly as if trying to stop herself from shaking, but she met his eyes. After a moment she said, "'Twas not your fault alone."

She looked so miserable, all remaining desire drained out of him. Contritely, he said, "We need not talk of fault. We simply shared a few kisses. 'Tis a common enough occurrence between a man and a maid.''

"Not between a maid and her sister's lover." Beatrice's tone was caustic, but Nicholas suspected that at the root of her harshness was shame. He tried to think of something that would relieve her, but he was feeling none too proud of his actions himself. He'd sworn, sworn on the holy battlefields of the Crusades, that if God willed him to return to England, he would give up all wanton behavior and lead an exemplary life.

"'Twas only a kiss, Beatrice," he said weakly. His words seemed to do little to soothe her ill humor.

"Aye," she said, backing away from him. "So if you've had enough amusement for the afternoon, I'll see to my father."

Her voice was strong and steady, but her trembling hands betrayed her agitation. "Wait!" he called to her as she reached the door of the shed.

She paused, and he searched frantically for a topic to keep her from running away with this thing unresolved between them. "I'd like to talk to you about your rents. I plan to see that they are lowered."

Beatrice froze and looked as if he had slapped her.

Nicholas realized at once that he had chosen the wrong approach. "If 'tis true that they were unjustly raised—" he began.

She suddenly seemed to grow in height as she straightened and stalked back toward him. "I imagine it has been your custom, Nicholas Hendry, to entice your *women* with all manner of payments, but I'm sorry to disappoint you. I'm not for sale, and, if I were, I'd sooner sell my body to Beelzebub himself than to you.''

"You mistook my—'' Nicholas let his voice trail off without completing the sentence. Beatrice was already gone.

More than likely, she'd been overly hard on the man, Beatrice had decided by the end of the day. And on herself, as well.

Owen was tucked away in his bed, sleeping soundly after his day of playing with little Nick. Phillip, too, had fallen into a restless doze. She'd insisted that he occupy her pallet in the same room with Owen so that she could keep watch over them both. She herself would bed down on the floor by the fire, that is if she decided to sleep at all.

For the past hour she'd sat staring at the flames, the warmth on her cheeks reminding her again and again of the kisses she'd shared with Nicholas in the brewing shed, of the heat of his flat, hard body against hers and the sensual trail of his lips along her neck. She shuddered, cold and hot all at once. She'd not known such sensations existed.

A log cracked in the fire and her father stirred, but stayed asleep. She knew that she should lie down and make an attempt to sleep herself. Tomorrow would dawn soon and with much to be done, as usual. But her mind and her body still raced too fast for drowsiness.

It was just as well that she'd treated him so rudely, she told herself. Perhaps now he would make his visits to the inn less frequent. From all accounts, Nicholas Hendry was a man used to having his way with women. Now that he'd seen she would not be the next one to fall under his spell, perhaps he'd give up the idea of somehow becoming a father to Owen and stay away altogether.

But somehow she knew that he would not give up that easily—either fatherhood or…the other.

Now that he knew about Owen, she could not keep him from coming to visit the boy, and, if she admitted the truth to herself, life had become much more stimulating since Nicholas Hendry began his daily visits. That was what was really keeping her from sleep this night. Even before the kisses he had bestowed on her that afternoon, it was becoming obvious that if she wasn't careful, the charming master of Hendry Hall would soon number two Thibault sisters among his conquests.

With a grimace of disgust, she stood, pulled a crushed gillyflower from inside her bodice and hurled it into the fire.

"'Twill do you no harm to visit with Winifred, Nicholas," his mother said firmly. "Baron Hawse has been generous in allowing you time to reaccustom yourself to life at home before he pushed the matter again. But the problem is not going to resolve itself."

"There would be no problem to resolve if the baron would simply agree that the deathbed papers are no longer valid since I did not die abroad as my father thought." Nicholas tried to keep the impatience out of his voice. It was unfair to blame his mother for his father's actions, but he wished she didn't always seem to be championing the baron's cause.

They were waiting in the great hall for the baron

and Winifred to arrive. Nicholas was most definitely not in the mood for the meeting. He had little desire to see anyone, but in particular he was not looking forward to spending the evening trying to carry on a conversation with Baron Hawse's shy mouse of a daughter.

The castle retainers were milling about the room, waiting to be seated until the guests of honor arrived. Nicholas recognized Mollie and gave her a wink. For just a moment, he wished that he were a youth again, when his only preoccupation was which pretty maid he'd choose to share his flirtatious games for the evening. He'd thought nothing of estate matters and fatherhood and responsibility. 'Twas no wonder his father had regretted ever producing such a son.

He'd not known in those carefree days, that such a woman as Beatrice could exist—a woman who combined intelligence, competence and spirit, and could yet make him forget those attributes and every other vestige of sense when their bodies came into close proximity. Would it have made a difference if he had met Beatrice back then?

He sighed. Perhaps it was as his father had said and he'd been born without virtues. It had been wrong for him to kiss Beatrice. He'd loved her sister and left her with child. What woman could forgive a thing like that?

"My dear Constance!" Baron Hawse's voice boomed across the room. Nicholas's mood turned gloomier as he noticed how the sound of it seemed to make his mother's face brighten.

She moved toward the visitors, her hand extended. The baron bent to kiss it, holding it quite a bit longer than necessary. Then he turned to Nicholas. "Well, lad, your mother tells me you've decided to stay in England for the time being after all."

Nicholas nodded, shook the baron's hand and turned politely to Winifred, who had ducked her head and was scraping first one foot, then the other. She looked like a nervous serving girl, Nicholas thought. When he reached for her cold hand to bring it to his mouth in the European fashion, she shrank back and blushed painfully. Nicholas regretted the gesture at once, but took her hand and lifted it quickly to his face before releasing it without letting his lips touch her.

Baron Hawse frowned at the couple, and barked, "Straighten up, Winifred. You look like a servant bowing your head like that."

Winifred lifted her eyes to Nicholas's face, the misery at her father's words obvious. Nicholas felt immediately ashamed, since he had had the exact same thought. In reality, the girl was not so uncomely, he decided. The blush actually favored her, giving her pale skin some color and making her soft blue eyes seem brighter.

He tried to think of some way to take the sting from her father's words. "By the saints, baron, most fathers would be pleased to have such a daughter—both modest and *pretty*."

The baron stared at his daughter as though she had suddenly sprouted horns, but recovered quickly and said, "Of course, she's a fine daughter, though she tends to the quiet. Which most men would consider a virtue in a wife, hey?" He gave Nicholas's shoulder a slap.

Constance cleared her throat. "Shall we sit down to sup? The roast will be cooling."

Nicholas turned to Winifred and nodded toward the dais at the end of the room, but carefully refrained from touching her as she moved ahead of him to take her place at the big table.

Winifred held tight to Nicholas's arm as they made their way across the rough courtyard to the Hendry stables. She had either gotten over her resistance to any contact with him or she was too worried about ruining her slippers in the muck of the stableyard to refuse his assistance.

The dinner had seemed as interminable as he had feared. She had answered all his questions with one or two words. It had only been at the end of their conversation that he had seen some sign of animation in her. Baron Hawse had asked how he had come by his current mount.

As he had recounted the tale of obtaining Scarab in the Holy Lands, Winifred had sat up straighter on her bench and there'd been a sparkle of interest in her eyes.

"Winifred likes horses," the baron said, "though she hasn't the gumption to ride them. She's inherited her mother's timidness, I fear." His glance at his daughter was disdainful.

"I like horses, too," Nicholas told her gently. "Would you like to visit Scarab when we finish the meal?"

Winifred had agreed and, to Nicholas's relief, the baron and his mother had declined to accompany them. The girl seemed much more relaxed when not in her father's company.

"'Tis true, then? You are fond of horses?" he asked her.

She met his gaze, her face alight. "Aye. I spend time in the stables. When my father's not around, the stable boys let me help with the grooming."

"But you don't ride?"

"Nay. I simply like being with them." She hesitated as if wondering if she should reveal something of her private self, then she said, "Sometimes I talk to them."

Nicholas grinned. "Do they answer you?" But he was immediately sorry for the joke when he saw the girl's embarrassment.

They were at the door to the stable. He stopped and grasped her shoulders to turn her to face him. "I talk to Scarab, too. All the time."

She looked up at him in amazement. "Truly?"

"Aye. What's more, during the Crusades I'd be willing to swear that there was a time or two when he *did* answer me."

Winifred laughed at that, and the sound of it was pleasant, almost musical. He smiled down at her. "You should laugh more often, Winifred. It makes your face bloom like a lovely rose."

She blushed, but this time she did not immediately lower her eyes. "You are a very nice man, Nicholas of Hendry," she said.

He released her shoulders and stepped back. The words lifted his spirits, but made his thoughts go immediately to Beatrice. *She* would have some argument with Winifred's soft-spoken statement.

She seemed to sense his change of mood. "You need not worry that I'm trying to convince you to accede to my father's wishes. I've no desire to wed you."

Her bluntness took Nicholas aback. "Why not?" he said, before he could help himself.

She smiled briefly. "I've met no man nicer or who has put me more at ease, but I'm not yet ready to wed any man. Mayhap I never shall be."

Nicholas weighed his words more carefully this time. "Winifred, I think the time will come when you will be ready, and the one who wins you will be a lucky man."

Her gaze did not waver. "And the one you choose will be a lucky woman, Nicholas."

They looked at each other in silent companionship for a long moment, then Nicholas turned his gaze to the western sky. "'Twill be dark, soon. Let's go talk to Scarab, and see if he has any advice for us about dealing with your father's matchmaking schemes."

Chapter Eleven

Nicholas was surprised to discover that the hour he and Winifred spent at the stables put him in a much better humor. The girl was more relaxed than he'd ever seen her. She insisted on being "introduced" to each horse in the stable, and then proceeded to talk with the animals as if they were human.

Without her father there to monitor and criticize her every mood, she began to speak freely and even to laugh at some of Nicholas's quips. Earlier, he'd been trying to be kind when he'd told her that her future husband would be a lucky man, but by the end of the evening, he realized that he had spoken the truth. He suspected that if Winifred could free herself from her father's domination, she could be a bright and even merry young woman.

But as soon as they rejoined his mother and Baron Hawse in the solar, her demeanor changed. His pleasant companion of the past hour disappeared and the timorous girl was back.

His mother changed, too, in Baron Hawse's presence. She did not appear intimidated by him the way

Winifred did, but she seemed to lose some of her usual serenity.

All in all, Nicholas decided, it would have been better if Baron Hawse would have no more to do with Hendry, but, of course, that was not likely to occur, as the baron himself had reminded Nicholas at his departure.

"'Tis time for us to have a discussion about how to combine the Hendry lands with the Hawse holdings," he said curtly, when Constance was occupied saying her farewells to Winifred.

"I believe the estate is managing just fine," Nicholas replied.

"'Tis no criticism of your management, boy. It's just that now that the mourning for your father is passing, we should see that his wishes are carried out."

Nicholas stiffened, but preferred not to engage his guest in an argument. "I'm willing to discuss the matter, baron, but not while the ladies are present."

"I'll send my steward to arrange a convenient time."

Shortly thereafter the Hawses left, and Constance retired to her room. Nicholas lingered for a time outside, watching the spectacular array of summer stars begin to fill the darkening sky. He had a sudden memory of sitting on the deck of the ship back from the Holy Lands, watching a darkening sky with his comrades-in-arms.

They'd had high expectations for their homecoming. After all, they were heroes returning from the Holy Crusade. But in Durleigh, Simon had been met with stunning news and treachery. Nicholas had come home to find himself a father and much of his world changed. Bernard was undoubtedly still recovering from the broken leg he had suffered during the skirmish outside of Durleigh. He wondered how Gervase, Guy and Hugh were faring.

When the night began to grow chill, he went inside and walked up the steep stairs to his bedchamber where he pushed the tallow-dipped reed he carried into a wall holder. It would burn for awhile longer before the room would be plunged into darkness. He hoped by then he would be asleep, hoped that this would not be one of the nights when his memories of black, rotting corpses at the siege of Damietta or the nagging ache in his leg would keep him awake until nearly dawn.

He lay on his pallet, not bothering to undress, and closed his eyes, remembering Winifred's face as she'd approached Scarab. She'd had the same look as Owen when Nicholas handed him a sweetcake. The usually high-strung horse had stood still as a lamb and let her stroke him.

He'd offered to take her for a short ride before sundown, but she'd refused.

"I don't ride horses," she'd said, with a nervous little laugh. "They're just my friends."

She was a strange girl in some ways, he decided, but sweet, and not as fainthearted as he had thought her at first.

The candle on the wall sputtered, but sleep wouldn't come. He opened his eyes and stared at the ceiling, remembering the baron's parting words. The showdown was approaching. If he wanted Hendry, for himself and for Owen, he'd have to fight for it. Or accept the baron's offer of marriage to his daughter. The prospect was not as disagreeable as he had first thought it. It would allow him to continue to manage Hendry and it would make his mother happy.

He closed his eyes once again and finally let his mind fill with the vision he'd been avoiding all evening—the vision of Beatrice, her lips swollen from his kisses and her eyes wide in the first stages of passion. His body hardened at the mere memory.

In a sudden moment of clarity, he realized that marriage to Winifred of Hawse was not possible for one simple reason. He was in love with another woman.

"His mother is too much under his influence. She's not been as receptive to me since his return." Baron Hawse was grumbling more to himself than to Leon, who'd been standing patiently in the baron's bedchamber for the past quarter of an hour while the baron, sitting on the edge of his bed, mulled over different approaches to dealing with Constance's stubborn son.

"'Tis unlikely that marrying him to Winifred would lessen his influence," Leon said.

The baron looked up, his expression dark. "Nay, 'twould merely put him underfoot for the rest of my life. Blast the boy for coming back to Hendry."

"'Tis his home. Where else would he go?" Leon asked. Everything about the Hawse Castle steward was unremarkable. He was of medium stature, medium build, ordinary features. It was impossible to tell if his hair had once been black or blond or if it had always been its current dull gray. His nearly gray eyes seldom showed expression. He was a man who had been underestimated by just about everyone, which had made him one of Gilbert Hawse's most valuable servants.

The baron shook his head. "Hendry's supposed to be mine now, and I'm beginning to see that it will be a constant struggle to keep it so while Nicholas remains here."

Leon stood without shifting, showing no sign of weariness from being kept standing for so long. "Then we'll have to deal with him after all?" A glint of satisfaction lit his gray eyes for an instant, but was gone before anyone could have noted it.

Hawse looked up at his steward. "It would break Constance's heart. Could it be made into an accident?"

"Of course."

The baron passed several moments lost in thought. Finally he said, "I've another idea. We'll try this course first." He told Leon of his plan.

Leon's face was inscrutable. "Whatever you say, milord."

Baron Hawse stood to pull back his covers, then dropped heavily onto the bed. Leon waited.

"You may go," the baron told him. "But come again first thing in the morning. I think 'tis time for you to pay a visit to Nicholas's bastard brat."

Beatrice held the door to the inn and looked out at the nondescript man who was paying such an early call. "I'm Leon, steward to Baron Hawse, your liege lord," he said without expression.

"The Hendrys are lords of this village," she answered curtly. She was not in the mood for pranks.

She'd had another night of little sleep. When she'd not been up to check on her father's labored breathing, she'd been tossing on her makeshift pallet by the fire and thinking about Nicholas Hendry and the brewing shed.

"Nay, they are not any longer. Baron Hawse is the new lord here."

She shook her head, trying to clear her wits. "By whose authority?"

"'Tis not your place to question, mistress. I've come to speak with your father."

"My father is ill. You'll deal with me or not at all."

The man peered over her shoulder. "Very well," he said. "We'll talk inside." Then he walked past her into the taproom. He appeared to be examining the room. "Where's the little boy?" he asked.

Beatrice was beginning to grow alarmed. She didn't know who this man was, but he had the air of someone who knew that he had the right to be obeyed. What did he want of her? And what did he know of Owen? For the first time she considered that it might have been a mistake for her to allow Owen's connection to the Hendrys be known.

"What exactly is your business here, sir?" she asked sharply.

Leon strolled over to the staircase and looked up toward the second floor. "You say your father is ill? What's the matter with him?"

"I don't intend to answer any questions until you state your purpose in being here."

"Baron Hawse likes to become familiar with all his tenants. He'll want to know what ails your father.

And how the boy is faring with no father to care for him.'' He glanced at her out of the corner of his eyes. ''The baron makes it his business to know these things about his people.''

Vaguely, Beatrice recalled that at the time of Arthur Hendry's death, there had been rumors that the estate had been deeded to a nobleman from another district, but when nothing had changed in the management of the estate, she'd discounted the tale.

''What proof have you that Baron Hawse is the new lord of Hendry?'' she asked.

''You'll see the proof soon enough when the Baron's men begin collecting the rents a month hence. 'Twould seem that the Gilded Boar payments have oft come past due.''

There was no denying the man's air of authority, nor that he was familiar with the inn's financial affairs. But that didn't give him the right to question her about Owen.

''If the rents are due within a month, we shall pay them,'' she said. ''And if that concludes your business here, I'd ask you to allow me to return to my father. He'll be wanting help to rise from his bed.''

Leon walked toward her and, for the first time, smiled. His expression made a shiver go down Beatrice's back. ''So your father is ill enough to be bedridden? My dear, 'tis tragic to see a comely woman like yourself without a male to protect her.''

''My father's condition is a temporary one.''

Leon regarded her for a long moment, his gray eyes looking suddenly like a wolf's. ''You'd do well to look for another protector before his condition becomes permanent, mistress.''

This time the shiver reached all the way to her toes, but she drew herself up and said, "I protect myself, sir. I need no one to do it for me."

Leon took two quick strides to bring himself directly in front of her. She stood with her back to one of the trestle tables, her hands gripping the wood behind her. He was so close, she could smell the breakfast ale on his breath.

"I'd heard you were a spirited one, Mistress Thibault. By good fortune, 'tis exactly the way Baron Hawse likes his women. Perhaps I should test for myself to see if you might be worth his attention."

Suddenly he lunged toward her, grabbing the back of her neck with his right hand and her breast with his left. He bent her backward over the table with his body and moved to kiss her.

After a moment when she was too startled to react, she began to struggle, pulling her head from his grasp and turning it so that his mouth landed on her ear instead of her lips.

She fought the instinct to cry out, not wanting her father to hear. If he tried to come down the steps to her aid, he would surely injure himself.

The steward took hold of her hair, wrestling her head back into position for his kiss. The lower part of his body pressed on hers, pushing her legs painfully against the edge of the table.

Desperately, Beatrice pounded at the man's back with her one free hand. He seemed not to notice the blows.

"What's going on here?" a voice boomed from the doorway.

With immense relief, she recognized Nicholas.

Leon dropped his hold on her head and moved a few inches away from her. "'Tis none of your affair, Hendry," he said calmly. "This is between Mistress Thibault and myself."

Nicholas stalked across the room, put his hand on Leon's shoulder and shoved him backward with all his might. The steward took a step back, then regained his balance. "Are you all right?" Nicholas asked Beatrice.

She rubbed her upper arms where Leon had held them. "Aye," she said. "But I'm glad to see you."

Nicholas looked from her to Leon. "If you ever touch this lady again, you'll answer to me."

Leon appeared unperturbed. "The lady is no longer your tenant, Master Hendry. I came here at the request of Baron Hawse, who is her rightful liege."

Beatrice could tell from the look on Nicholas's face that the steward's words bothered him. "Is it true?" she asked him. "Are you no longer lord of Hendry?"

"There are matters yet to be decided," he answered, obviously annoyed. "But no matter who your landlord is, this worm has no right to molest you in this way."

Leon gave one of his cold smiles. "You're mistaken, Hendry. 'Twas the lady who offered. I merely decided to accept."

Beatrice gasped in outrage, but before she could say anything, Nicholas drew back his fist and smashed it against the steward's thick chin. It was a shattering blow, but Leon hardly moved.

Nicholas was about to repeat the action when suddenly the steward gave a sideways kick of his leg against Nicholas's leg and the knight went crashing to the floor. Beatrice looked on in astonishment. She looked frantically around the room for some kind of weapon, but Leon dusted his hands together, stepped over Nicholas's legs and walked toward the door.

"We'll continue this discussion at a later date, my dear," he said to Beatrice. "As for you, Hendry. You'd do well to remember your position in this shire. You live at Hendry Hall on my lord's sufferance."

Then he turned and left the inn before either Beatrice or Nicholas had a chance to reply.

Nicholas sat in stunned silence. Somehow the steward had managed to strike a deadly blow exactly at the point of his old wound. The pain had made him crumple immediately, and still came in great throbbing waves, momentarily robbing him of speech.

Beatrice stood bracing herself against the table, but after a moment she straightened up, shakily, and adjusted her overgown. She could still feel the imprint of Leon's hand against her breast. For a moment, she thought she was going to be sick to her stomach, but she swallowed heavily and fought back the sensation.

She looked down at Nicholas. His face was distorted with pain. It must be his old wound, she decided, since the Hawse steward had not used any kind of weapon.

After their devastating meeting in the brewing shed yesterday, she had hoped to be able to avoid Nicholas Hendry for awhile. She'd lain awake in the predawn planning how she would help her father get settled downstairs and leave him to greet the knight when he came for his visit with Owen. But things had not gone quite as planned. And she'd never been able to over-look suffering on any human's face.

"Are you able to move?" she asked him.

He nodded and said, "'Tis nothing. Just give me a moment." But his voice was strained.

She reached her hands toward him and said, "Hold tight."

After a moment's hesitation, he took hold and let her pull him upright. Once he was on his feet, he regained his balance and gave a forced laugh. "You'd never believe I fought in the Holy Lands after that display of valor, would you?"

Beatrice sniffed in disdain. "Women are much less concerned with displays of valor than men think they are, Nicholas. In truth, we care little for the subject and would be just as happy if our men would find better ways to occupy their time."

This made Nicholas grin. The pain was subsiding and he could stand normally on two feet. Soon he'd be able to ignore the ache entirely. He'd been through this before. But as his own pain ebbed, he was aware that Beatrice herself was still shaking. "Are you all right?" he asked, his smile fading.

She nodded. "'Twas fortunate you arrived when you did."

"What was he doing here?"

She looked at him sternly. "I know not. Mayhap you know more of the matter than I, Master Hendry. What is this about Baron Hawse being our new landlord?"

Nicholas rubbed his leg. "'Tis a business matter. I thought the baron was giving me time, but now it appears that I must get this thing settled at once."

"'Twould seem so. Rents are due in a month."

"I care little about the rents," Nicholas said. "But I'll not have the baron sending his steward around to molest my tenants. He has no right to do so, even if he is the liege lord."

Beatrice rolled her eyes. "You've been away from home for a long time, Master Hendry. Perhaps you forget how things are in England. Landlords and their retainers have the right to do anything they please. 'Tis the tenants who have no rights."

Nicholas frowned. "'Tis not as it should be."

Beatrice's expression had turned hard. Instead of the flushed, flesh-and-blood woman he'd held in his arms the previous day, she was once again the haughty beauty who had taken his breath away the first time he'd glimpsed her. "Forgive me if I feel that you, of all people, are a poor one to be championing that cause."

They both knew that her implication was unfair. Nicholas had never taken advantage of his tenants in the way Leon had just attempted. His relationship with Flora had been nothing at all like that. However, he *had* been the son of the lord and Flora *had* been his tenant. Beatrice had a right to her bitterness.

He searched for a reply, but Beatrice had already moved past him toward the stairs. "Sit on that bench and don't move until I come down," she said.

Her tone was so much like a mother scolding a naughty child, that it brought a smile back to Nicholas's lips. "Aye, Mum," he said and dropped with some relief onto the bench, his bad leg straight out in front of him.

She paused at the bottom of the stairs, evidently

realizing that she'd barked the order. She smiled briefly, then said, "I need to attend to my father and Owen. Then it will be your turn, Master Hendry."

"My turn?" Nicholas was puzzled.

She gave a determined nod. "Aye. I intend to see to that troublesome leg of yours." Then she turned and hurried up the stairs.

She was gone nearly an hour, but Nicholas didn't move from the bench. For one thing, his leg still throbbed. But mostly he stayed because he wanted to see her again, to hear her voice, to assure himself that she suffered no ill effects from the morning's misadventure. His rage returned every time he thought about the scene he had witnessed upon his arrival at the inn—Leon pressing her back against the table. He'd like to wring the steward's thick neck, though legally he could do little. Beatrice was right, tenants had virtually no rights over landlords. It was not uncommon for the lord or his steward or bailiff to be the first to deflower a comely village maid, and the families could do nothing about it.

He'd just spent four years trying to wrest the Holy Lands from the rule of heathens and put them under the control of good Christians, yet now that he was back in his own land, he wondered if the real enemy was not a race of people but rather the injustice that was as rampant in England as anywhere else on earth.

Nicholas expected to hear Owen clattering down the stairs along with Beatrice, but she was alone. "I told Owen he had to play upstairs and take care of his grandpa," she explained. "Father is sitting up and doing well this morning. I'll take them up a tray of breakfast and be down directly.''

This time she disappeared for only a few minutes before he heard her steps on the stairs. When she appeared, she was carrying a white linen pouch. Her face looked tired in the harsh morning light and Nicholas once again felt that uncharacteristic wave of protectiveness. She was all alone to care for an infirm man and a young child. And now she wanted to take on the problem of his old wound as well. He struggled to stand, determined not to look like an invalid.

"If everything's fine here," he said, "I'll take my leave and come back to see Owen later in the day."

She gave him one of her piercing stares. "You're not going anywhere until I've seen that wound. Now that you've managed to make your visits the thing Owen most looks forward to each day, I'll not have you dropping dead on us."

Her tone was contentious, but the words gave Nicholas a warm glow. He kept his expression neutral and said, "As you will."

"Can you walk?" she asked, her voice still cold.

He nodded.

"Then follow me."

She led him back through the taproom and the pantry to the room at the rear of the inn where Phillip had slept before Beatrice moved him up to her own bed.

"Lie down here," she said, indicating the pallet that took up most of the tiny chamber.

Nicholas felt ill at ease as the realization dawned that showing Beatrice his wound would involve intimacies he would not normally have shared with a maiden, that is, unless it was for purposes far removed from nursing.

But Beatrice did not seem embarrassed as he sat on the bed and looked up at her uncertainly. "You'll have to remove your hose," she said briskly. "I'm going to fetch a stool." She laid the pouch on the end of the bed and left the room, returning shortly with a low wooden seat which she set down close to the bed. Nicholas had not moved.

"I'm a healer, not a sorcerer, Master Hendry," she said. "I can't tend your wound if I can't see it."

"'Tis not a pleasant sight."

"Festering sores are rarely pleasant to look upon. 'Tis not my purpose to enjoy myself."

In spite of her matter-of-fact tone, he was reluctant to undress in front of her. Her manner was impersonal, like any healer, but he was sure that she remembered as vividly as he that only the day before he'd been kissing her.

Finally he lay back on the pallet and rather awkwardly stripped off the wool hose and short breeches he wore underneath his tunic and surcoat, leaving his body exposed from the waist down. He pulled the tunic down to cover his private parts, but Beatrice's eyes were on the puffy red gash that extended the length of his thigh. Where it ended just above the knee, the wound gaped open. A trickle of blood had started down his leg.

She sucked in a breath. "How long has it been like this?"

Nicholas shrugged. "Months. It seems to heal, then something happens to start it up again. The last time was in Durleigh." He stopped. It would do his cause

with her no good to go into the matter of the widow
who had caused him to delay in Durleigh after the
knights' return, even though the woman's attentions
had been totally unsolicited.

"Well, you've reopened it. This blood is fresh."
She reached into her pouch and pulled out a roll of
torn linen. Pulling off a piece, she wiped the blood
from the lower part of his leg, then she dabbed gently
at the wound itself. Nicholas winced. "The baron's
steward did part of our work by cracking it apart,"
she continued, pressing a soft hand on his upper thigh
where the wound was closed, but swollen and an angry red color. "'Twill make it easier to open the rest
of it."

Nicholas's mouth dropped. "Open it?"

"Aye. 'Tis full of poisons. We need to root them
out and pack it with marjoram. That will let it heal
clean this time."

The thought of someone deliberately opening the
wound he'd been battling for so long gave him a sudden urge to turn over the side of the bed and lose his
breakfast, but as he did not want to appear a total
coward, he said meekly, "Are you sure you know
what you're doing?"

She nodded, paying little attention to his sudden
pallor, and went about preparing herself for the duty.
She pulled a small bone knife from her pouch and
tore off several more strips of linen. Then, while
Nicholas averted his eyes, she proceeded to open and
clean out the wound. The treatment stung, but her
hands were so gentle and quick that the whole process
was finished quickly and, to Nicholas's amazement,
with very little pain.

"We'll dress it again on the morrow," she said. "And the next day after that. Then it will stay tightly bound for a week. If we're lucky, when we remove that binding, the redness will be gone and 'twill finally begin to heal correctly. You should be comfortable meanwhile. I've added herbs that will numb the pain."

Nicholas shook his head in wonder. "The only other nurse I've had was my fellow knight, Bernard, who helped me just after I was wounded. By the time he finished with me, I had fainted from the pain."

"Women are better at bearing pain than men," Beatrice said, putting away her healing supplies.

Nicholas fought his annoyance. She had as well called him a baby, but his leg already felt worlds better and he was grateful. He also was once again conscious that he was lying in front of her half-naked.

"I'm in your debt, mistress," he said.

"Aye," she agreed, to his surprise. She stood and picked up the bag and the stool. "You may dress, but have a care not to move the bandage. You're to come again on the morrow to have it changed." She started to leave the room.

"Wait," he said, sitting up on the bed. When she paused, he asked her with an attempt at his usual smile, "How would you like me to pay my debt, mistress?"

"I haven't decided," she said. Then she was gone.

Chapter Twelve

"I think you should take Owen and go to York," Phillip said, his voice full of concern.

After Nicholas had departed, Beatrice had helped Phillip walk down the stairs, but had insisted that he sit without stirring while she cleaned the taproom. There was little to do, for they'd had few customers since the Midsummer's Eve fair. The inn had been her father's dream, but with few overnight travelers, the Boar served mostly as an outlet for sales of Phillip Thibault's ale. When there was a drop in demand for the ale, the inn revenues suffered. Beatrice wondered if her father, too, was wondering how they were to pay the rents that were due the following month.

"I'll not leave you to manage the inn by yourself, Father," she said firmly. "I'll not run off just because of some ruttish estate manager."

"If you'll not think about yourself, what about Owen?" Phillip argued. "You say this man asked specifically about the boy. No doubt that means that Baron Hawse knows all about Owen's connection to Nicholas Hendry."

Beatrice put the stick broom in its place beside the chimney and turned to her father. "Owen has nothing to do with the squabbles of noblemen," she said. "He's our child—yours and mine."

"He's Nicholas Hendry's child, and we'll never be able to forget that."

She walked over to her father and kissed his cheek. Phillip's ailment seemed to go in cycles, and she hoped that they were now entering a good cycle that would last a long time. In spite of all her healing arts, she'd been able to do little to help him, but her instincts told her one thing. Her father would stay healthier for a longer time if he could continue living in Hendry and running his inn. If she took him away to live closeted in a tiny room in the city, his decline would be sure and quick.

"I'm not as afraid of Owen's high connections as I was once. I believe I can manage Nicholas Hendry."

Phillip smiled. "There's little you can't manage, Beatrice, but even you can't change the rules under which we live. And those rules say that the rich usually get what they want."

"Aye, but when two of those rich want the same thing, 'tis their problem to work it out. This Baron Hawse and the Hendrys can battle over their land rights and leave the rest of us in peace."

She disappeared into the pantry as Phillip muttered to himself, "Aye, let them battle, as long as neither my daughter nor my grandson is in their line of fire."

Nicholas stopped only to inform his mother of his destination before riding for Hawse Castle. She did her best to persuade him to wait until his temper had died and until his leg felt better before confronting the baron, but her pleas were in vain.

"Beatrice said that Leon asked specifically about the boy, Mother," he told her. "I intend to find out exactly why the baron is interested in my son."

He'd ridden hard, but his leg had stood up remarkably well thanks to Beatrice's poultice. It had been worth the momentary embarrassment. A smile danced around his lips as he remembered how she'd ordered him around as if he'd been a naughty pageboy.

But his smile faded when he rode across the dry moat around Hawse Castle and through the open gates into the bailey beyond. A number of men-at-arms came up to greet him, courteous but wary. When he asked to be taken to the baron, a captain, whom Nicholas had met on his previous visit, stepped forward.

"Is the baron expecting you, Sir Nicholas?" he asked politely.

"Nay. Nor will he be glad to see me, I suspect. However, we have business to discuss."

The captain looked as if he was trying to decide what he should do about the intruder when Winifred emerged from the castle keep and ran across the courtyard toward him.

"Nicholas!" she called. "How kind of you to visit. 'Tis glad I am to see you." Unlike the first time he had called, her voice held genuine warmth.

He swung off the saddle and stood holding Scarab while Winifred put her cheek up against the horse's muzzle and said, "Don't be jealous, Scarab. 'Tis glad I am to see you as well."

The horse held still, seemingly content with the attention. "You've won his affection, Winifred," Nicholas observed.

She looked up at him with a bright smile that made her appear a totally different girl from the shy creature he'd first met. "Aye, and he's won mine. He's got a noble spirit," she added, stroking the horse's flank.

Since Scarab's courage had saved his life more than once, Nicholas heartily agreed. But, though he would happily have lingered a time in Winifred's company, he had a less pleasant duty to attend.

"I must see your father, lass," he told her. "Would you like to see to Scarab while I wait?"

She nodded and led the horse away while the captain-at-arms, who'd been patiently waiting while Nicholas had talked with Winifred, led the way to the baron's antechamber. Evidently the man had decided that if the daughter of the household was receiving Nicholas with such warmth, he'd best not question the visitor further.

The baron was seated at a table looking at some scrolls with numbers etched on them. He looked up when Nicholas entered. The captain followed two steps behind and gave a little bow. "Sir Nicholas has requested an audience, milord," he said, quickly, as though afraid he'd be blamed for the interruption.

But the baron smiled pleasantly and waved the man away. "Good afternoon, Nicholas. This is a surprise," Hawse said when the man had retreated.

"I doubt it, Baron. You must have been expecting me after you sent your man sneaking around, asking after my son."

"Your bastard, you mean," the baron said smoothly. "There's a difference."

"Nay, there is not," Nicholas said firmly. "The boy's my son."

Hawse nodded his head a little in acknowledgement. "So be it. Though you might have some trouble convincing your *wife* of that fact when you do decide to marry, which you will have to do one of these days. How else does a landless knight find a fortune? 'Tis fortunate you're a well-favored lad. You should be able to find some wealthy widow who would want you."

Learning from his lesson with Leon in the morning, Nicholas was determined to keep his temper in check. "Not a month ago you were offering me your own daughter, Baron."

"Aye, 'twas a foolish notion. I don't hold it against you for not wanting the poor girl. She's lacking in spirit and not good for much more than a nunnery, I'm afraid."

"Your daughter is a fine young woman, and shows plenty of spirit when not overwhelmed by her father's bullying," Nicholas said, regretting the words before they were out of his mouth.

The baron merely smiled, baring his yellow teeth all the way to the gums. "I trust this doesn't mean that you've come here to accept my earlier offer to marry the chit, Nicholas, for you see, I've changed my mind. I'd thought to be generous for your mother's sake, but since you've continued to oppose me, I've decided to keep Hendry for myself. Both you and I shall be happier if you seek your fortune elsewhere."

"Then I'm to understand that you have no intention of being reasonable about the circumstances of my father's death?'' The baron seemed to jerk a little at the question, but relaxed as Nicholas continued, "That he signed over his estate thinking that his only son was dead?''

Hawse shrugged. "'Twas done of his own free will, Nicholas. As I've told you, your father had often expressed his doubts about you, so who's to say that he would not have done exactly the same thing even if he knew you were alive?''

In spite of their differences, Nicholas was certain that his father would never have disinherited him, but there was little point in arguing the case with the baron when he had no proof of his father's state of mind.

The walls of the antechamber seemed clammy and close around him. He wanted to be out of Hawse Castle and out of sight of the baron's oily smile.

"I can see that we'll never come to a point of agreement on this matter," he said. "So I intend to take my case before the king."

The baron looked surprised. "Do you now?" he asked softly.

"Aye. 'Tis said he's a just man despite his faults."

Hawse laughed. "Take your case to the Pope for all I care, Hendry. 'Twill be of little avail. I have the papers your father signed, and I have an unimpeachable witness to the deed."

Nicholas straightened up. "And who may that be?"

"Why, the lady Constance, lad. Your very own mother."

Nicholas felt his mouth grow dry. The baron would call his mother to testify against his case? The idea made him cold inside, but he was determined not to show the baron that he had any fear about the eventual outcome of the matter.

"'Twill be up to my mother what she wants to say and when, but this matter will be settled." He took a step closer to the table and leaned across it to bring his face close to the baron's. "In the meantime, hear me well on this. If you or any of your underlings go anywhere near my son or his family again, you'll answer to me."

Then, without taking his leave, he turned around and stalked out of the room.

"This is much better already!" Beatrice said with unmistakable delight. "See how the redness is nearly gone?"

Nicholas braced his hands against the pallet so as not to flinch when she prodded the wound. "'Tis kind of you to be so concerned about my health," he told her.

She lifted her gaze from the wound. "'Tis merely the normal pride of a nurse over a successful healing," she said, but there was a glint of teasing in her eyes.

"So is it unimportant to whom the flesh is attached?" he teased back.

She turned her attention to the wound and said, "Nay, 'tis not important." The nonchalance of her tone was a little too deliberate.

"Does it make a difference if the flesh is attached to a man or a maid?" he persisted.

Her fingers prodded a little more deeply into the wound and he grunted at the sudden pain. "Not to true nurse,'' she said crisply. ''Now be still, lest I lose my concentration.''

He remained quiet while she finished dressing the wound as she had on the previous day. '''Tis done,'' she said finally. ''Mayhap we'll leave it two days this time.''

''In truth, I do thank you, Beatrice. 'Twas a wondrous thing to awake this morning with hardly any pain.''

''Soon the pain should be gone entirely. If the wound had been tended correctly from the first, it would have healed long since.''

'''Tis not an easy thing to tend a wound on the field of battle.''

Something in his voice made Beatrice look up sharply. He was gazing straight ahead, unfocused, as though suddenly seized by the memories of that faraway land. ''It must have been a horrible thing. You and your companions were brave men.''

''Nay, we were lucky men.'' He turned his gaze toward her. The memories made his eyes intense, and all at once she felt so drawn into the dark depths of them that she almost fell off her small stool.

It was happening again, she thought with a kind of panic, just as it had in the brewing shed. And this time she was sitting next to him...and he was half-naked.

She had lied when she'd told him earlier that tending a wound was impersonal. She'd been utterly conscious that it had been Nicholas's bare legs that were stretched out in front of her, that his most private parts were mere inches from her fingers. She turned away from the close scrutiny of his gaze and began to pack up her materials.

"It takes more bravery to face the everyday adversities of life," he said.

Beatrice looked up blankly. She'd already forgotten the mention of the Crusades.

"As you have here," he added, misreading her confusion.

"Aye," she answered vaguely. She had to get out of the tiny room before she made a fool of herself. Her father was upstairs sleeping and Owen was once again with the Fletchers. She and Nicholas were as good as alone, and all at once she was afraid of what that might mean for them both.

"So, we're finished here," she said, standing and still avoiding his eyes. "I'll go so that you may dress yourself and then we'll do this again in two days."

She turned to leave, but Nicholas swung his bare feet to the floor and reached out to grasp her hand. "Don't leave yet. I've not properly thanked you."

She looked down at him waiting.

"Stay a moment more. By the saints, I think looking into those blue eyes of yours cures a man of what ails him more surely than all the healing herbs in Christendom." He gave a tug on her hand, pulling her to sit beside him on the pallet.

His flattery smacked of the Nicholas Hendry of old and helped steel her to resist his plea. "I've work to do, Master Hendry," she said curtly. "What's more, you're half-naked, and 'tis not proper for me to be sitting here now that the nursing is done."

Nicholas cocked his head. "So that harridan Nurse

Thibault is gone and 'tis merely the fair Beatrice who sits beside me?''

He accompanied the words with a grin so engaging that even she found it impossible not to give a small smile in return. ''I thought you were grateful to Nurse Thibault,'' she said.

''Aye, I am. But she can be just a bit of a shrew, don't you think?''

He had not let go of her hand, and now his thumb was making slow circles in the middle of her palm. She pulled her hand away and said, ''Mayhap she is that way with difficult patients.''

Nicholas let her hand go free, but leaned closer to her. ''The last thing this patient wants is to be difficult,'' he said.

The cockiness was gone from his voice, replaced by a husky sincerity.

She leaned back slightly so that she could look him directly in the eyes. ''You're not a difficult patient, Master Hendry, but you make me uncomfortable.'' She looked around the room. ''*This* makes me uncomfortable—being here with you.''

He was quiet for a long moment, then said, ''I'm uncomfortable, too, sweetheart, but only because I'm remembering what it felt like to kiss those red lips of yours.''

The words slid into her midsection. Without thinking, she must have tipped her head back, because all at once his hands were in her hair and his face was above her, his mouth seeking hers.

He claimed her lips softly, nibbling around the edges and teasing her with his tongue. It was exquisite, and she gave a small moan of surrender, but still he continued the delicate kisses until she felt as if her lips had turned to warm honey.

"Beatrice," he murmured, dropping his hands. His eyes were huge dark pools and once again she had the feeling that she could drown in their depths.

The linen bag of healing supplies had fallen to the floor. Nicholas slid back on the pallet until he was braced against the wall, then pulled her more fully onto the bed and into his arms. She heard him give a small grunt as she slid against his wound, then he picked her up entirely and lifted her to the other side so that she was touching only his good leg. His *bare* good leg, she realized vaguely, though her mind had gone into an odd kind of haze.

The kisses started again. She was half reclining and now felt the pressure of his body on top of her. His one arm pillowed her head, but the other hand was free and began a gentle exploration of her body. His fingers traced the line of her jaw, then the slope of her neck, then trailed down above the rough linen of her overgown to reach the peak of a breast. Even through the cloth, she could feel how hard her nipple grew in response to his caresses.

His lips were wandering as well, to her eyes, then, playfully, the tip of her nose. He was smiling at her now, that charmer's smile with his white teeth and full lips and dancing eyes. His hair was mussed and his eyes were slightly hooded with desire.

Growing up with the nuns, and then caring for her father and Owen, Beatrice had had no opportunity and little inclination for such man-woman play. The sensations that were coursing through her body were new. Her limbs felt heavy, as though she had drunk too much mead, and she could feel an urgent, almost sharp pulse from where his hand lingered on her breast straight through to her private woman's area between her legs.

Somewhere deep in the recesses of her mind, she knew that allowing this to continue was the height of folly, but her body refused to move and her mouth refused to tell him to stop. Instead, her treacherous hands began their own exploration. She'd touched many bodies, both male and female, in the course of her healings, but this was different.

She smoothed her fingers over the rough whiskers of his chin. He rewarded her with another smile and with a return of his mouth to hers. As his kisses continued to send waves of signals straight through her middle, she moved her hands underneath his tunic to his back. She could feel each ridge of his warrior's body and she wondered what it would look like to see him with no clothes at all.

Suddenly she looked down. His garments had ridden up so that he was bare from the waist down, revealing his manhood in flagrant arousal. Beatrice looked away quickly at first, but then found her eyes drawn back to the sight. Almost unconsciously she slid one of her hands around from Nicholas's back and touched him there, directly on that proud masculine hardness, and was surprised to learn that it was so hot and so silky.

Nicholas gasped when her fingers found him. For a moment she thought she'd hurt his leg, but then she realized that the gasp was one of pleasure. His head had gone back and his eyes were closed. It gave her a curious feeling of power.

Emboldened, she closed her fingers around him, eliciting another startled sound. She smiled to herself and explored further, moving her hand and testing his reaction.

Then he opened his eyes, reached down to take her wrist and pulled it up, pinning her against the bed. His mouth came down on hers again, but this time the onslaught was deep and passionate. She forgot about her explorations, forgot about the feel of his back, forgot everything but his mouth. And her body melted against the bed like warm honey.

"Ah, sweetheart," he murmured.

Beatrice could no longer distinguish her mouth from his. "Aye," she whispered.

As suddenly as it had all begun, Nicholas abruptly pulled away with a muttered oath. Beatrice's senses returned slowly, but as the air of the room cooled her burning cheeks, she sat up and looked at Nicholas, who had turned away from her on the bed.

"Did we hurt your leg?"

He shook his head.

She sat in puzzled silence.

Finally, he turned to her, took her hands, and said, "Forgive me, Beatrice. I'd not intended to take things this far. I'm no longer the man I was before I left England." He appeared to be struggling to come up with the right words. "I'm done with the days of easy dalliance," he said finally.

Easy dalliance? Beatrice stiffened as her puzzlement turned to hurt.

Nicholas seemed to realize that he was stating his case badly, but he did little to rectify matters as he continued, "I never should have started such a thing. Especially not with *you,* of all people."

Beatrice clasped her hands in her lap to keep them from shaking. With her of all people, he'd said. Was the memory of her sister that hard to banish, then? She gave a painful swallow and with as much dignity as she could muster, she pushed herself off the bed and stood.

"Get dressed," she said without looking at him. "That binding can stay on for a sennight, so I'd prefer it if you would refrain from visiting here until that time."

Feeling dizzy and out of balance, she walked carefully out of the room.

Chapter Thirteen

In spite of her admonition that he not return for a week, she spent the entire next day looking for him to come. She felt the need to talk with him. It simply did not seem logical to her that Nicholas Hendry could have inspired those feelings inside her if he had been all the while thinking of her sister. Yet he did not appear, and by midafternoon her spirits drooped.

Her father was weaker again. She was horrified at the possibility that he was *willing* his own decline because he realized that it was his presence that was keeping Beatrice and Owen in Hendry.

She argued with him. "I want to raise Owen here. I'd prefer to do it with you, but with or without you, this is his home and now it is mine, as well."

Phillip looked at his beautiful daughter sadly. "Now that you've drawn the notice of the nobles, 'twill be safer for you to be away from this place. You and the boy could start a whole new life in York, daughter. Your aunt will aid you."

Beatrice remembered his words when she looked up from her candlemaking to see the bulky form of

Baron Hawse filling the doorframe. She stood, wiped her hands on her leather apron and waited for him to speak. It was possible that the baron had stopped by the inn for a flagon of ale, but she thought it not likely.

He stepped into the room, looking around as his steward had on his earlier visit. Finally, his eyes rested on her. "Good day, Mistress Thibault. Business is slow at midweek, hey?"

"'Tis slow at all times, Baron. The Gilded Boar is not like the inns of the big cities, nor the busily traveled highways."

"Not flocking to your doors, hey? What d'ye live on then? You and your father and that boy of yours?"

She supposed he had a right to his questions, if it was true that the Hendry lands had been passed to his estate, but she felt uncomfortable facing his interrogation. "We manage. My father's always been the brewer for Hendry and still is."

"Well, then, mayhap I should try myself a sample, mistress." He sauntered over to one of the tables and sat down, throwing his voluminous cloak back over his shoulders. When she did not move, he said, "What are you waiting for, girl? Bring me some ale."

Beatrice went into the pantry to draw a mug of ale, then brought it out to him. His eyes never left her as she approached his table. "With barmaids as comely as yourself, 'tis a wonder the men of the village have not worn a path to this place," he said.

The words were a compliment and decent enough, which didn't explain why she felt somehow diminished by them. She placed the mug in front of him, then turned to leave.

"Stay, mistress," he ordered. "In truth, I came not for the Gilded Boar's ale, but for a chat with its mistress."

"My father is proprietor of this inn."

"I'm told your father does little these days. 'Tis the palsy, is it not?"

She had no intention of discussing her father's condition with the baron. "He does well enough."

"Where is he, then?"

Beatrice sighed. She could not afford to be rude to such an important man, but she wished she could simply turn around and walk away. "My father is upstairs occupied with other matters."

The baron nodded as though he knew the full extent of her father's condition. "And the boy?" he asked.

Beatrice felt the beginning of the same chill she'd suffered with the baron's steward. It appeared that her father was right in at least this. The baron did have an unusual interest in Owen.

"Owen is visiting with friends," she said. "'Twas to give me the afternoon free to get some chores done, baron, so if you'll forgive me—"

He held up a hand to interrupt her. "All in all, your prospects are not the brightest, Mistress Thibault. My steward tells me that you claim your rents are too high."

His words made Beatrice pause. Perhaps she was misjudging the man because of her unhappy experience with his steward. Could it be possible that he actually was concerned about her welfare as one of his tenants?

She moved back toward the table where he was

sitting and addressed him earnestly. "Aye, Baron Hawse. I do believe when the tax keepers heard the term 'inn' they thought my father would soon be collecting money by the fistful, but, as you can see—" she gestured to the empty room "—'tis not the reality. He's asked the Hendry steward for an adjustment, but so far they've paid him no heed."

"'Twould seem an injustice has been done," the baron said with a pleasant smile.

Beatrice's hopes rose. It actually appeared that Baron Hawse was lending her a sympathetic ear. "Aye. We'd be willing to have your men look over my father's ledger." Words she'd been wanting to say to someone in authority for quite some time began to tumble out. "'Tis not that we're unwilling to pay a fair rent. I've tried suggesting a plan whereby we would pay a portion of the tax in barrels of ale. This would be easier for us to come by each tax day and—"

Once again the baron held up his hand to stop the flow of her words. "My dear, I'm not interested in your ale, nor in whatever paltry amount this place pays in taxes."

Beatrice looked confused. "Did you not come here today to talk about the rents?"

"Nay, I came to talk about *you*, Mistress Thibault, and your family."

The shiver was back. "I don't understand…." Her voice trailed off.

"I'd like to relieve you of this place. As you, yourself pointed out, 'tis not a thriving establishment."

She frowned. "Nay, but 'tis our home and our livelihood."

"Aye, such as it is." For the first time, the baron lifted the mug of ale to his lips, then grimaced a little, as if the brew was not up to his standards. He put the mug back on the table and pushed it to one side. Beatrice sensed that his insults were deliberate and calculated.

"We find it satisfactory," she said through stiffening lips.

He looked up at her sharply. "I'm willing to make a proposition. Sit down, girl. I'm tired of cranking my neck up to look at your face."

Angry and wary, Beatrice sat on the bench across from him. "What kind of proposition?" she asked.

With his gaze stabbing directly across at her, he looked much less pleasant and much more dangerous. "It has come to my attention that the boy who lives with you is Nicholas Hendry's bastard."

"Owen is my sister's child."

"Aye, planted by Nicholas, as I understand. Do you deny it?"

There was little point, with Nicholas himself trumpeting it around the shire. "Nay," she said.

The baron nodded. "For reasons that don't concern you, I'd prefer to have the boy gone from here. I assume that you would want to go with him."

"I go where Owen goes, but—"

"I'd be willing to help you with such a move, get you established in a city somewhere, as long as it's far from here. 'Twould relieve you of the burden of this place."

Though she'd been considering the very same possibility with her father all week, she had the urge to throw the baron's words back in his smiling face.

"I've no desire to leave Hendry," she said. "This is Owen's home and mine. We intend to stay here."

The baron's smile stayed firmly in place as he said, "I'm not offering you a choice, my dear. As your landlord, I can make life sufficiently unpleasant so as to force you to leave."

"You'd raise our rents even higher?"

"That or…" He folded his hands carefully in front of him on the table. "There are a number of ways. Landlords have interesting rights over their tenants, as I'm sure you're aware, m'dear."

Though he had not made a move toward her, nor given her any of the lascivious looks of his steward, he left no doubt that some of the "ways" he was contemplating had to do with her personally.

She pushed back the bench and stood. "Tenants may have few rights under the law, Baron, but my father and I have many friends in this village. I'd advise you to think twice before you attempt to bully us."

The only evidence of his anger was the sudden bulging of a vein at the side of his nose. His reply was restrained. "Does this mean you'll not accept my offer of help?"

"We've no need of help with any move, since we'll not be leaving this place."

The baron stood slowly, the smile still on his face. "Then I'll bid you good day, Mistress Thibault. I regret that we could not come to an understanding."

She stood still while he turned and walked out of the inn. He had not paid for his ale, but she was not about to call him back to render account. Instead, after she saw him mounted on his horse and headed down the road, she took the nearly full flagon, marched to the door, and flung the contents outside.

"Never did I think to see the day," Harold Fletcher said with a grin at his boyhood friend. "'Twas always you who did the breaking of hearts, Nicky, not the other way round."

Nicholas did not return his smile. "She's not broken my heart."

"Nay, but she's captured it, which is the first step toward feeding it piece by piece into the gristmill, if I know Beatrice. She's not your typical village maid, Nicholas. She's too smart to be enticed by a charming smile and flattering words."

Nicholas had not told his friend all the details of his last meeting with the brewer's daughter. He'd not told him that it had been Nicholas himself who had broken off the encounter, not Beatrice. He doubted that Harold would have credited such a tale, knowing the old Nicholas as he did.

The two friends had gone up into the hills north of Hendry where they'd often hunted as boys. Harold's father had used to give them arrows on the condition that they chase down as many as they could and return them to him at the end of the day. The few that found their mark in an unlucky rabbit or partridge were also retrieved and cleaned up for reuse.

The hunting was a pretense this day, though they carried bows and each wore a quiver over a shoulder. "'Tis no longer legal to hunt these lands," Harold had warned when they had started walking from the village. "If 'tis true as they're saying that they belong to the Hawse estate."

"Let him arrest me, then," Nicholas had answered, but neither man had fired a shot all afternoon.

"I'm not concerned about my heart, Harry, 'tis hers and Owen's. Beatrice was right, you know, that first day I ever saw her. I *did* cause her sister's death, and left my son to live without a mother or father all these years."

Harold snorted. "And I suppose you singlehandedly lost the Crusade, my friend, for you might as well add that to your penance bag."

Nicholas gave a humorless chuckle. "Nay, not singlehandedly. I had some help."

"'Tis not like you to take such a gloomy view of things, Nicky," Harold said. They were seated under a large oak tree, leaning up against the broad trunk and looking down at the road below. "If I did not think 'twould anger you, I'd say you're sounding a bit like your father. He was ever the gloomy one."

"Oh, he could be cheerful enough. 'Twas only when it came to his son that he turned morose."

Harold didn't argue the point, but after a moment, he asked, "Have you told Beatrice how you're feeling?"

Nicholas shifted on the damp grass. "After a fashion."

Harold shook his head. "Well, now there's your mistake. 'Tis one thing Jannet has taught me well. You have to tell them direct, else it counts for nothing. All these things that men would as soon left unsaid, women like to hear them."

Nicholas laughed. "So you've become an expert, have you?"

"Nay, I've just become a husband."

They turned their heads as both heard a horse in the distance. They could see a cloud of dust far down the road, but could not yet identify the rider.

"'Tis your nemesis, the baron," Harold observed after a moment.

Nicholas frowned. The baron was coming from the direction of the Gilded Boar. He voiced his thoughts aloud. "I wonder where he's been?"

"Viewing his ill-gotten estates, no doubt. He's coming from Hendry lands."

"Aye." The idea made Nicholas uncomfortable.

"Does he know about Owen?" Harold asked.

"I've not kept it a secret."

"Mayhap 'twas a mistake to broadcast it so widely, at least before things were settled with Hawse."

"Mayhap, but 'tis done."

They watched in silence as the horse passed beneath them and headed west toward Hawse Castle. Then Harold said, "So are you going to talk to her?"

"What would I say?"

Harold gave an exasperated grunt. "By the saints, Nicky, you never had to ask what to say in all the years you were seducing girls behind every shrub in the shire."

Nicholas looked thoughtful. "This time it's different."

"Well, then, you say, 'Beatrice...'" Harold paused and started again. "No, you say, 'Darling Beatrice, you must know that I've developed an affection...'" He jumped to his feet, put his hand over his chest and started a third time. "You say, 'Darling Beatrice, it cannot have escaped your notice that...'"

Nicholas stood more slowly and clapped a hand on

his friend's shoulder. "Thank you anyway, Harold. Mayhap I do remember a thing or two about how to talk to the maids."

Harold let out a breath. "Well, 'tis glad I am to hear it, Nicky, for I do believe I've forgotten the art entirely."

It was late. Her father and Owen had long since retired, but Beatrice had no desire for sleep. She sat gazing into the fire in the taproom. She glanced at the candles she'd left unfinished that afternoon and decided that they'd keep till the morrow.

She'd not told her father about Baron Hawse's visit. It would only have worried him. She'd resolved to ignore the baron's words. As vast as were the Hawse estates, she found it hard to believe that the baron would spend much time on the matter of an innkeeper's daughter and the illegitimate son of the former landlord. He'd been annoyed because obviously he was a man used to having his way, but she didn't think much would come of his threats.

Still the incident nagged at her. She didn't want to take any chances where Owen's welfare was concerned. In some ways, it might have been smarter for her to accept the baron's offer. Her father certainly would have been relieved. The nuns in York had always accused her of having a stubborn streak, and she supposed it was that characteristic that made her so adamant about staying in Hendry.

Well, she admitted to herself with a sigh, it was her stubbornness and something else as well. For as much as she told herself that she was staying for her father's health or Owen's happiness, she knew there

was another reason she was reluctant to leave, and
that was the most absurd reason of all.

The fire popped, startling her. The flames danced
as brightly as Nicholas Hendry's black eyes. She
closed her eyes, trying to banish the vision. If she had
the brains of a sparrow, she would accept Hawse's
offer precisely in order to get *away* from Nicholas.

He'd made it clear the previous day that he didn't
want her, not, at least, as he had wanted her sister.
Yet she couldn't stop thinking about those moments
with him on her father's bed. She couldn't erase the
memory of his kisses from her treacherous thoughts.

Then, suddenly, as though conjured by a wizard,
he was there, just behind her, his hand gently touching her hair. She jumped, and had to catch herself to
keep from falling off the stool.

"Forgive me," he said hurriedly. "Your eyes were
closed and I thought you might be sleeping."

He steadied her with a strong hand on her shoulder.
He was flesh and blood, then, not a sorcerer's spell.
"What are you doing here?" she asked, still un-
steady.

"'Tis late, I know, but I wanted to talk to you."

He moved around her to the other side of the fireplace. Gesturing to another low stool, he asked, "May
I sit with you?"

She nodded. Since she'd not been able to banish
him from her thoughts, it would seem pointless to try
to banish him from her home. "What did you wish
to talk about?"

He sat, leaning his hands on his knees and staring
into the fire, much as she had been doing earlier. After

a long moment, he said. "I saw Baron Hawse riding from this direction. Did he come here?"

Beatrice did her best to hide her disappointment at his words. He'd come because of the baron. No doubt he was concerned for his son's safety. She'd been foolish to think that his visit might have something to do with her. She answered coldly. "Aye. He offered to help me move."

"Move?" He sounded completely puzzled.

"Move away from Hendry. With Owen and Father," she added.

"Whyever would he make such an offer?"

"To keep us away from you, I suspect."

He looked astonished. "'Tis absurd. You can't leave Hendry. Owen's my son and you..." He stopped. "Surely you've never entertained such a notion?"

"In truth, my father says he would feel safer if we left Hendry. He believes it would be safer for Owen, as well."

Nicholas stood and began a restless pacing back and forth in front of the fire. The rest of the taproom was in darkness as she'd not bothered with candles. "I'll not allow it," he said. "Owen belongs in Hendry."

She bristled a little at his tone of authority, but was not in the mood to argue an issue that did not even exist. "I didn't say that I intend to go. I declined the baron's offer."

He seemed to relax at that and came back to drop down again on the stool. "What did he say?"

She shrugged. "'Tis not important. He wasn't

happy about it. I believe Baron Hawse is a man who is used to having his way in all things.''

Nicholas gave her an admiring look. ''Until he met up with mistress of the Gilded Boar.''

Beatrice gave a reluctant smile, but said firmly, ''I'll do whatever is best for my family.''

The admiration in his eyes shifted subtly to something more intimate. Through the flickers of the firelight, she felt it as surely as if he had reached out and touched her.

''I didn't really come to talk about the baron,'' he said.

The husky timbre of his voice made her breath stop halfway down her throat. She wet her lips. ''What did you come to talk about?''

''I came to ask your forgiveness.''

''My forgiveness?''

''Aye.''

''For what?''

He stood again and took a step closer, towering over her. ''For being a bloody fool.''

Chapter Fourteen

*T*alk to her, Harold had said, but now that he was here with her, words didn't seem adequate. He lifted her from her seat and drew her against him. He'd speak first with his kisses, since he already knew that in those, at least, their communication was near to perfection.

He'd expected resistance after the inexcusable way he'd halted their lovemaking the previous day, but she made no protest. Her body melded instantly to his as if the hours since they'd been together did not exist.

"Ah, sweetheart," he murmured, after he'd softened her lips with several tender kisses. "I've thought of nothing but this for the past day. I've scarce eaten. I've not slept...."

"Nor have I," she whispered.

His head was clearer than it had been the previous day when he'd been half-naked and her fingers had been wreaking their innocent havoc on his private parts. He'd been embarrassed then by the immediacy of his arousal. This time, he was determined to go slow, though already his manhood had grown hard.

"'Twas ill done, yesterday," he said against her cheek. He stopped as he considered how to explain the conflicting emotions that had made him halt their lovemaking. "Since Flora—" he began. But when she stiffened in his arms he stopped, biting back a curse. Could he have found a more indelicate moment to mention her sister's name? he berated himself. Had he no brain left in his head?

He began again. "I took a vow that if I returned to England, I'd never again take advantage of a maid. It seemed that I was breaking that pledge."

"By taking advantage of me?" she asked, pulling slightly out of his arms.

"Aye. I've more experience in these things than you. You couldn't resist me."

Beatrice smiled. "Oh."

He smiled back, uncertainly. "I was about to seduce you, lass."

"Mayhap I was the one doing the seducing, Sir Knight."

In all his many liaisons with females from fourteen to forty, such a thing had never occurred to him. "'Tis the man who does the seducing," he said, a little indignant.

"Ah, is that what you believe? Even after my obvious tactics in getting you to remove your breeches?"

He felt his cheeks grow warm. It was true that it had been a novel experience for him to lie half-naked with a fully clothed woman. He studied her to see if she could possibly be serious. Her smile was devilish...and irresistible.

With his mind in such a muddle, actions were safer

than words, he decided. He began to kiss her again, and the stiffness dissolved. Her body felt pliant and warm, but he wanted to be closer to her, wanted to make his way through the layers of stiff clothes to the sweet flesh underneath.

"Your father and Owen are asleep?" he asked.

She nodded.

He lifted her then, smiling at her look of surprise. Tall as she was, she was still an easy armful for his battle-hardened arms. Just to be sure that they would have privacy, he asked, "They'll not come downstairs?"

Her arms had crept around his neck. Her eyes, usually so sharp, looked dewy and unfocused. "Nay," she answered.

He grinned at her. "I have you at my mercy, then?"

She nodded happily.

He carried her back to Phillip's old bedroom, and found the bed in the darkness. "I want to see you, sweetheart," he whispered, setting her down. "I'll be right back."

He returned to the taproom and took two candles in their holders from the tables, lit them in the fire and returned to the bedroom. To his surprised delight, Beatrice had removed her stiff overgown and sat on the edge of the bed in a soft undergown that revealed every curve of her upper body. He stood a moment, just looking at her.

There was no table in the room, so he placed the candleholders carefully on the floor at each end of the bed. Beatrice watched him with some amusement.

"'Twill make this look like some kind of pagan ceremony," she said.

He laughed and even to his own ears, the sound of the laugh was happier than he'd heard since the days of his youth. "'Tis a ceremony of sorts when two people decide to come together in love. I know not whether it be pagan."

When he finished placing the candles, he stripped off his surcoat and boots and placed them to one side. He hesitated a moment, then pulled off his tunic as well, leaving his chest bare. She was watching him with an expression that, if not pagan, was at least ages old. It made his blood race.

He joined her in the bed and took her in his arms. Gently, he laid her back and began to kiss her again, taking his time. Her eyes closed and he kissed them, then her chin, her cheeks, her forehead, her neck and back to her mouth.

She gave a lazy murmur of contentment, but he was ready for more. His hands explored her body through her gown, then he said, "I want to feel you against me, sweetheart. May I?" At her nod, he helped her remove the rest of her clothing. For a moment she looked uncharacteristically shy. He leaned on one elbow and with his other hand simply stroked her, slowly, reverently, until she relaxed under his touch and the smile came back to her lips.

In the candlelight her body looked like a lushly endowed alabaster goddess, but she was no statue. Her skin was warm and vibrant and responded to his fingers like a fine-tuned lute.

He took special time with her breasts, teasing the little nubbins into hard pebbles before he bent to take each one in his mouth. She gave a little gasp that subsided into a moan of pleasure.

He waited until she'd begun to toss restlessly, moving her thighs against each other, before he quickly disposed of his hose, then drew himself over her and let their private parts touch. She was already moist and needy, but he lingered still, touching her with his hands and his body until she gave a kind of begging groan. Then he entered her, as slowly as he could bear.

Her strong, lean body took him easily and soon they found the rhythm to move together. She touched the bandages on his leg at one point, but his wound did not hamper him in the least. The room around him faded as all his sensations suddenly centered on the place where their two bodies had become one. She cried his name and he clasped her more tightly as she tumbled over the edge.

He pulled himself away from her and took his own climax outside her body. Then he gathered her back in his arms and kissed her, smoothing back the damp tendrils of hair from her face. His own body was covered with a sheen of sweat that made him shiver in the chilly room. Beatrice lay limp.

"Are you all right, sweetheart?" he asked her.

She looked up at him, her eyes sleepy and sensual. "Aye."

"Are you cold?"

"Nay."

But she, too, had begun to shiver, so he moved to find a blanket and cover them both. They lay snuggled together without speaking for such a long time that he thought she must have fallen asleep, but finally she said, "'Twas even better than I'd imagined."

He gave a surprised chuckle. "What kind of admission is that? Are you telling me that you've spent some time thinking about what this might be like— you and I together? 'Tis not something I would suspect of a proper maid."

"I warrant that proper maids spend as much time thinking about such things as do their men," she replied.

Her smile was saucy with a touch of silliness and made her look totally different from the practical, competent woman he'd come to know.

"Are you such an authority on the subject, then, missy?" he teased.

Her laugh was infectious and young. "I'll admit I've spent some considerable time thinking on…these matters. But I have little practical experience, as you yourself must have just divined."

He grew serious. "I suspected that I was the first with you. 'Tis true?"

She nodded. Her cheeks were still flushed from their lovemaking, but he had the feeling that she was blushing as well. He leaned over to her and kissed her gently once on the mouth. "You honor me, sweetheart," he said.

She moved out of his arms and sat up, pulling the blanket with her to cover her nakedness. "We honored each other. 'Twas a mutual choice."

The playfulness was gone from her voice, he noted wistfully. She was in control again, more the woman he'd seen before. In an effort to recapture the spirit, he sat up beside her and took a little nip of her ear.

"'Twould not be too soon to honor each other one more time," he whispered.

But somehow the mood had changed. She was shivering in earnest now, in spite of the blanket, and had bent over the edge of the bed to search for her clothes. He stopped her with a hand on her shoulder and turned her to face him. "Beatrice?" he asked soberly. "Is aught amiss?"

She freed herself from his hand and resumed her search. "Nay. I'd dress before my father or Owen should happen upon us."

He frowned. "I thought you said they sleep the night sound."

She avoided his eyes. "Aye, usually. I'd rather not take any chances." She'd found her shift and pulled it over her head. Once again Nicholas tried to discover what had made her turn away from him so abruptly.

"There *is* something wrong," he insisted. "Have I hurt you?"

She shook her head and stood, lifting one of the candlesticks from the floor. Then she took a deep breath and turned to face him. "Nay, you didn't hurt me, Nicholas. In fact, 'twas one of the most truly wonderful moments of my life, but now I need some time to think on what this means. 'Tis not something I'd ever thought to have happen to me."

Slowly he began gathering his own clothes and dressing himself. He was not totally satisfied with her answer. This was not like the aftermath of any lovemaking he'd ever had. In his experience the woman usually wanted to be held and praised for a spell, then he would leave her with whispered promises of future bliss. This had been the pattern even with Beatrice's own sister. But Beatrice was not like any woman he'd ever known.

"Shall I come on the morrow?" he asked uncertainly. "I've not seen Owen these two days past."

"Come if you please."

Her seeming indifference pricked his ego. "It matters not to you whether I come or stay away?"

They were both now fully dressed, she holding the candlestick tightly in front of her with two hands. "Owen is always happy to see you."

His gaze held hers for a long moment. "Ah," he said dryly. "I'll come to see Owen, then."

"We all look forward to your visits."

It was the most he was going to get out of her, he could see. "So you'll talk no more about leaving here?"

Beatrice shifted restlessly, obviously wanting the meeting at an end. "I intend to do what is best for Owen and for my father."

"Which is to stay here in Hendry."

"For the present, aye. I think 'tis the best place for us."

He nodded. That much, at least, was settled. As for settling what had started between him and Beatrice, it would evidently take longer. Patience was a virtue he had never possessed as a young man, but it was another one of the lessons he'd carried back from the wars. He could be patient, especially when the reward was worth waiting for. "Then I'll take my leave and see you in the morning," he said lightly, though it was not the way he wished to end the encounter.

"Aye. But we'll…" her voice faltered. "Of course, we'll say nothing of this night to my father."

Nicholas gave her a look of exasperation. "For a maid who's spent some considerable time thinking about 'these matters,' you appear to have a few things yet to learn."

She gave a small smile, but then turned and led him back into the taproom and across to the door. "Till the morrow," she said, opening it.

He stepped across the threshold, then turned back to her, but before he could even lean over to give her a kiss goodnight, she had shut the door behind him, leaving him standing alone in the dark.

Had it been what she had expected? Beatrice wondered, resuming her seat by the taproom fire. She had no desire to sleep.

It had come on her like some kind of madness. The minute he had appeared beside her at this very spot, she'd known that the moment had come for experiencing that ultimate gift a man and woman give to each other. Physically, it had been all that she could have hoped.

But she was a practical woman. Once sanity returned, she'd had to assess the truth of this thing. Nicholas had loved Flora, perhaps still did. He'd mentioned her name tonight while holding Beatrice in his arms. And even if he'd never laid eyes on her sister, he was a noble, out of her station.

She closed her arms around herself and rocked back and forth, crooning tunelessly. She squeezed her eyes shut, trying to blot out the image of his eyes looking down at her in the candlelight as his body stoked her passions.

Flora was the sweet and gentle one, everyone always used to say. Beatrice was smart and capable. At the moment, she felt neither.

She buried her face in her hands and still the images came. She could no longer deny what she'd been fighting almost from the time she first saw Nicholas Hendry's dancing black eyes. She was in love with him. And now what in the devil was she supposed to do about it?

I should have learned my lesson, dearest Flora, she whispered. *I should have learned from you that the price of giving away one's heart is sometimes too high to bear.*

Baron Hawse gave his daughter a distracted smile as she entered his antechamber and glided noiselessly across the flagstone floor to stand in front of his table.

"I'd thought you retired by now," he said, looking up from a map he was studying.

"I was in the kitchens discussing the week's menus with the cook," she said.

The baron looked thoroughly bored with this account of her domestic activities. "Well, what is it you want?" he asked.

She wrung her hands together nervously, but her gaze did not waver as she looked at her father and said, "I've changed my mind."

He blinked at her direct tone. "About what?"

"I've decided to consider marriage to Nicholas Hendry after all, if 'tis favorable to him."

The baron pushed back his chair and stood. "What brought about this change of tune?"

Winifred shrugged. "I find him gentle. He's not like some men I've known."

"No doubt you're smitten with his devil's looks, just like half the women in the shire, from all reports. But never mind. 'Tis too late, for I've changed my mind, as well." He walked around the table to tower over her. "I've decided 'tis not worth giving up Hendry just to get you off my hands."

She flinched, but she answered him with more insolence than she'd ever before dared. "Am I such a burden to you then, Father?"

He frowned at her tone. "Daughters are ever a burden. First they must be protected, then they must be dowered. And what does a father receive in return?"

Winifred drew herself up, her usually dull eyes flashing. "Some receive a great deal in return, I'm told. Though 'twould be hard for you to understand such a thing, some fathers actually receive *love*."

Then she spun around and fled from the room.

Nicholas looked at the grease floating on top of his suet pudding and pushed it away with a grimace.

"'Tis the fifth mug of ale you've called for since you came in this evening," his mother observed in her even-tempered way. "Do you think 'twill be enough to free you of whatever demons are biting your tail?"

"If you're trying to ask whether I intend to get sopping drunk, I do."

"Will it be to good purpose, do you think?"

"Nay." He shook his head, then winced as the

movement made him feel as if he might fall off his seat.

"Mayhap I could help."

"Only if you can tell me how to understand women."

His mother gave a surprised laugh. "Now there's a new one. Is this the same son of mine who charmed so many women that he had to run off to the Holy Crusades to escape from them all?"

"The very same," he said. "Though it seems with my advanced years, I'm losing my touch."

"Whoa, now. If you're in your advanced years, what would that make me?"

He grinned weakly. "As young and fair as ever, Mother. 'Tis only hard living that makes one grow old."

"Hard drinking, mayhap. Are you going to eat your pudding or not?" she asked in the tone of a mother impatient with her child's nonsense.

He shook his head. "Forgive me, Mother. I've not the stomach for it this evening."

She leaned toward him across the table and took his hand. "Tell me about it, son. Is it Winifred?"

He looked up, surprised. It had been days since he'd even thought about the baron's offer of marriage. But, of course, his mother knew nothing of his infatuation with Beatrice. Though she'd known about his light affairs, she'd probably be shocked by the idea that he'd actually fallen in love with one of the village maids.

"Nay, Mother. Winifred is a sweet girl who will no doubt find herself a worthy husband some day

without the manipulations of her father. It will not be
I.''

"Then what is it?''

Nicholas pulled his hand away from his mother's
grasp, lifted his mug of ale, and took a large swallow.
"'Tis not important since it appears the lady is no
longer interested. No doubt she's too intelligent to
link herself with a rogue like me.''

"I'd listen in any event. Sometimes talking things
out can help clarify the mind.''

Nicholas shook his head. "I'll handle this in my
own fashion. But there is something I would discuss
with you, Mother, and I fear 'twill not be what you
want to hear.''

"I'll listen to anything you want to tell me, son.''

"I need to know how you feel about Baron
Hawse.''

His mother sat back on the bench. "Why?'' she
asked after a moment.

"Because Hendry belongs to me—to *us*—and I intend to fight him for it.''

"Surely you don't mean to...you're not talking *violence?*''

"Nay, I intend to plead my case in court.''

"But the court is presided over by the ruling baron,
which is Gilbert.''

"I'll go to York to the assizes or, if necessary, I'll
take my case all the way to the king.''

"The baron is a powerful man, Nicholas. He has
many friends, both at court and here in the north.''

"That's why I need you, Mother. As Arthur Hendry's widow, your testimony would hold major influ-

ence with the courts. But if you side with the baron, I hold out little hope.''

He hadn't expected his mother to be happy about his decision to fight the baron, but, in spite of the baron's words to him, he'd been certain that his mother's loyalty would remain with her son. His heart sank as he saw that she was struggling with her answer. Evidently the baron had come to wield more influence over her than he had suspected.

After a long silence in which she seemed to sense her son's disappointment, she said, ''Nicholas, I'd like to see you here at Hendry, see you choose a wife and raise fine grandchildren for me, but I'd also like to see you at peace with Gilbert. As I've told you, he's been wonderfully kind to me.''

''He's had reason enough to be kind as he steals our lands out from under our noses, Mother. I wish you'd wake up and see the kind of man he really is.''

There was pain in her blue eyes as she said gently, ''Nicholas, Baron Hawse has asked me to become his wife, and I've agreed.''

Nicholas reeled back in surprise. When he could recover his voice, he asked, ''I thought you said you had no desire to remarry.''

''I've changed my mind. Gilbert, as you know, has been attentive and a great comfort to me.''

''Are you in love with him?''

She answered slowly. ''You are an adult now, son, so I'll speak frankly. He makes me feel wanted, and I've decided that I rather like the feeling.''

Any embarrassment Nicholas might have felt over the implications of his mother's words was overshadowed by the larger consideration. If she did go through with this marriage, it would surely cement the baron's claim to the Hendry lands.

He studied his mother's face. In a lifetime of tempests with his father, she had always been the port of calm. If this marriage was what she wanted, shouldn't he step aside?

After a moment, he shook his head. "Mother, I can't believe this marriage would bring you happiness. Hawse is a tyrant who would bully anyone he encounters, starting with his own daughter. Even you become intimidated in his presence."

"I do not."

"Mother, the man has blinded you."

Constance pushed herself back from the table and rose. "I'm sorry you and Gilbert have not been able to become friends, Nicholas. But I have my own life to lead now, and I intend to do so."

He watched her as she walked out of the room, graceful and straight as a woman half her age. Yes, his mother deserved to find a good life for herself, Nicholas thought, but she'd not find it with Gilbert Hawse. Of that he was more certain than he'd ever been about anything in his life.

It was near midnight and Leon had had to be awakened by his page, but he showed no sign of irritation as he walked into the baron's antechamber and gave a small bow. "You sent for me, milord?"

"Aye. I paid a visit today on the innkeeper's daughter. 'Tis as you say, she's...delectable."

"I believe I said she appears ripe for plucking, milord," Leon corrected.

"Aye. I intend to be the one to bring in that particular harvest."

Leon's expression did not alter. "Very good, milord. Did you want me to have her brought here?"

"'Tis complicated by Hendry's involvement with the family. If aught happens to the wench, Hendry will know about it, which means that his mother will, too."

The baron's inner circle had long been used to dealing with his peculiar obsession for Constance Hendry. Leon merely nodded and waited while the baron tapped his fingers on the table, lost in thought.

"I tried to convince her to let me set her up away from Hendry," Hawse continued. "'Twould be more convenient not to have her so close, and that way we'd get rid of Hendry's brat as well."

"I take it she did not favor the plan, milord?"

Hawse shook his head. "She'd not hear of it."

Finally the baron looked up and said, "Blast me, say something, man. What do I pay you for?"

"Mayhap the lady needs to be persuaded to be cooperative. If Hendry is no longer an agreeable home for her, she should be willing to accept your patronage to relocate."

The baron smiled. "I believe you've hit it exactly, Leon. In fact, I know precisely the leverage to use to make her amenable."

"The boy?" Leon asked.

"Aye," Hawse answered. "The boy."

Chapter Fifteen

It was a rare summer day. The sun had dawned red and by midmorning it was hot and the air was heavy and still enough to hear the drone of insects in the trees. It was going to be too hot to work, Beatrice decided, so she walked into the village to ask Jannet if she and little Nick would like to join her and Owen on a walk in the hills.

"What of your father?" Enid asked, looking up from her spinning.

"He's feeling better. The palsy's hardly noticeable today. I'd not let him walk with us, but he's good enough to be on his own for a few hours."

The old woman stood and replaced the bobbin on the wheel. "I'll take a wee stroll over to the inn to see if Phillip needs anything while you young ones have your day in the country."

"'Tis not necessary—" Beatrice began, but she stopped when she saw Enid's eager face.

"Father would be pleased for the company," she said with a smile.

She and Jannet exchanged a glance as the older

woman carefully patted her hair into place and fastened on her best wimple before heading out the door.

"'Tis not possible that a woman of her age could be having romantic feelings for a man of your father's age, is it?" Jannet asked.

Beatrice smiled. "Enid has a lot of life in her yet, Jannet. More than my father, perchance. It would be wonderful to think that the two might have some life to share together. They've each been without a mate for a long time."

Owen and Nicky had been playing on a barrel in the corner of the room, rocking it from one side to another, when it suddenly tipped over with a great crash. Little Nick started wailing at once and Owen looked frightened. Jannet and Beatrice rushed to comfort them.

"We'd best get them outside before they destroy your household," Beatrice observed when the commotion had subsided.

"Aye. I'll put some pasties in a basket and we'll be off."

The procession of the two women and two boys made its way around the back of the house to tell Harold their plans for the day, then set off to the north, walking straight through the fields rather than staying to the road.

"Can we climb a tree?" Owen asked as he and little Nick darted back and forth, running three steps for every one taken by the more sedate grown-ups.

"Tree!" Little Nick echoed his friend.

"We'll see if we find one with low branches," Beatrice answered. She'd learned to put qualifiers on her promises.

"Hurray, tree!" Owen yelled and ran forward in a burst of energy, followed several paces behind by little Nick.

Jannet and Beatrice laughed at their exuberance. "Mayhap you and I should climb a tree as well, Beatrice," Jannet suggested.

Beatrice shook her head with a smile as the two women picked up their pace to keep up with their charges.

Neither one saw the two horsemen watching them from a nearby grove of trees.

Nicholas tried ignoring the knocking on his door, but the caller was insistent. Finally, he stumbled out of his bed, fought off the waves of nausea from too much liquor the previous evening, and crossed the room to throw open the door.

Mollie stood on the other side with a tray of food. "'Twas your mother's idea, milord," she said with her usual brazen smile. "She said ye'd taken nothing of food yestereen and if ye did not eat, ye were likely to wither away that magnificent body of yours."

As always, Mollie's impudence drew a smile. "Somehow I can't imagine my mother saying such a thing."

She cocked her head. "I may have mistook some of the words," she admitted. "Though 'tis the truth. A soul's got to eat."

She pushed the tray toward him, backing him into the room. "Now sit down like a good boy and have some pottage," she coaxed.

"Honestly, Mollie. I thank you, but I'm not hungry."

"Nor would I be with half a barrel of ale under me belly. But that stuff'll pickle yer brain, Nicky. 'Tis food ye need."

He let her push him backward until he was sitting down on the bed. She placed the tray beside him. "Very well, I'll try to eat something," he said, to be rid of her. "Thank you for bringing it."

"Oh no, my boy. Ye'll not be getting off that easy. I'm standing here until I see you down a good few swallows."

She crossed her arms and stood watching him like a master-at-arms.

He looked up at her, and even that slight motion set off waves of pain behind his eyes. "I'm not sure I can without tossing it right back up again."

At that, she picked up the tray and sat on the bed with the tray on her lap. "Sure ye can, Nicky," she said, her voice coaxing. She took a spoonful of the stew and held it to his mouth. "Come on. Give it a try."

Nicholas laughed. "I've been drunk, Mollie, not sick. I can feed myself, at least." He plucked the tray off her lap and put it on his own, then proceeded to take several large bites of stew. After the first couple of swallows, the food started to taste almost good to him.

Mollie watched in silent approval while he finished about half the bowl. Finally he said, "There. That should be enough to satisfy both you *and* my mother."

She leaned over and eyed the bowl. "'Tis better than nothing." She took the tray from his lap, but instead of standing to leave, she set it on the floor.

Then she turned back to him on the bed and tucked her legs up underneath her like a child. "Hot food's the best comfort for a gloomy heart, Nicky. I used to have another remedy. Do ye remember it?" She cocked her head at him suggestively.

Nick had not the slightest idea how old Mollie was. She'd lived at Hendry as long as he could remember. She had a kind of ageless earthiness that made it impossible to pin her to a certain number of years.

"Your remedies have served me well in the past, Mollie," he acknowledged.

She gave an exaggerated sigh. "'Tis a pity I had to get reformed in me old age. Though methinks the likes of Mollie be not what ye're needing anymore. Is it not so, Nicky?"

He hesitated, not wanting to hurt her feelings, but finally told her, "Nay."

Mollie put a calloused palm against his cheek. "Ye've grown up, Nicky. I always told yer father that ye'd be a fine man one day, and so ye are."

Nicholas blinked. The drink was still clouding his head, and Mollie's words seemed to make little sense. When would Mollie the serving maid ever have held a discussion with the arrogant and distant Arthur Hendry? He must have misunderstood her.

"I'm a man, now, Mollie. That much is for certain. As to the kind of man, I'm still learning about that. Did you know that I've a son now?"

Her smile was warm. "Aye, I've seen him, Nicky. He's a bonny boy, just like his father."

Nicholas smiled back. He'd not seen Owen these past two days and suddenly he missed the boy. Whether Beatrice wanted to see him or not, he was not going to stop his visits with Owen. Unlike Nicholas himself, he was determined that Owen would grow to manhood with the help and support of a father who loved him. "Aye, the lad's bonny. And brighter than most, I'd wager."

Mollie looked amused. "I'd wager, Nicky."

Nicholas looked down at the tray of food on the floor. "You can leave this, if you like. I may finish it, then I'll return the dishes to the kitchen."

Mollie gave a satisfied nod. "The color came back into yer face when ye began to talk about yer boy, Nick. Mayhap ye should go see him today. I warrant the young lad's the best remedy of all for whatever's eating at ye."

Nicholas leaned over and gave Mollie a kiss on the cheek. "You continue to be wise as well as warm, Mollie luv."

She jumped up with her usual energy and started toward the door, saying, "If Clarence ever proves me false, I just might try to make ye change yer mind, Nicky." He was surprised to see that when she turned back, her smile was sad, as if she knew full well that the days were past when Nicholas would be likely to seek her out in her quarters behind the kitchen.

"Thank you, Mollie," Nicholas said gently.

She bobbed once, and then was out the door.

After she left, Nicholas sat for a moment, then lifted the tray of breakfast and finished the contents of the bowl. In the bright light of morning, things were clearer than they had been the previous evening as he'd ridden home from the inn in dismayed confusion trying to figure out what had gone so wrong after he and Beatrice had made love.

Beatrice had long resented him for having left Flora, but he'd had the feeling that she had at least begun to forgive him for that. However, she might still be feeling guilty for making love with the man who had wronged her sister. She may be worried about Phillip's reaction.

All things considered, it was not so shocking that she had had conflicting feelings on the matter. But Beatrice was one of the brightest women he'd ever met and, by all standards, the most independent. She wasn't the kind of woman to let the ghosts of a past tragedy keep her from living her life to the fullest. He would just have to be patient until she had time to work things out for herself.

By the time he had finished dressing, he found himself whistling a ballad one of the traveling minstrels had played for him and Beatrice on Midsummer's Eve, just after he'd kissed her. His humor was almost totally recovered, though his ringing head was a reminder of his gloomy thoughts of the previous evening.

He'd seek her out, he decided. It was going to be a hot day. The walls of his perpetually chilly bedchamber had turned clammy. Perhaps he could take both Beatrice and Owen for a ride in the countryside. Then they would find a place to spread a blanket on the grass, and when Owen was occupied with his playing, he'd steal a kiss from her. He'd tell her that things were going to be all right between them. He'd tell her that Flora, so sweet and generous while on earth, could only be rejoicing from her heavenly post in the happiness they had found.

Rehearsing the little speech made him jittery, like

a young swain courting his first maid. He continued whistling the tune all the while as he hurried down the stairs, called a farewell to his mother, who was still at the dining table, and raced out to the stables.

They'd decided to give the boys a project to help them run off some of the limitless energy of their stubby legs. Beatrice and Jannet sat on a small hillock while Owen and little Nick scurried back and forth bringing them wildflowers which the women were weaving into two wreaths.

"Have a care that ye don't run too far," Jannet hollered as the two tiny heads disappeared over a slope down the hill. Both women stopped their work and craned their necks, but in a minute, the heads bobbed into view again.

"Beatrice, ye won't admit it, but your voice tells me that you're smitten with the man."

"Ah, Jannet, how could I possibly be smitten with a man who was in love with my sister? A man whose baby caused her death?"

Jannet tucked a flower stem into her garland before she answered carefully. "Don't be angry, Beatrice, but I'd not be so sure that Nicholas was in love with Flora. From the way Harry tells it, before Nicholas Hendry left for the wars, he *loved* many women, but was *in* love with none of them."

Beatrice felt a curious twinge of satisfaction at Jannet's pronouncement, but she was not sure that the idea that Nicholas may not have loved Flora should assuage her guilt. Even if Nicholas hadn't been in love with Flora, Flora had definitely been in love with him. If he'd convinced her sister to love him, who was to say he wasn't using the exact same empty charm on Beatrice? It would serve her right if she ended up abandoned and pregnant the way her sister had.

"That only shows what a scoundrel he is, Jannet," she said, trying to keep her voice light. "I'd be a fool to trust my heart to such a one."

"Harry says he sees him changed since he's come back."

"Aye, war always changes a man, and he's the man of the house now with his father dead. But where ladies are concerned..." Beatrice jumped as she pricked her finger on the stiff end of a flower. Then she sighed. "A rogue is a rogue, for all that. I don't think 'tis something you can change."

Jannet looked at her friend out of the corner of her eyes. "I believe the right woman can change a man like that."

Beatrice shook her head. "Nay, I'd best stay ten leagues away from Nicholas Hendry if I want to keep my sanity. For, in truth, he is devilish handsome."

Jannet grinned. "Ye'd make a handsome twosome."

"Even if he were the kind of man to fall in love, 'twould not be with me. He's a knight and a landowner. I'm but a brewer's daughter."

"You're running the inn now, like a real businesswoman. 'Twould not be unheard-of."

Little Nick ran up to his mother with four crushed flowers in his hand, which he presented to her proudly.

Beatrice looked behind him down the hill. Sud-

denly she felt cold in the pit of her stomach.
"Where's Owen, Nicky?" she asked.

Jannet's expression grew serious as she turned
around, searching for her son's friend. "Owen!" she
called.

Beatrice jumped up, the flowers falling around her
in disarray. She shaded her eyes from the sun and
turned in a circle, looking every which way and calling Owen's name.

He had simply vanished.

She crouched down and took little Nick's hand.
"Where's Owen?" she repeated.

The little boy looked worried. "Owen runned
away," he said. Jannet repeated the question, but that
was as much as they could get him to say on the
subject.

"He's an adventurous little tyke, Beatrice." Jannet
tried to sound reassuring. "He's just wandered off.
We'll find him."

"You search down there, and I'll go down this
way," Beatrice said, her voice revealing nothing of
her alarm. "He may be in those trees down there."

Jannet scooped little Nick into her arms and started
down the east side of the hill while Beatrice headed
west. She tried to slow her racing heart by telling
herself that Jannet was probably right. Owen loved to
explore and had no doubt just ventured a little farther
than he had intended.

The hillside where they had been sitting was fairly
open, but halfway down the hill there were quite a
few bushes and trees. Owen might be just behind any
one of them.

She traced a zigzag pattern down the slope, not

wanting to miss any possible hiding place. Every minute or so she called Owen's name, and she could hear Jannet doing the same from the other side of the hill.

She'd almost reached the bottom and there was still no sign of Owen. Once the ground leveled out, the trees became quite thick. If he'd wandered into the forest, she thought, holding down a sob of panic, it could take hours to find him. She and Jannet would have to return to the village to seek help.

"Owen!" she called again, the desperation cracking her voice.

Suddenly a man stepped out from behind a tree just below her. "'Tis shocking how easy it is to lose an active little lad like that, is it not?" Baron Hawse's voice was frighteningly calm and solicitous.

Beatrice gasped. "Where is he?"

The baron put up a hand. "I tried to warn you, m'dear. I tried to get you to see that another clime might prove to be *healthier* for your family."

He had that superior half-smile on his face again, but Beatrice was too afraid to be angry. Her knees felt weak and it was all she could do to keep her voice steady. "What have you done with my child?" she asked.

The baron took a couple of steps up the hill toward her. "So you want to claim the bastard as yours?"

"Owen's my nephew by birth, but my very own child for all that."

"Just so." He stepped closer, his big nose almost directly in her face. "And of course, you want to keep him safe, which is why I'd ask you to consider my offer of, shall we say, *protection?*"

"I want nothing from you but my child, safe and sound."

"'Tis a cruel world, Mistress Thibault, especially for a young child with no father to protect him."

"Owen has a father."

"And you think he will protect the boy? Nicholas Hendry has never thought of anyone but his own self and his own pleasures. He may be momentarily amused by the idea of having a child, but once he marries my daughter, he'll—" He stopped and cocked his head sympathetically as Beatrice went white. "Ah, you didn't know? My Winifred is quite in love with Nicholas, it appears, and, of course, 'tis an excellent match for him."

His expression became sympathetic as he continued, "Ah, m'dear, I hope he's not been trifling with *your* affections. Nicholas Hendry is not a man to be trusted by any woman."

Beatrice took a step backward up the hill to get away from the baron's fetid breath. "I care not who Master Hendry marries," she said. "I just want Owen. Where is he?"

"He's safe, Beatrice. You see, I've kept him safe for you." He followed her up the hill and put a hand on her cheek. "I'm a powerful man, m'dear, and I can do a great deal for the people who are nice to me."

His voice was oily and the touch of his hand made her skin crawl, but she didn't dare escape until she found out about Owen. "Please, baron." Her voice was a near whisper. "Where is he?"

The baron put two fingers to his lips and gave a shrill whistle. From a grove of trees at the very bottom of the hill, Leon emerged with Owen squirming in his arms. He set the boy down, and he ran up the hill and into Beatrice's arms.

"Don't like that man, Aunt Beady," the boy said.

She clasped him to her, closing her eyes and letting out a breath of relief. "You're all right now, Owen. Don't worry about it."

She turned her gaze back to the baron. "'Tis a despicable trick to use a child this way."

The baron smiled. "'Twas merely to show you how vulnerable a woman and child can be when they have no one to look after them."

Jannet called down from the top of the hill. Beatrice turned to wave up at her and was surprised to see Nicholas standing alongside her.

The baron seemed surprised as well, and none too pleased. "I'll let you get back to your flower weaving, Beatrice," he said, speaking a little more quickly. "But I trust you'll consider my offer carefully. As you saw from today's little demonstration, 'tis an easy thing for children to find themselves suddenly in harm's way. With my protection, you'll never have to worry about Owen's safety again. I promise you."

Now that Owen was back safe in her arms, Beatrice's fury rose. "I've no need of protection from you, Baron, nor from any man. But my father and I have many friends in this village, and, by the saints, if anything happens to Owen, you'll know what it is to have enemies."

The baron listened to her words, admiration and something more primitive kindling in his eyes. "By God, but you're a fine piece, m'dear. We'd make a match, you and I."

She sucked in a breath. "Not in a dozen lifetimes," she spat.

His expression clouded for a few seconds, then his bland smile returned. "We shall see about that," he said softly.

Then, as Nicholas and Jannet, with little Nick in her arms, started down the hill toward them, the baron turned and strode away. By the time Nicholas reached her, both he and Leon had disappeared.

"Is Owen all right?" Jannet asked as they drew near.

Beatrice still held the boy tightly in her arms, but he wiggled to get down when he saw Nicholas. She let him go and watched as he ran into his father's embrace.

"He's fine. He just wandered a little too far off," she told them. She wasn't sure she wanted to reveal the details of her conversation with the baron, at least until she'd had time to consider his words and what his veiled threats might mean to Owen.

But Nicholas had seen the baron and demanded more information. "What was Hawse doing here?" he asked with a frown.

"Passing by, I suppose," she said.

"Ugly, bad man," Owen said, burying his face against his father's chest.

Nicholas looked from his son back to Beatrice. "What's he talking about?"

"The baron's steward scared him, I believe. 'Tis not surprising. The man would scare a hobgoblin."

To her relief, Nicholas did not ask for further explanations. Instead he turned his attention to entertaining Owen and little Nick. Soon he had the two boys laughing, the misadventure forgotten.

But when they all had walked back to the Fletchers' cottage, Nicholas turned to Jannet and asked, "When we reach the village, could I trouble you to look after Owen for a spell?" He stopped and looked over at Beatrice. "I have a few things I need to discuss with his aunt."

Chapter Sixteen

After the initial scare over Owen had passed, Beatrice's head kept whirring with the other things Baron Hawse had said to her, in particular, his statement that Nicholas Hendry was affianced to the baron's daughter. Nicholas had never mentioned such a thing, but, of course, she thought bitterly, why would a landed knight bother to mention his marriage plans to a mere villager, one of his very own tenants?

Walking back through the fields to the Fletchers' she watched him romping up ahead with Owen and little Nick, at times seeming as much a boy as they. The incessant giggling of the boys punctuated by Nicholas's deep, rich laughter, floated back to the two women.

Beatrice felt an ache in the middle of her chest. This was exactly what she had feared. She'd acted no more responsibly than her sister. She'd fallen in love with Nicholas Hendry, and would be left with nothing but a broken heart to show for it. At least, she thought grimly, she had fared better than her sister. Even in the midst of the new sensations of lovemaking, Beatrice had been aware that Nicholas had taken care not to repeat the mistake he'd made with Flora. There'd be no illegitimate baby to reveal her humiliation.

By the time they reached the Fletchers' she'd decided that the only help for it was to stay as far away from Nicholas Hendry as possible. He could have his visits with Owen when she was not around. She'd ask for a warning when he was going to be at the Fletchers' so that she would not encounter him there. And she'd never walk anywhere near Hendry Hall again.

They'd reached the Fletchers' cottage and Jannet was asking, "Is it all right with ye, Beatrice?"

"Is what all right?" she asked blankly.

"To leave Owen here so you and Nicholas can speak privately together."

"Nay!" Then she lowered her voice when both of the little boys looked up at her in alarm. "I've nothing to say to Master Hendry," she said, shooting him a scathing glance.

Nicholas looked hurt for just an instant, then his expression clouded into anger. "Then I'll have to insist, for I've things to say to you, mistress."

Jannet looked from one to the other uncertainly. "Ah...shall I just run along with the wee ones and you two can work this out?" she asked with a nervous smile.

Nicholas and Beatrice spoke at the same time.

"Aye."

"Nay."

Jannet folded her arms and waited.

Owen came running up to Beatrice and tugged at her dress. "May I stay with little Nick, Aunt Beadie?

We're going to ride our horses.'' The elaborate hobby horse that Nicholas had given Owen had been duplicated at the Fletchers' so the boys could ride together. Though the horses consisted of little more than two stout sticks, the boys seemed to enjoy them every bit as much as the finely crafted one that had belonged to Nicholas.

"We've had a long day—" she began, but as Owen's face fell with disappointment, she relented. "You may stay until supper. Then I'll come back to fetch you."

The boys ran off with a whoop. Jannet gave a small sigh of relief and said quickly, "Well, then. I'll just go around and see if Harry has missed us." Then she bustled around to the back of the cottage.

Nicholas and Beatrice stood looking at each other warily.

"Will you not even talk to me now?" he asked finally.

"I'm not sure we have anything to talk about."

"If nothing else, we'll talk about my son."

"What about him?"

Nicholas shook his head. "Not here." He pointed to Scarab, who was tethered nearby. "Will you ride with me?"

Beatrice looked around. There was no sign of either Jannet or Harold. She could hear the shouts of the boys from behind the cottage. With a sigh, she agreed, and followed him over to his horse in silence. "I've not done this before," she murmured, as he held his hands cupped for her to mount.

He flashed a smile. "I'm not worried. I've found you to be capable in all things, tried or untried."

Beatrice knew that he was referring subtly to their lovemaking, but she ignored the remark and concentrated on positioning herself awkwardly at the front of the saddle as he swung up behind her.

Once they started to move, it was not an unpleasant sensation. She slid back a little to end up nestled in his arms. If he hadn't been such a scoundrel, she'd quite like it, she decided.

After a few moments, she realized that they were riding in the direction of Hendry Hall. "Where are we going?" she asked sharply. "I must get back to my father at the inn."

She couldn't see his face, but she could hear the smile in his voice as he said, "Your father's doing just fine, sweetheart. I went to the inn looking for you and discovered him sassy as a kitten while Enid fussed over him."

The news made Beatrice happy, but she said, "I'm not your sweetheart, Master Hendry."

He made no reply, and they continued riding in silence.

They had not ridden as far as Hendry Hall when Nicholas turned off the road and onto a path worn in the grass.

"Where are we going?" Beatrice asked again.

"Just a place where we can talk uninterrupted—neither your home nor mine."

The place turned out to be a small cottage tucked away in the forest that occupied the lands just behind Hendry Hall. The small house was not visible from the road and did not appear to be inhabited. An old path leading to the door was now covered with brush.

"I discovered this place when I was a boy," Nicholas told her, as he dismounted and held out his arms to help her off the horse.

She jumped down, and he held her there long enough for them both to feel the instant heat of their connection.

"I should not be here alone with you," she said, stepping out of his way.

One of Nicholas's black eyebrows went up. "'Tis late to worry about propriety between us, wouldn't you say?"

She'd spent the entire night awake, reliving their lovemaking. She'd called herself a fool a hundred times and had resolved that a momentary weakness of the flesh was not going to make her the latest in Nicholas Hendry's long string of conquests. She'd forced herself to relive the long hours at Flora's bedside listening to her sister sing the praises of the very man who had caused her death.

Baron Hawse's news that afternoon of Nicholas's engagement had hardened her resolutions into pellets of steel.

None of which explained why she was this moment staring at Nicholas's cocky grin and feeling the pulse beat at the side of her neck.

"I've never been overly concerned with propriety, Master Hendry, nor, I'm sure, have you. I am simply trying to avoid a meeting that might be disagreeable for us both."

Nicholas's smile faded. He grasped her arm and leaned close to her. "This is what has me puzzled, mistress. Unless 'twas some faerie's dream planted in my head after too much mead, you and I spent endless moments yestereen that were far from disagreeable.

And now I want to know what went wrong and why you've been looking at me all afternoon as if I'd just kicked your favorite dog.''

She felt his gentle grip on her arm as if it were a burning cloth. With some weariness in her voice, she said, '''Twould be easier on us both if it had been a faerie's dream.''

Nicholas shook his head, obviously angry. "It *was* magical, Beatrice, but it was no dream.''

Beatrice bit her lip and looked away from him. "Why did you bring me here, Nicholas?" she asked.

He looked around as if surprised to realize where they were standing. "Come," he said curtly, and, acting as if he would brook no argument, took her hand and led her inside the little cottage. There appeared to be only one room. Most of the space in the center was taken up with a table and four chairs, one tilting crazily on a broken leg. A small chest was sitting on the floor near the door, but there were no cupboards, no wardrobes. The only other piece of furniture was a rather large bed, pushed up against the opposite wall. It was made up with linens, but there was a musty smell that permeated the whole room.

"Does no one live here?" she asked.

Nicholas shook his head. "Nor ever has, as far as I know, though it belongs to the estate. Sometimes I'd play here as a child and wonder about it. If I'd not known my father so well, I'd have thought it a trysting place.''

Beatrice shot him a glance. "No doubt it was convenient as you grew older," she said sharply, then wished she'd bitten back the words. Had he brought Flora here? she wondered.

Nicholas was studying her face with a slow dawning smile. "Is that what our problem is all about, sweetheart?" He took hold of her shoulders to move her over to the bed, then gently pushed her to sit down and sat beside her. "Is that why you turned so suddenly cold last night? The other women?"

Beatrice looked away from him. His assessment was far too simple. But how could she expect to explain to him the feelings that had assailed her—the mixture of jealousy and guilt and fear of heartbreak? "A woman would be a fool to entrust her heart to such a one as you, Nicholas Hendry," she said finally.

Nicholas winced at her words, but they did not entirely dismay him. This was something he could understand. She was jealous. His unusual ability to attract the fairer sex and his reluctance to disappoint any one of them had made him something of an expert on the subject.

He twisted around on the bed so that his eyes were looking directly into hers. "I want you to listen to me. I've never before brought anyone to this place." He put up a hand to stop her as she seemed about to interrupt. "Though mayhap 'twas only because there were always other likely locations for our games, for I'll not deny that before I went to war I was not living the life of a monk."

Beatrice gave a reluctant laugh at the absurdity of the image of Nicholas Hendry in any kind of holy orders.

"But war can wreak many changes," he continued, his voice low and persuasive. "I'm not the same man who rode off to battle four years ago."

She seemed to be paying some heed to his words,

or at least was no longer trying to interrupt, so he continued to press his case. "I'm no longer interested in the kind of casual love affairs of my early days. The idea no longer intrigues me. Since my return—" he paused for a moment as the attractive face of the widow back in Durleigh danced before his eyes. He'd resisted the ardent woman's attentions for nearly a week before succumbing in one moment of ale-driven weakness. "Since my return to *Hendry*," he amended, "I've been with no one but you. I've not looked at another woman, nor have I wanted to."

At first Beatrice was reluctant to listen to his words, but the sincerity of his tone finally began to soften her. She couldn't believe it possible that he could sound so earnest if he was lying to her. Which meant that Baron Hawse had lied about Nicholas and his daughter. And this was not at all difficult to believe. She'd be a fool to credit a single word of what the baron told her with that slimy half-smile of his.

She thought of telling Nicholas about the baron's tale, but became distracted when he moved closer to her on the bed and reached for her hands. "Tell me you won't let my past sins ruin everything for us, Beatrice," he said. "I know 'tis asking much, since your very own sister—"

He stopped as she put her hand against his lips and spoke softly, "Hush, Nicholas. We'll not talk of Flora just now." She stopped and looked around the room warily. "You're certain you never brought her here."

Nicholas's laughter was relieved and hearty. "Nay," he told her, snatching her fully into his arms. "Not her, or anyone, you jealous wench. You're the first I've cared to bring to this trysting place."

''I'm glad,'' she murmured, as he rolled them both back on to the bed.

She was hoping that he would add that she would also be the last, but he had occupied himself with removing her clothing and had no more words for the moment.

Soon she had no desire for words as his lips found hers and his hands began their skillful exploration of her body. His fingers played about her breasts, teasing first one nipple, then the other, into rigidity. Then his hand sought an even more tender area below.

He stopped kissing her for a moment to watch her face as he found her most sensitive spot and massaged gently. She closed her eyes and gave herself up to the sensations, unembarrassed that he was observing the effect his ministrations produced on her. In only a few moments, the waves began and chills ran along her limbs. She opened her eyes and smiled up at him.

He grinned, then bent over to kiss her, murmuring, ''You are so responsive, my love. 'Tis incredibly erotic.''

She let him gather her into his arms, her body limp and momentarily sated. He held her quietly for several minutes without moving, but soon the feeling of his naked hardness against her made her begin to shift, restlessly. He chuckled without speaking and began to kiss her again.

All at once, his kisses seemed harder, deeper, with a greater sense of urgency. ''I'd thought to keep this a slow fever, sweetheart,'' he said, his voice suddenly hoarse. ''But I find myself suddenly unable to wait.''

She gave a moan of encouragement as he shifted their positions and entered her. This time she knew what to expect as he moved within her. There was a sense of oneness about their joining that went beyond the physical sensation to a place deep inside her that she hadn't known existed.

"My love," he whispered to her, his lips directly over her ear. The words echoed all the way into her core as she felt his rhythm increase and the intensity build between them. When they reached the pinnacle together, he said her name, over and over, and made the word sound like the closing line of a love poem.

Gradually the world came back into focus—the four walls of the tiny cottage, the musty odor of the linens, the chill of the dank air on her skin. Nicholas lay halfway on top of her, still and heavy.

She made a tentative move and his eyes flew open. His lips turned up in a lazy smile. "Will you tell me that this is another dream planted by the midsummer wood sprites?" he asked. "For I'll believe you."

She gave a happy giggle, and did not recognize the sound as her own voice. "'Tis you who've enchanted me, not the faeries."

He kissed her for that. "I'm glad. Though I may have had some help from those otherworld creatures, else I doubt I'd have been able to win you."

She pulled away to ask, "That sounds like an unlikely bit of modesty from a man of your reputation."

He laughed. "Do you forget what my reception was from you the first time we met?"

She flushed and answered more seriously. "I was prepared to hate you, Nicholas. Indeed, I already did."

His expression sobered as well. "Aye, you had your reasons. 'Tis not something we'll ever forget, nor should we. But I'm glad you've been able to change your feelings about me.''

He pulled her into his arms again, but the sober words and the memory of Flora had changed the mood. After a time she said, ''I really should be getting back to the inn. Father will wonder what's become of me.''

He didn't argue as she sat up and began to retrieve her clothes. After a moment, he followed her example. They dressed in silence until he said, ''Before I take you back, there's a matter I'd like to settle.''

She looked up, surprised. ''I thought we'd already settled the matter rather well,'' she said with a smile, pointing to the rumpled bed.

He returned her smile only briefly. ''Aye, we settled that part of it, but this is in regards to Owen.''

Beatrice frowned. ''What about him?''

''I didn't like to see him today in the arms of the baron's steward. I don't want Baron Hawse to have anything to do with my son.''

She felt a prick of misgivings. ''Nor do I. So we are agreed.''

''I've decided the best for all would be to bring him to live at Hendry Hall.''

Beatrice almost lost her balance as she finished the last fastenings of her gown. ''To live?'' she gasped.

''Aye. Things between the baron and me are likely to get…'' He paused. ''I'd feel better if I knew Owen was safe in my own home.''

The last remaining lethargy of passion disappeared as Beatrice felt her temper rising again. ''What makes you think he'd be safer with you than with me and his grandfather? It appears to me that you are the one who has a quarrel with the baron. Taking the boy to your home will only involve him in your disputes.''

He took a step toward her, evidently realizing that his suggestion had once again upset her. ''Of course you and Phillip could come to see him whenever you like.'' He tried to make his voice soothing. ''And at Hendry Hall we have servants who can be watching out for him at all times—''

''At the Gilded Boar he doesn't have to be watched by *servants*. He has an aunt and a grandfather to take care of him and love him.''

He reached out his hand and gave a little flip to her tangled curls. ''I'm not trying to make you angry, sweetheart, 'tis just—''

She interrupted again. ''Well, for not trying, you're doing a mighty good job of it. Owen's home is the Boar, and there'll be no more discussion of the matter.''

She knew her face was set in stubborn lines and she could see that Nicholas was becoming irritated, as well. ''Owen's my son,'' he said, his voice growing soft. ''I am his closest born kin. And I shall say what is best for him.''

Beatrice threw her arms out angrily. ''Is this why you brought me here to your trysting place, Nicholas? Did you think that your lovemaking would convince me to give up the rights to my child?''

''Owen's not your child.''

She could not believe the cruel words were coming from the man who only moments before had been kissing her with such tenderness. The baron's words came back to her. *Nicholas Hendry is not a man to be trusted by any woman,* he'd said. Mayhap he'd been right after all. She pulled away as he reached for her once more, trying to soften the harshness of the statement.

Her feet planted firmly apart, she faced him and said, "You're wrong, Nicholas. Owen is ten times more my child than yours. I was there at his birth. I walked the floor with him each night as his mother lay dying. I've fed him and cared for him and dressed him and taught him and played with him, while his father was off waging war in a faraway land. Owen's mine, Sir Knight. And I intend to keep him."

She was breathing hard by the end of her speech and felt the closeness of the room around her. She wanted nothing more than to flee, to run back to the Fletchers to find Owen and clasp him in her arms to assure herself that her words were nothing but the truth. But she was not entirely sure she could find her way out of the forest from this hidden place, so she was forced to wait while Nicholas calmed himself and tried to calm her as well.

"Sweetheart," he began, then, when she stiffened at the endearment, he changed it to, "Beatrice. You've been everything to Owen, you and Phillip. You've been both mother and father. And you've done a wonderful job of raising him. I'm not trying to separate you. I just want to take him where he'll be safe, especially now. There are things I need to do—" he stopped as he saw that she had turned her face away from him and was obviously not listening to his arguments.

"Will you take me home now," she said coldly, "or do I have to walk?"

He gave a great sigh. "I came today to put things right with us."

She looked at him then, and asked bitterly, "And you thought to accomplish it by taking my boy away from me?"

"Nay, I thought to accomplish it by doing just as we have done—by making love."

"Of course. 'Tis the way you've settled things your whole life, is it not? Once you've introduced a woman to those particular talents of yours, she can refuse you nothing."

He shook his head. "'Twas not my purpose."

She looked him square in the eye. "I don't believe you." Then she turned her back and walked out of the cottage. It might take her half the night to find her way home, she thought as she ran headlong into the forest, but it was worth it not to spend one more minute in Nicholas Hendry's seductive, treacherous company.

Chapter Seventeen

By the time Nicholas had caught up to Beatrice, she'd worked herself into a fine fury. Still trying to figure out how he once again appeared to be losing a battle he'd thought won, he'd tried talking to her, but she had only icily asked him to take her back to the Gilded Boar.

After he left her at the inn, she without a word of farewell, he'd ridden slowly back to Hendry Hall and found himself talking to his horse.

"'Tis like this, Scarab," he said to the back of the hulking animal's head. "Females think differently than males. I used to consider myself an expert in understanding such matters, but with this particular female I seem to take the wrong fork at every turn."

Scarab gave no sage reply, but neither did he turn shrewish and argue, so all things considered, he was probably better company at the moment than the inn-keeper's daughter.

In earlier days, Nicholas might have confided in his mother, but after her admission that she was going to marry the baron, there'd been an estrangement between them. In particular, he was quite sure she would not be able to understand the kind of peculiar panic he'd had when he'd seen Owen at the bottom of the hill that afternoon in the arms of Leon.

Simply put, he did not trust Baron Hawse or his steward, and he did not want either man anywhere near his son.

But perhaps he'd been too abrupt in bringing his suggestion up to Beatrice. He should have put it to her slowly, in stages. Perhaps he should first have explained to her about the war he was about to wage with the baron over the rights to Hendry. Now she was too upset with him to listen.

He reached the hall and rode his horse around to the stables. It was almost dinner time and there were no grooms in the yard, so he dismounted by himself and led Scarab inside.

"How long should I give her, Scarab?" he asked the horse as he removed his saddle and began to rub him down. "Will she be calmer by morning, do you think?"

Scarab tossed his head and turned away.

"You'd wait, eh? That could be the wiser course. Or the delay may simply fuel her anger with me. Beatrice can mount quite a fury, you know."

He pulled the horse blanket off the horse's back and paused, as if actually expecting some kind of answer.

Finally he gave a rueful chuckle, and pitched a forkful of hay into Scarab's trough. "Ah, you're a wise one to refuse an opinion," he told the animal. "In matters of the heart, 'tis best to let the protagonists muddle through it themselves."

He gave the animal an affectionate slap on the rump and turned to leave the stables.

Winifred Hawse was standing in the doorway, her face pale and grave. She gave a shaky smile. "So you really do talk to your horses."

He was startled, but recovered quickly. "Aye, particularly when I have questions that have no answers."

She nodded her head sadly. "I find myself with many of those questions myself."

He smiled and walked toward her. "You may ask them of Scarab, if you like. He's a good listener."

"So are you, Nicholas."

He was surprised at her words and a little uncomfortable. He decided to keep his reply light. "I'm always a good listener when 'tis a pretty girl doing the talking."

She laughed. "Ah, well, *sometimes* you're a good listener and other times you're an outrageous flirt, Nicholas Hendry, but in all cases I've found you easier to talk with than any man I've known."

The directness of her statement was unlike anything he'd have expected to hear from the shy girl he'd once thought her. "I'm sure there are many men who would like to hold conversation with you, Winifred, if you'd but give them the chance."

"Mayhap. I usually have little chance to find out when my father's around. I've only recently gathered the courage to consider how good life could be if I'd break away from him, but it appears I'm too late."

"Too late?"

"I'd thought you might be my savior, Nicholas. That idea of my father's for us to marry."

Nicholas blinked in surprise. "But we talked about this, Winifred." He searched for the right words. "We agreed that there is no love between us."

Her smile was sad as she reached out and put a gentle hand on his sleeve. "Don't worry, Nicholas. I know that I was not the woman you were discussing so earnestly with your horse. She's a lucky lady, your Beatrice."

"'Tis nothing against you, Winifred. Any man would be lucky to win you as well."

She shook her head. "You don't need to try to comfort me, Nicholas. Though my father tells me regularly how little use I am to anyone, I know that I have value. One day a man will come along to discover that fact, and it will be to him that I give my heart."

Nicholas sought desperately for more words of reassurance. Winifred had become stronger before his very eyes, just in these past few days. She was right, she'd make some man a wonderful partner in life, if her father didn't entirely crush her spirit before that man appeared.

Unfortunately, he was afraid that he was only harming her fragile confidence. He could read the disappointment in her—he'd seen it before in the girls he'd discarded. At one time he'd been callous about it, but now the look in Winifred's soft brown eyes made his heart ache.

"If you need help standing against your father, Winifred, I want you to know that you can call on me. I'd like to be your friend."

She winced at the word, but said, "Aye, I'm grateful to you, Nicholas. I'll be your friend as well. Now I'd best get back before they begin to miss me.''

He looked around for some sign of her litter. "How did you get here?" he asked.

She pointed to a small bay mare munching some grass at the edge of the yard. "I rode."

"On a horse?" he exclaimed.

"Well, 'twasn't on a donkey." She grinned. "Granted, Chestnut's not much of a horse compared to Scarab. She's pokey and gentle, but just fine for me as I'm still learning."

"Congratulations," Nicholas told her. "'Tis quite an accomplishment."

She seemed pleased. "But I still talk to them," she said over her shoulder as she walked over to the horse.

He followed her and helped her mount. She rode well for a beginner, he thought, as she made her way out of the yard. She was a smart lass to have turned out so well in spite of her overbearing father.

He turned toward the house with a sigh of frustration. The last thing he wanted to do was add to her burden. He told himself that it was the escape from her father she wanted, not Nicholas himself. Her disappointment would be short-lived. Still, he'd come back from the Holy Lands determined to show his worth to all who knew him. It was a vow that so far had been thwarted at every turn.

Enid had already prepared dinner for Phillip by the time Beatrice got home. The couple was seated next to each other on a bench, eating their meal from a shared trencher. The old woman did not appear to be the least bit tired from her day at the inn. In fact, Beatrice noted, she looked merry and a touch mischievous. Phillip, too, was wreathed in smiles.

Their good humor helped Beatrice let go of her sour mood. "Has everything been fine here, today?" she asked, coming to a halt opposite them.

"Aye," Enid answered with a cackling laugh. "I sent Gertie home, told her if any handsome gentleman travelers should pass by, I'd serve them myself."

Beatrice smiled. "And did any pass by?"

Enid made a long face. "Nay, though some of the village lads came for their afternoon ale, and I served that up."

"Prettiest barmaid we've had in quite a spell," Phillip put in, and Enid blushed a bright pink.

Beatrice looked from Enid to Phillip in amazement. If the older couple did not muster nearly six score years between the two of them, she would swear that they had the faces of a young maid and young swain in the first stages of courting.

She sighed. It was probably an absurd notion, and she'd long held the opinion that romantic love was an overrated concept. Her most recent adventure had only served to confirm the matter.

Likely as not, Nicholas actually *was* affianced to Baron Hawse's daughter and had simply inveigled Beatrice into his love nest that afternoon in order to…well…*have his way with her,* softening her up for the announcement that he was about to rob her of her child.

"I must go fetch Owen," she said, suddenly anxious to have the lad in her arms again. "Would you have me wait to walk back to the cottage with you, Enid?''

Phillip shook his head. "I shall escort Mistress Fletcher home."

Beatrice stared at him. "You've not walked farther than the brewing shed in over a week."

Phillip grinned. "I've had a near miraculous recovery. Enid, here, is a witch."

Enid blushed again and gave him a weak shove. "Go on with you, Phillip."

Phillip? Enid? Beatrice turned to leave, a little dazed. Perhaps those mischievous wood sprites Nicholas mentioned had moved on to the Gilded Boar to cast their spell over her father and the fletcher's widow. That, she thought with a sigh, would explain why the lovemaking imps had so thoroughly abandoned *her.*

Constance Hendry and her serving maid exchanged a look of exasperation. Nicholas had just spilled an entire pitcher of ale, the second he had ordered that evening.

"Shall I just tell the kitchens not to bother with the roast, since ye'll be drinking yer dinners from now on?" Mollie asked.

Constance gave the girl no rebuke for her insolence, partly, Nicholas was sure, because she shared the sentiment herself. But also because, ever since Nicholas could remember, Mollie had never been like any normal serving wench. She was used to speaking her mind, and his mother never seemed to have a problem with her nonsubservient behavior.

Mollie was looking quite pretty to him tonight after

his sixth or seventh mug of ale. Age had only added more lushness to her buxom figure. When he'd been young and Mollie had been the first to introduce him to the delights of lovemaking, her ample breasts had seemed to him the most magnificent creations in all of Christendom. Now, after all his travels, he decided drunkenly, he'd still count them as one of the world's wonders.

"'Tis all a man really needs, Mollie luv," he told her with a silly grin. "A measure of ale and the heart of a good woman. Isn't that what the bards sing?"

Mollie gave a huff and began to clean up the spilled drink which was running all over the table and dripping onto the floor. "They sing no such thing, ye big lug." She looked up with a shake of her head at Constance who had jumped up from her seat to avoid getting soaked by ale. Nicholas remained seated, heedless that the brew was dripping onto his lap.

"Get up, Nicholas," his mother told him. "Help Mollie with the mess."

Slowly he got to his feet, weaving slightly. "I'm sorry, lass," he said to Mollie. "I'm feeling none too steady for some reason."

"For good reason," Mollie said, picking up the empty pitcher and showing it to him. "And 'tis the last of this stuff ye'll be drinking this night."

Nicholas reached out and caught Mollie's wrist. "If I can't have my liquor, I'll take my comfort in other ways."

Constance was watching him with a pained expression. "Son, mayhap I should call one of the servants to help you to bed. I know not what demons have been eating away at you since your return, but

I know that they'll not be banished by drink, nor by reckless living."

Nicholas sat heavily back down in his chair and planted his elbows on the sopping table. "'Tis not the demons, Mother," he said bitterly. "'Tis the real people who are bedeviling me. 'Tis my neighbor who robbed me of my lands when I was off fighting a holy war. And my mother who has given that neighbor her loyalty above her very own son." He reached for the mug of ale, found it empty, and slapped it back down on the table. "'Tis one maid who wants me one minute and spits at me the next."

Both his mother and Mollie were looking at him with expressions that combined sympathy with distaste. Ah, if his righteous father could only see him now, he thought bitterly. He'd be vindicated in every dire prediction he'd ever made about his son's prospects.

Nicholas blinked to clear his vision and put his hands, palms down, on the wet table to push himself up. His leg did not even give a twinge as he stood. It was one thing that had gone right, but, of course, he owed the thanks for his healing to Beatrice.

Once he was standing and sure of his balance, he made an exaggerated bow to his mother. "Forgive me," he said. "I'm not the best of company this night." Then he walked as steadily as he could out of the room.

The two women stared after him for a moment, before Mollie said, "Do ye want me to go to him?"

Constance shook her head. "Nay, Mollie. I know you care for him, have even loved him in your own way, but I think you understand that you are not what Nicholas needs anymore.''

''Mayhap not, but he needs something. He's a man now, but nothing's changed. He's still flogging himself over the things his father used to say to him.''

''Aye. I should have talked to him about it long before this.''

Mollie looked surprised. ''Are ye going to tell him about his father?''

''''Tis time he knew the story.''

''The whole story?'' Mollie asked, her eyes suddenly wide.

Constance gave a rueful laugh. '''Tis time he knew, Mollie, though I regret any embarrassment it may cause you.''

''Lord luv ye, mistress. Ye could shame me in the public square every day of me life and I'd still not be paying ye all I was owing.''

Constance shook her head. ''You owe me nothing, Mollie. But if you feel indebted, then pay the debt by staying clear of Nicholas. You're still a tempting lass, and I see Nicholas in a state to be tempted.''

Mollie bobbed her head. ''Ye may be right. I'll stay clear of the lad for the nonce.''

''Thank you,'' Constance said.

''Ah, mistress, ye do know that if ye told me to walk into the gates of hell with me eyes open, I'd do it in a trice.''

Constance smiled sadly. ''You've already been there and back, Mollie. I'd not set you on any such path again. Nor do I want to see my son head toward the flickering fires.''

"If I found my way back, 'twas due to your graces, mistress, and I'll never forget it."

"Just help me on this one thing, Mollie. Stay far away from Nicholas until he's cleared his head about exactly what he wants to do with his life."

"Aye, mistress." Mollie gave a determined nod. "I'll do that very thing."

"For my money, you should forget about the trull, milord. Let me find you a nice ripe wench from the village to scratch your itch." Leon only rarely gave his master suggestions, but Baron Hawse had lingered over this particular problem longer than usual. They were once again in the baron's antechamber—Hawse seated at his table and Leon standing in front of him.

The baron rubbed his hands together as if they were chilled, though the evening was warm. "She's magnificent, you know. She stood there above me on the hill and practically spat the threats back in my face."

"I could find you a willing lass who'd devote herself to pleasing you."

The baron looked at his steward scornfully. "This is a lesson you've never learned. The pleasure is not in being satisfied, 'tis in the *conquest*. It would be the ultimate in pleasure to conquer a woman as spirited as Beatrice Thibault."

Leon sighed. "What about Lady Hendry?"

"Constance is a lady. She pays no heed to the scandals surrounding her son. And, of course, she turned a blind eye to exploits of that foolish husband until I did her the favor of killing him off. Even if she finds out about this, I don't think she'll cause much trouble over a quick affair with a mere tenant, even if that tenant is the guardian of her very own grandson.''

"Then you're determined to do this thing?"

The baron's eyes narrowed into two dark beads. "I've given my orders, Leon. Bring her."

"Aye, milord," the steward said with a bow. He shifted from one foot to the other. "Will that be all, milord?" he asked after a moment.

The baron waved his hand. "Aye, go."

Just outside the doorway to the antechamber, Winifred leaned against the cold stone of the hallway and tried to recover her breath. She'd been on her way to her father's chambers when she'd heard him talking with his steward and had paused. She'd come impulsively, after her talk with Nicholas, to ask the baron to send her away. But the words she'd heard drifting out from her father's room had made her freeze with shock.

What had her father meant about killing off Constance Hendry's husband? And this woman her father was lusting after—he'd called her Beatrice? Surely this could be no other than the Beatrice who had captured Nicholas's heart.

Along with everyone else in the shire, Winifred had heard the gossip about Nicholas Hendry's son, and was aware that the boy lived with his aunt at the Gilded Boar. She didn't know Mistress Thibault herself, but hearing of her father's plans for her made Winifred want to be sick.

She heard Leon's footsteps on the flagstones and forced her numb legs to move. Scurrying around the corner before the steward could emerge from her father's room, she ducked into a window well and hid herself in the shadows.

Leon passed right by without noticing, no doubt intent on his mission.

Her breath was still coming in shallow spurts, but there was no time to lose. She had to warn Nicholas of her father's intentions. She closed her eyes a moment and leaned her head back against the wall. She'd always known her father to be ruthless, but could it be true that he had actually killed Nicholas's father? She leaned over, her hand clutching her stomach, and wretched, dryly. But after a moment, she straightened up and took a deep, cleansing breath. She didn't have time to be sick, she told herself firmly. She had to find Nicholas.

Chapter Eighteen

There was no response to her knock but the door was not firmly shut, so Constance pushed it open, tentatively. Nicholas was lying on his bed, but had not gone to sleep. The candles in his room were still lit and the room reeked of ale.

"You've not changed out of your wet clothes," she said.

"I've slept in wetter on the march," he said.

"You're not at war anymore, Nicholas."

He sat up. "Not with the heathens, at any rate."

"Not with anyone," his mother said, walking over to sit beside him on the bed. "Unless it may be with yourself."

He stared at the dancing light of the candle on his bedstand. "Have you come to scold me, Mother? In truth I was hoping for softer words this night."

"From Mollie?"

"'Tis one age-old way to forget the world," he said with a weary grin.

"Aye, a romp under the covers would no doubt make you forget your troubles for a night, but what of her? Mollie's finally found happiness in her life. Would you destroy all that for your own selfish pleasure? Is it simply a male curse to be born without a conscience?''

Nicholas coiled back as if she had hit him. He'd never heard his soft-spoken mother talk this way. ''I'm sorry, Mother. I'm happy to see that Mollie has found a good man. I'd not do anything to spoil her marriage, I swear it.''

His mother sagged a little and all at once looked old. She patted a hand on his knee and said, ''Aye, son, I know. You have your father's looks, but nothing else about you is like him.''

Nicholas was confused by her answer. His father often enough had mentioned that Nicholas had inherited none of his attributes, but his mother had never before expressed a similar sentiment. And what did that have to do with Mollie?

His mother must have realized by his blank look that her words were not making sense. She gave a big sigh, settled back a little on the bed and said, '''Tis past time I talked to you about this, Nicholas.''

Thoroughly mystified, he asked, ''Talk to me about what?''

She paused a moment, then wrinkled her nose. ''Mayhap you should first change your tunic, then join me in the solar. It will not be easy for me to speak of these matters, but 'tis only fair that you know. I was able to forgive Arthur many things in order to keep peace in my household, but I never will forgive him for the way he treated his only son.''

He started to speak, but she stopped his words by rising from the bed and saying, ''I'll wait for you downstairs, son. Let me tell my story, then I'll answer any questions you still have.''

"I've decided that you're right, Father," Beatrice told Phillip as she sat down at the table in the middle of the big upstairs bedchamber. She'd already tucked Owen into his small bed.

"Now there's a novelty. Right about what, daughter?" His voice was amused, but slightly distracted. He was concentrating on whittling some barrel stops for the brewing shed.

"I think we should take Owen and move to York."

Phillip stopped the motion of his knife. "Well, this is a surprise."

"Aye. I've decided 'twould be best."

He looked up at her then, his expression grave. "And what do you think Nicholas Hendry would have to say about this change of heart?"

"I care not what he has to say. 'Tis my decision...*our* decision where we're to live."

"I grant you 'tis our decision where *we* are to live, but we might have an argument on the matter concerning Owen."

"Owen's our child."

Phillip put aside the knife and piece of wood and leaned across the table. "Nay, daughter, Owen is the child of Nicholas Hendry and your sister. You'd do well not to forget that."

Forget it? She'd thought of little else all evening. If Nicholas was determined to take Owen to live at Hendry Hall, there was legally little she could do to stop him.

She looked over to the small bed where only the

tousled black curls of Owen's head were visible above the blankets. "We are like parents to him."

"Aye," Phillip agreed calmly. "Which is why we must be sure that whatever we do is in Owen's best interests. Now tell me why you suddenly want to run away to York when you've been fighting the idea ever since I mentioned it."

She'd not planned to tell him about her conversation with the baron that afternoon, since he'd been so weak of late. But tonight he was looking much better, indeed, much like the strong father she remembered from her youth. She took a deep breath and let the words tumble out, concluding with Nicholas's threat to take Owen to live at Hendry Hall.

Her only omission was the interlude she and Nicholas had spent in bed at the abandoned cottage, which now seemed more like a dream than reality.

When she was finished, her father pursed his lips and said evenly, "I mislike that you and Owen have drawn the baron's notice. And there was a time when I thought the only solution for it was to flee, but now *I've* changed *my* mind."

Beatrice shook her head impatiently. "The threat now comes not only from the baron, but from Nicholas as well."

"Ah, but Nicholas has a legitimate interest in the child and, unless these old eyes are deceiving me, I believe he's developed one in you, as well. Can you deny it?"

Her blush belied any attempt at a denial, however she said, "He's a noble and I'm a tenant."

"Stranger matches have been made," her father observed.

"Nicholas is already pledged to marry the daughter of Baron Hawse."

Phillip's eyes widened. "Where did you get that information?"

"From the baron himself."

Her father gave a snort. "I'd not trust anything that man told me, daughter. Did you ask Nicholas for yourself if he is affianced?"

She gave a reluctant shake of her head.

Phillip reached to pick up his whittling. "Well, there you have it. I've seen the way he looks at you, Beatrice. 'Tis not the look of a man whose sights are elsewhere."

Could it be that her father was right and the baron's words a lie? A bud of hope began to grow inside her.

"You've never before been afraid of putting things direct," her father continued. "I'd suggest that now would not be the time to turn timorous."

This elicited a small smile from her. "You may be right. I should put the question to him before I judge."

Phillip nodded and began the rhythmic slice of his knife.

Beatrice looked toward the window where the midsummer sun still shone high in the sky. "Shall I go yet tonight?" she asked her father uncertainly.

Phillip continued whittling. "'Twill serve nothing to leave it to the morrow."

"Will you be all right alone here for a spell?"

His eyes came up from his work momentarily. "Go to him, daughter," he said.

She jumped up from her seat and went around to

drop a kiss on his forehead. "I'll return before dark," she said quickly, then fairly raced out of the room.

"Mollie was not the first," his mother said. The pain behind her words was not evident in her smooth face. "It started shortly after you were born, and for a time I did not hold Arthur totally to blame. The midwife who helped at your birthing told us that another child would surely kill me. After that, Arthur moved out of my chambers permanently. 'Twas too much to ask of any man."

Nicholas leaned against the straight back of the bench for support. He was still digesting his mother's stunning words. His stern, self-righteous father and *Mollie?* The generous and loving woman who had first introduced Nicholas himself to the delights of lovemaking had been the mistress of his very own father?

His mother continued her obviously painful account, but he interrupted her. "But Father was always so scornful and disapproving of my—what did he call it?—disgraceful behavior."

Constance nodded, her face hard. "Aye. I think 'twas his own shortcomings he was seeing every time he chastised you."

Nicholas shook his head, trying to clear it. The effects of the ale had dissipated, but he felt as if he was still drunk. "If Mollie...why is it that...?" He stumbled over the words.

"Why is Mollie still serving here in my home?" Constance finished the question for him. At his nod, she answered, "Mollie was but thirteen when she...when she caught your father's eye, an orphan with no family. I would not have held her to blame in any event.''

"'Tis strange that she would *want* to stay,'' Nicholas said, still puzzled by the odd twists and connections in a household he thought he had known.

"Strange, aye, but stranger still that she and I became, well, friends, I suppose you could call it. 'Twas after—''

She stopped, and when she didn't continue for several moments, Nicholas prompted, ''After what?''

Constance took a deep breath. ''I don't know if I'm doing right in telling you these things, son. Mayhap 'twas better for you to continue thinking that your father was the man he tried to portray himself as.''

"The perfect paragon of virtue who was burdened with a less than perfect son?'' he asked bitterly. "Nay, Mother, I would know the truth after all these years.''

She looked down at her hands. ''Mollie became with child, but Arthur could not face the scandal. He forced her to see an herbalist who nearly killed her while ridding her of the baby. The poor lass was scarcely more than a child herself.''

Nicholas put his head back and closed his eyes. "Poor Mollie,'' he said in a whisper. ''I never knew. She never spoke of it.''

"She's never spoken of it to anyone. But she's stayed on here at Hendry and now she has her baker and two fine, healthy babies. Over the years, I've offered to help her establish herself somewhere else, but she says this is her home.''

"And so it is,'' Nicholas said softly.

Both were silent for a long time. Finally Constance said, "I'm sorry, son. I've put a burden on you."

Nicholas straightened up from his seat. "Nay, Mother, you've *lifted* a burden from me. All the years I felt my father's disapproval, I didn't realize that he had sins as grave as mine."

"Graver," his mother said.

"Aye, graver. For no child of mine shall be lost through an herbalist's potions."

"Owen is a fine boy," Constance said with a wistful smile.

"Aye." Nicholas stood. "And if I can get that beautiful, stubborn aunt of his to stop arguing long enough to listen to me, I intend to raise him here at Hendry Hall."

His mother cocked her head in surprise. "I trow Mistress Thibault does not like that idea," she said.

"Nay, she needs convincing."

Constance smiled. "That's always been one of your specialties, son, but Mistress Thibault is not like most of the women you've charmed. How do you plan to convince her?"

Nicholas grinned and leaned over to her ear to say in a conspiratorial whisper, "I plan to marry her, Mother."

Nicholas had gotten no farther than the stableyard when he heard the sound of a horse approaching. Turning toward the road, he was surprised to see Winifred, riding fast. She looked anxious, but was doing a creditable job of staying in the saddle.

As her horse slowed, then stopped a few yards distant, Nicholas went to greet her with a smile. "Have you become such a rider that you give the horse no rest day and night?'' he teased.

She did not respond to his sally. Instead, she took a great gulp of air. ''I've come to talk to you, Nicholas. 'Tis about your son and your…your friend.''

Nicholas was surprised to learn that Winifred knew about Owen, though he supposed that there were as many gossipmongers at Hawse Castle as in the rest of the shire. Studying Winifred's face, he suddenly became alarmed. She was distressed over something more than village gossip.

He held up his arms to help her dismount. ''Calm yourself now, and tell me what has upset you.''

She was breathing heavily, though he couldn't tell if it was from agitation or the breakneck ride. Quickly, she repeated to him what she had heard from outside her father's antechamber. Nicholas's face grew dark as the account proceeded.

''The bastard!'' he exclaimed as she finished with the baron's assertion that it had been he who had caused Arthur Hendry's death. ''Forgive me, Winifred. I know he's your father, but he's a vicious man, now with lechery and murder to his credit.''

Winifred nodded, her eyes wide and miserable. ''Aye. It seems as if I've spent my entire life trying to love him, but I'm done with it. I'll no longer live at Hawse Castle, even if I must take vows to escape.''

''Somewhere there has to be justice in this thing— for you as well as me. You are welcome to stay here at Hendry for now while we see what is to be done. Are you willing to tell this tale to the courts, mayhap to the king?''

Winifred suddenly looked small and forlorn, but she nodded, her eyes filling with tears.

Nicholas gave her a smile of encouragement. "'Twould seem that neither one of us won the prize when they handed out fathers, Winifred, but we won't let it ruin the rest of our lives, now will we?"

Winifred looked uncertain, but shook her head in agreement.

"Before we see what action to take against your father, we must warn Beatrice. Will you ride with me?"

"Aye." She made a brave attempt to return his smile. "I'd meet this woman who has captivated both you and my father. Mayhap she'll give me lessons."

"You need no lessons, Winifred. I have a feeling that once you're free of your father's heavy hand, you'll be captivating men aplenty yourself."

He helped her back on her mount, then went to fetch Scarab. The sun was low in the sky, but he calculated that there should still be time to reach the Gilded Boar before dark.

Beatrice was not sure what she expected to accomplish by heading out at this late hour to Hendry Hall, but she knew that the hope that her father's words had inspired would not let her rest until she'd confronted Nicholas.

She would take the shorter route to the manor, up the hill and across the meadow, rather than staying to the road. That way she should be able to reach Nicholas's home before the sun fully sank below the horizon.

She stopped for a minute at the crest of the hill.

The exertion of the climb in the warm evening had her breathing hard and wiping moisture from her forehead, but the way down would be less strenuous and the breeze was picking up. She should look cool enough by the time she arrived at the gates of Hendry Hall.

She squinted down the hill toward the manor, avoiding the glare of the red sun that was setting just behind it. Two horses were leaving the gates. One of the riders was Nicholas. The other was a woman, and it took her only seconds to realize that it could be none other than the baron's daughter.

She raised a hand to block the sun from her view, willing her eyes to be mistaken. But there was no doubt. The couple rode side by side and, as she watched, Nicholas leaned over and adjusted something on the noblewoman's saddle. The girl seemed perfectly comfortable to have him attend to her.

Beatrice felt a plunge of disappointment through her middle. Disappointment and something more. As she watched, the girl laid a gloved hand on Nicholas's arm. He patted it with his own. So this is the green-eyed monster they speak of, Beatrice thought, with a touch of self-ridicule. This thing that can turn women into hags and drive men to murder.

She stood at the top of the hill and watched them until they disappeared around the bend of the road. Her expression was hard, her eyes dry. Evidently the baron had spoken the truth. Nicholas was affianced to his gently-born daughter, and it had been the height of folly for Beatrice to ever imagine that the time he'd spent with her had been anything more than a casual dalliance.

"So be it," she said aloud. Then she turned to walk back down the hill toward the inn.

The sun had disappeared over the horizon as Nicholas and Winifred reached the door of the Gilded Boar. Nicholas could see a light through the upstairs casement, but the taproom door was closed and the place appeared to be closed up for the night.

He slipped his hunting dagger from his belt and used the hilt to knock on the door. After a moment, the upstairs shutters were flung open and Phillip's head emerged. "Who's there?" the old man asked.

Nicholas took a few steps back from the door to look up. "'Tis Nicholas, Master Thibault. I beg pardon for intruding at this hour, but I must speak with Beatrice immediately."

Phillip looked surprised. "I'd have thought you'd already spoken with her, lad."

"I saw her in the afternoon, but—"

"Nay," Phillip interrupted, his expression suddenly concerned. "I mean tonight. She went to find you at Hendry Hall."

Nicholas exchanged a glance with Winifred, who had not dismounted. "When did she leave?" he asked, his face mirroring Phillip's worry.

"Well before sundown," he replied, scanning the darkening sky. "I'd not have let her go after dark."

Nicholas felt as if someone had pressed cold fingers on his throat. "She never arrived at Hendry," he said. "Nor did we see her on the road."

"I'm coming down."

Phillip started to close the shutters, but Nicholas shook his head and called up to him. "Nay. She probably went over the hill. We'll look for her. You stay there with Owen. He's sleeping?''

''Aye.''

''Will you be all right with him by yourself or shall I ride to the village to fetch Gertie?''

Phillip gave an agitated wave of his hand. ''I'm fine. Owen's fine. You just concentrate on finding my daughter.''

They'd picked their way up the hill in the dark, but had seen no sign of Beatrice. Winifred had volunteered to ride directly to Hawse Castle to see if her father knew anything about her disappearance, but Nicholas had refused to let her go.

''I'll not have another lady wandering alone this night,'' he'd said, his uneasiness growing by the minute.

They checked the road to the village, then stopped briefly at the Fletchers' to see if she had stopped there.

''Poor Phillip must be out of his mind with worry,'' Enid had said. ''I must go to him.''

It was agreed that Harold would escort Enid to the Gilded Boar while Nicholas and Winifred rode to Hendry Hall to see if Beatrice had arrived there in their absence.

''After I see my mother safely to the Boar, I'll join you at the Hall,'' Harold told his friend, and Nicholas clasped his hand in gratitude.

Night had fallen in earnest by now, but there was a half moon in the eastern sky that illuminated the road as Nicholas and Winifred returned to the manorhouse. As they entered the stableyard, Nicholas jumped off Scarab while the horse was still moving and took off toward the house at a run.

The great hall was brightly illuminated. Since it was past his mother's usual hour for retiring, something must have kept her up. He stopped and took a breath of relief. No doubt he would find Constance in the solar entertaining Beatrice. He and Winifred had simply missed her somehow in the gathering twilight.

But when he crossed the hall and made his way back to the smaller receiving room, it was not Beatrice who his mother was addressing with her usual perfect lady-of-the-house manners. It was his old colleague from the wars, Bernard.

Chapter Nineteen

Bernard leapt awkwardly to his feet at Nicholas's entrance, a big smile on his face.

Nicholas regarded his friend with astonishment. "So your broken leg has healed," he exclaimed as Bernard started toward him across the room, his gait nearly normal.

"Aye, 'twas a mere flea bite compared to what we went through rescuing Hugh in Jerusalem."

The big man looked as though he would willingly launch into a series of reminiscences, but Nicholas interrupted him. "Forgive me if my welcome is stinted, my friend. 'Tis glad I am to see you up and about, but there's a pressing matter I must see to." He turned to ask his mother, "You've seen nothing of Beatrice Thibault this night?"

Constance stood, looking perplexed. "Beatrice here? I thought you'd gone in search of her."

"I did, but her father claims that she was at the same moment on her way to find me."

"'Twould not be the first time a lady seeks out your son in the middle of the night," Bernard joked, not understanding the gravity that lay behind the polite conversation.

At that moment, Winifred walked up behind Nicholas. "We should have passed her on the road," she added.

Bernard's glance slid from his friend to the newcomer and lit with admiration. "Why, good evening, fair lady," he said with a little bow. Then he turned to Nicholas, raised an eyebrow and asked, "Two, Nicky?"

Nicholas shook off his friend's jesting and made the introductions. "Bernard, this is Winifred, daughter of Gilbert, baron of Hawse. Winifred, this lout is my comrade-in-arms, Sir Bernard."

Bernard bowed again. "Formerly of the Knights of the Black Rose, milady, at your service."

"'Tis good that you're here," Nicholas said tersely. "I may have need of you."

Finally Bernard seemed to become aware of the tension in Nicholas's voice. "What's the problem?" he asked.

Nicholas's reply was grim. "I seem to be missing a lady."

"Now there's a new one," Bernard observed dryly, but then he added, "I'm here for you, Nick—whatever you need. You know that."

Nicholas nodded and the two men exchanged a look of the kind of understanding that is only possible between those who have shared the worst that life has to offer. "Aye," he replied simply.

"What's going on, son?" Constance asked. Her usually serene expression was gone and her hands were clasped tightly at her waist.

Nicholas turned to her. "Sit down again for a moment, Mother. And you, Bernard. Winifred has a tale to tell the both of you."

Beatrice tugged at the ropes that bound her hands behind her back. She knew that she was somewhere in Hawse Castle, but the room was dark and dank and appeared to be little used. She could hear no activity outside the door.

She had not seen the face of the men who had captured her. It had begun to grow dark, plus she had been able to struggle only for brief seconds before some kind of hood had been slipped over her head. It had only been removed when she'd been shoved into whatever this place was that was currently serving as her prison.

But she had no doubt who was behind her abduction. Any minute she expected to see the door creak open and hear Baron Hawse's oily voice. Well, she thought to herself, she wasn't about to wait around idly until that happened.

They had not bound her feet, so she was free to walk around the room, but the only light to guide her was a tiny sliver that shone through underneath the door. Mostly she would have to explore by feel, which wasn't easy with her hands tied behind her.

They'd shoved her onto a narrow bed, which filled most of one wall. Beatrice skirted along it, then started inching along the second wall which appeared bare of furniture. After a few cautious steps, she stumbled over something on the floor. She knelt awkwardly and reached behind her to feel that it was a chest, held shut by a metal clasp. Maneuvering carefully, she opened it. She hoped to find some kind of weapon, but was disappointed to feel nothing but cloth. Evidently it was nothing more than a chest of old clothes.

She sat for a minute, then ran her finger along the edge of the cover. Then for the first time since she'd been captured, she turned her lips up in a smile. The metal clasp was sharp as a knife.

It took her a long time to cut through the ropes, and by the time she was finished, her shoulders were aching with the effort, but at last her hands were free. Immediately she sprang to her feet and began to explore the room blindly for anything that might serve as a weapon. She was not sure exactly what would happen when the baron decided to make his appearance, but she intended to be prepared.

Constance had urged them to wait until morning. But Nicholas had insisted that if Beatrice was at Hawse Castle, he was not going to let her pass the night there at the baron's mercy.

Bernard had agreed. "I think we should go tonight, but we'll go prepared, my friend." Then he'd disappeared upstairs into the chambers where Constance had settled him upon his arrival. When he emerged, Nicholas stared up at him in surprise. His friend wore chain mail, and over it the striking tabard of the Black Rose, the same that Nicholas and his comrades had worn into battle as they took the city of Damietta.

In his hand, Bernard held a wicked-looking scimitar. When he'd lost his sword in battle, the big knight had seized the curved saber from the hands of a fallen enemy. It had become his trademark as he earned his reputation as one of the fiercest fighters of the group. The sight gave Nicholas a surge of confidence.

For a moment, neither man spoke. Then Nicholas said, "One last battle, my friend." And Bernard answered with a grim nod of agreement.

Nicholas, impatient, was not sure he wished to take the time to costume himself as Bernard had done. But finally, at his mother's urging, he, too, donned the mail and resurrected the worn tabard that he'd never thought he'd take from the chest where he'd gratefully stored it upon his return home.

The two knights were a formidable sight as they took their leave from the two women. Both big men, they looked even broader with their armor and silver tabards, lined in red and black with the distinctive black rose that had been the symbol of their unit.

Winifred had offered to ride to Hawse Castle with them, hoping to be able to reason with her father, but Nicholas had refused.

"'Tis too dangerous, lass. I'm afraid if your father has taken things so far as to do this thing, the situation will be beyond reasoning."

"Then take me with you, Nicholas," Constance urged. "Gilbert will do nothing to harm me, I would swear it."

Nicholas shook his head. "Nay, Mother. I'll not risk it."

Constance looked from one knight to the other. "You can't think to go up against the baron and all his soldiers with just the two of you."

Nicholas and Bernard exchanged a grin. "There were only five of us, Lady Constance, when we hauled Hugh out of the most heavily guarded fortress in Jerusalem,'' Bernard said. "I warrant two ought to be enough to handle one English baron."

Both women shook their heads at the masculine bravado, but when they could not convince the men to wait or to recruit help from the servants at Hendry or the men of the village, they gave up and wished them Godspeed.

It was like the olden days, riding through the night on their two big chargers, their Black Rose tabards flapping in the breeze. Like old times, too, when Bernard leaned toward Nicholas and asked in a nonchalant tone, "So what exactly *is* our plan when we get to this castle, comrade?"

Nicholas laughed. "I was hoping you had one."

Bernard shook his head. "I'm just along for the ride. Plus, my leg's still none too steady, remember?"

Nicholas rolled his eyes. "Now you tell me."

Bernard gave a whoop. "Oh, the devil take it. We'll just ride in and demand that they give us back the woman. In the name of the king. We look fierce enough, I warrant."

Nicholas's expression was doubtful. "Hawse might simply say that he knows nothing about Beatrice's disappearance."

They rode in silence for several minutes, then Bernard said, "'Tis already the middle of the night. There probably won't be more than one or two guards at the castle gates. We could dispatch them, then sneak into the castle, find your lady, and spirit her away before anyone's the wiser."

"The castle's a veritable catacombs. We'd never find her."

Bernard sighed. "What we need is some of that black powder from the Orient that we used in Jerusalem. Now, *that* was pretty fighting."

Nicholas shook his head in frustration. "Do you think I'd risk blowing up Beatrice in the bargain?"

"Oh, aye. Mayhap 'twould not be a good plan."

The moon was high in the sky now, illuminating the dirt road like a silver ribbon. Nicholas stood in his stirrups and looked down it as far as he could. "Well, my friend," he said to Bernard. "We'd best think of something quick, for just around the bend at the bottom of this hill is Hawse Castle."

In the end they'd simply relied on their instincts, honed from their years as comrades in battle. Without asking, each seemed to know what the other was thinking. Bernard sensed when Nicholas needed help before Nicholas knew it himself and vice versa.

If the garrison had been awake, their bold approach would have been disastrous. But, as Bernard had said, most of the men were asleep. There were two drowsy guards at the castle gate and one other, also half asleep, just inside the bailey. Taken by surprise, the guards put up little fight. Nicholas tied and gagged the two at the gate, while Bernard stood over the third, who was lying on the ground with the edge of Bernard's scimitar at his throat.

"Did you ever see me cleave a man's head from his shoulders, Nicky?" Bernard asked casually.

"Aye, I saw it a time or two in Damietta, did I not?" Nicholas's voice was equally nonchalant.

"Do you recall that it was not pretty?"

"Aye, that's the way I recall it."

Bernard leaned over the prone guard. "Do you doubt, my good man, that if you so much as breathe wrong, they will have to bury you in two separate pieces?"

The man shook his head, quaking.

Bernard backed away and motioned for the soldier to get to his feet. He held him with his scimitar poised while Nicholas, having finished tying the other two, asked the man, "A woman from Hendry village was brought here tonight. Where have they taken her?"

The man shook his head and started to speak, but Bernard stopped him with a nudge of the scimitar. "No words, my friend. Just take us there. We'll follow you. If we see anyone or hear any noise from you, then you'd best make the sign of the cross quickly while your head is still perched on your shoulders."

They followed the shaken man into the castle, walking as quietly as possible in their armored suits. A few torches lined the hallways, but to all appearances, everyone in the castle was asleep.

Nicholas's anxiety was growing. It had been hours since Beatrice had disappeared. If Baron Hawse had harmed her...

They skirted around to the back of the great hall, and there the guard halted, looked uncertainly at Bernard's scimitar, and shook his head.

"What is it, man?" Nicholas whispered frantically. "Where is she?"

"I swear, yer lordships, I know not. I saw them bring her, 'tis true, but I didn't see where they took her."

Nicholas and Bernard exchanged a look of exasperation. "Shall I lop his head off just for good measure, Nicky?" Bernard asked with a grin.

The frightened guard's gaze followed the curving line of Bernard's scimitar.

Nicholas pulled a length of rope from under his tabard and threw it to his friend. "Tie him. I'll start searching for her."

He felt a moment of panic as he looked down the corridor from the back entrance to the great hall. It was getting close to dawn. Before long the rest of the castle guards would be stirring. How was he going to find her among the maze of halls and rooms?

The rear of the great hall appeared to be full of sleeping soldiers. Gentle snores came from the length of the rear wall. Nicholas crept carefully along the corridor just behind the sleeping men. Deciding that it was likely that the family slept higher up in the round castle keep, he found a circular stairway and started up.

The dim light from the corridor below faded as he wound his way up the steep stairs into total darkness. For a moment he considered going back down to find himself a torch, but time was too precious. He'd find some kind of light at the next level.

Using his hand along the wall to guide himself, he continued up, taking care that his mail did not scrape against the cold stone. The ability to move quietly in spite of his armor had proven useful in the Holy Lands, especially when the Black Rose knights had rescued Hugh from the Jerusalem prison.

Suddenly in the silence, he heard the unmistakable sound of steps above him on the stairs. He tensed and noiselessly took hold of his sword with both hands.

The steps neared. He lifted his sword, ready to strike, but at the last moment, held the blow. The steps were light. Perhaps they belonged to some hapless milkmaid whose duty it was to be up before dawn. Whoever it was, he'd have to keep the early riser from calling out.

He shifted his sword back to one hand and stretched out his free arm just as the dark form reached him. It was unmistakably a woman. He wrestled her to the ground and covered her mouth.

With unusual strength, she pulled away from his grasp and gasped, "Let me go, you oaf!"

Nicholas's sword dropped on the stairs with a ringing clatter. "Beatrice!"

"Nicholas!" she answered, equally astonished.

He pulled himself upright and her as well. "How did you get here?"

"The latch was rusted. I worked it loose after I freed my hands with—"

He interrupted her with a kiss that hit her mouth unerringly in the dark. "You're priceless, sweetheart," he said buoyantly. "But we still have to get out of here."

He felt in the darkness to retrieve his sword, then took her hand and led her down the stairs. Bernard was waiting at the bottom, and greeted him with an angry whisper. "I don't think you made quite enough noise to wake the entire garrison, Nicky. Shall I call in some minstrels as well?"

Then the knight caught sight of Beatrice just behind Nicholas. His tone lightened. "Ah, you've found your lady, I see."

"Aye. The battle's half won, my friend. Now all

we have to do is get ourselves out of here with our skin intact.''

There was no time for introductions. Bernard gave Beatrice a nod, then the three made their way back down the corridor and past the sleeping men in the great hall. Bernard stopped a moment to check that the bonds were still secure on the guard they had tied.

As they emerged onto the bailey, the first hint of daybreak was streaking the eastern sky. Nicholas turned to Beatrice and grinned. '''Tis the dawn of a new day for us, my love.''

She gave him an answering smile, but there was a sadness at the base of it that he did not have time to decipher. ''Come on, let's leave this place.''

They'd almost reached the outer gates when Beatrice gasped at the same moment Bernard said, ''The guards we left here are gone.''

From inside the gate tower, the two gate guards rushed out at them, accompanied by a third man—the baron's steward, Leon, holding a broadsword.

''He's mine,'' Nicholas shouted.

Bernard grinned and said, ''I'll take these two.''

Leon's advance was relentless. He appeared to have no fear whatsoever of Nicholas's sword as his weapon and the knight's came together in blow after blow, ringing out in the empty courtyard like cathedral bells.

Bernard made short work of the two guards, leaving both unconscious in the dirt, then he stood back and smiled as he watched his friend.

''Should you not help?'' Beatrice asked him.

''He needs no help, mistress,'' he replied.

But it appeared that in moments they would all

need a great deal of help as shouts arose and doors began to open around the castle. A group of half-dressed soldiers emerged from the keep.

"Could you hurry it up a little, Nick?" Bernard asked calmly.

Nicholas glanced briefly at his friend, allowing Leon to strike with the flat of his sword along his opponent's ribs. Nicholas staggered with the blow, but stayed upright.

There was a gleam of triumph in Leon's gray eyes. Behind him, the soldiers had reached the middle of the courtyard.

"Help him!" Beatrice cried, but Bernard stood without moving.

Nicholas gritted his teeth, drew a deep, painful breath and lunged. The dull point of his sword hit Leon at the base of his throat. The gleam in his gray eyes died suddenly, like a doused candle.

Nicholas stood for a moment, dazed, as the steward toppled into the dust. Bernard grabbed his arm and urged, "Come on, Nick. They're not coming to invite us to stay and break fast."

Recovering his wits, Nicholas reached for Beatrice's hand and together the three fled through the gates to their waiting horses.

Constance and Winifred ran out the front door to greet them as Scarab and Bernard's big mount clattered into the stableyard. Nicholas lifted Beatrice to the ground, then slid off the horse, holding his side.

"Are you all right?" his mother asked anxiously.

He winced. "The knave may have broken a rib or two, but I'll live."

Constance's hand flew to her mouth. "The baron?" she asked.

"Nay, his steward, Leon."

"His ex-steward," Bernard corrected. "By now he's keeping old Lucifer's accounts in hell, thanks to Nicholas's fine skewering."

All three women looked faintly sick, and Bernard looked around as if wondering what he had said wrong.

Constance put her arm around Beatrice. "And you, my child," she asked. "Gilbert—" her voice broke "—he did not hurt you?"

Beatrice returned the woman's embrace. "Nay. I escaped before any harm could come to me and met Nicholas and Bernard on the way out of the castle." She looked over at Nicholas. Winifred had come to stand next to him and had placed her hand gently on the side of his Black Rose tabard over his sore ribs.

The sight made Beatrice stiffen. With a touch of bitterness, she said, "No doubt I could have gotten out of the castle quietly by myself without bloodshed if these two hadn't come riding in with armor clanking."

Instantly, she was ashamed of her churlish statement. She blinked back tears and amended, "But they risked their lives for me, and I'm grateful."

She walked over to Bernard. "I am Beatrice, milord. And I thank you for coming to my rescue." She made a wobbly curtsy that revealed her exhausted state.

Bernard took her arm to steady her. "'Tis all in a day's business for a sworn knight, mistress. I was glad to be of service."

Nicholas's expression had gone dark when he'd heard Beatrice's sharp words. It had been that green-eyed monster again, she thought ruefully. The sight of the baron's fine daughter giving him sympathy had twisted inside her like a sharp blade. As he turned his gaze to her, she looked away.

Constance was saying, "You all are overtired. We'll go inside for some food and wine and then let you get some sleep. Unless—" she looked over to the road "—you are being pursued?"

Bernard shook his head. "No one came after us. We'd have heard them on the highway."

Constance nodded briskly. "Well, then. If you will all go into the great hall, I'll see to the food."

Nicholas was still looking at Beatrice. In a dull voice, he said, "I'm not hungry, Mother. I'll send word to Phillip that we've found his daughter, then I'm going to bed."

"But, son, you should take nourishment and we must see to your ribs."

He shook his head. "Forgive me, Bernard," he told his friend. "After we both get some sleep, I'll show you how appreciative I am to you for this night's work."

Then he stalked off toward the manor.

There was a moment of awkward silence. Then Constance turned to Beatrice. "Mayhap you should go to him, my dear."

Beatrice looked from Nicholas's mother to the baron's daughter. "*I* should go to him?" she asked in astonishment. "Surely...?" She tilted her head toward Winifred.

For a moment, all three women looked confused.

Bernard said to Beatrice, "Seems to me a man's lady should be the one to tend him, mistress. From what I understand, that would make you the candidate."

"But Nicholas is affianced to this lady—" Beatrice began.

Both Constance and Winifred interrupted her at the same time.

"Nay, he is not."

"Nay, we are not."

Beatrice blinked, letting the denials sink in. "Truly?" she asked after a moment.

Constance gave her a gentle smile. "Nicholas is in love with you, my child. He told me plain that he plans to wed you."

"And you would countenance such a match?" Beatrice asked, not quite ready to believe what she was hearing.

"I can think of no better way to bring happiness to both my son...and my grandson."

Beatrice swayed slightly and once again Bernard put out a hand to steady her.

Winifred spoke, her voice warm. "'Tis true. I, too, have heard him speak of his love for you."

"But your father told me—"

Winifred gave a sad smile and said, "My father is not an honorable man. He says whatever he pleases with no regard for truth."

As she finally accepted what they were telling her, Beatrice began to tremble with something more than the early morning chill. "I must go to him," she said hoarsely.

Constance reached out and took her hand. "Come, child. First you need some warm food inside you and a mug of mulled wine. Then you can see to my temperamental son."

Chapter Twenty

The Black Rose tabard lay crumpled on the floor beside Nicholas's bed. Pieces of his chain mail were scattered about the room. At least he had had someone help him remove his armor, Beatrice thought, as she cautiously moved into the room and shut the door behind her.

He lay on the bed still dressed in his hose and tunic. Though he was asleep, he tossed restlessly and there was an expression of discomfort on his face.

She went to his bed and sat beside him, placing her hand on his forehead to see if he was feverish. To her relief, the brow felt cool. But the broken ribs would not profit from his fitful movements.

"Nicholas," she whispered.

His eyes opened at once, but took a moment to focus on her face. When he recognized her, he closed them again and said, "I'm asleep."

She chuckled. "Aye, but I've brought linens to bind your ribs. Sit up and take off your tunic."

He opened his eyes again. "You need not trouble yourself, Mistress Thibault."

"You're angry with me, and you've a right to be. It was wrong and ungrateful for me to criticize your manner of rescuing me."

He closed his eyes. "You were probably right. You could have handled the situation by yourself as you seem to be able to handle everything else in your life. I have always considered you an eminently capable woman."

Beatrice sighed. "Aye, I was the capable one. Flora was the sweet one. And the one to catch a man's eye."

At this, he frowned and his eyes blinked open once again. "You are jesting, of course?"

Beatrice twisted the roll of torn linens in her lap. "Jesting?"

Nicholas put a hand on his side and sat up, wincing. "Surely you can't think your sister was more appealing to a man than you?"

Beatrice was taken aback. "She seems to have been more appealing to you at least."

Nicholas looked at the ceiling and rolled his eyes. "The woman has taken leave of her senses," he said.

"Can you tell me that you are not still partly in love with my sister, that you have not thought of her when we have been…*together?*"

Nicholas shifted on the bed so that he was facing her directly. "Beatrice, your sister was a sweet, bright flower who honored me with her company as I left for battle in what could have been my last springtime. She was not and never would have been my great love and the partner with whom I want to share my life. There is only one woman I have ever met who would seem to fit that role. However, she has been infuriatingly difficult to win.''

''And I suppose this woman is *not* Winifred Hawse?'' Beatrice asked warily.

Nicholas's gaze went to the ceiling again and he shook his head in exasperation.

''Mayhap you've not been direct enough with this woman,'' she said. ''Most ladies like to be told things clearly.''

Nicholas studied her, his expression softening. ''For some time now, I've been trying to tell her that I love her, but she keeps running off or getting herself kidnapped or—''

''Say that again,'' she ordered.

''That she keeps running off or—''

Beatrice gave a little stomp of her foot. ''The other part.''

Nicholas gave a slow smile. ''I love her,'' he said.

She looked into his eyes with tears brimming her own. ''I have no station—'' she began.

He put a finger to her lips. ''You are mistress of the Gilded Boar, the most magnificent inn in Hendry. And you are aunt and guardian to the finest little lad in all of England. While I, at least for the moment, am a shattered former Crusader with no lands or riches to his name.''

She smiled. ''Mayhap I should look for a better bargain.''

''No doubt you should, mistress, but you won't, for I know a secret about you.''

''And what might that be?''

He plucked the roll of linen from her hands, leaned toward her and whispered in her ear, ''You profess to be a nurse, but one way or another, you keep trying to get me to take my clothes off.''

For two days they awaited retaliation from the baron. Bernard, though anxious to be riding to Dasset Castle on his own business, insisted on staying at Hendry in case further help was needed.

Nicholas, when he and Beatrice finally emerged from his bedroom a full twelve hours after she had gone there to bind his wounds, sent Mollie to bring Owen and Phillip back to Hendry Hall.

She returned with Owen in her arms, but reported that Enid Fletcher had installed herself at the inn and that she and Phillip would be staying there.

''The old man said 'twas to give his daughter time alone with ye, Nicky, but if ye ask me, 'tis he that wants the time alone with the Widow Fletcher,'' Mollie had told him with a wink.

Nicholas had thought about saying something to Mollie about the things his mother had revealed to him, but when she continued to treat him with her usual brusque affection, he realized that Mollie neither wanted nor any longer needed sympathy from him.

He was careful to make all his comments to her, to Winifred and to every other female under the age of eighty as innocent as possible. Now that he and Beatrice had finally found their happiness, he was not about to let anything spoil it.

Even the knowledge that the baron was still to be reckoned with could not mar the couple's delight in each other and in Owen, who was wild with glee exploring every nook and cranny of his big new house.

Their joy was infectious, and the household fairly hummed with it. But still they waited.

The reckoning came on the third day, and in the most unexpected form. Bernard, looking out the shutters of one of the solar windows, was the first to see him. He ran from the room and shouted up the stairs at Nicholas who had disappeared into his chambers with Beatrice for the third time that day.

"'Tis Simon, Nick!" he bellowed. "Riding this way!"

After a moment, Nicholas appeared at the top of the stairs, hastily dressed. The two men made their way out to the courtyard where, Simon of Blackstone, Knight of the Black Rose, was riding up to the stone gates of Hendry Hall.

They strode out to meet him, all smiles. Nicholas shouted, "Welcome to Hendry," but the words faded as he drew near and saw Simon's grim expression.

"What kind of sour face is this to greet old friends, Sir Sheriff?" Bernard asked, trying to stay jovial. After several misadventures upon the knight's return, Simon had been appointed sheriff of Durleigh.

"I've not come for a greeting," Simon said as he pulled his horse to a stop between the pillars. He looked at Nicholas. "I'm here to arrest you in the king's name for the murder of Leon of Ryminster."

Nicholas and Bernard looked at each other in astonishment. Then Nicholas looked back up at Simon and said, "I'm no murderer, Simon, as I'm sure you know."

Simon swung off his big horse. "'Tis not what I believe to be true that matters. There are witnesses, and Baron Hawse has ordered a writ against you from the king." After a moment's hesitation, he took a step toward Nicholas and extended his hand. "By the saints, Nick, I feared one of your female affairs had finally gotten you in trouble, but I see from your eyes that you are telling the truth."

"You can see it from my eyes, too," Bernard snorted, and stepped up to take Simon's hand after Nicholas.

Then all three looked down the road as a number of riders approached. "I asked to come in first," Simon explained. "To avoid violence."

Most of the riders wore the livery of Hawse Castle. The baron rode at their head. Nicholas looked at Simon, questioning.

"My men are at the rear," Simon assured him. "No one will take justice into their own hands this day."

By now Beatrice had come out to join them. "You don't have to be here," Nicholas murmured.

She glared without flinching at the baron who sat huffing in his saddle at the exertion of the ride. "I'll stay," she said simply.

Nicholas slipped an arm around her waist, then turned to Simon and said, "Here is the man you should be arresting. For the murder of my father, Arthur Hendry."

The baron's florid face grew a shade paler, but he said scornfully, "The villain will spout any fool story to save his neck. Do your duty, Sheriff."

"I can testify to his innocence," Beatrice said loudly. "Nicholas killed the baron's steward in self-defense while rescuing me from this man." She pointed to the baron. "The man who kidnapped me."

Simon turned to look at Hawse. ''Look at them,'' the baron ranted. ''She's the murderer's lover. Her testimony is worthless.''

From the door of the manor house a strong female voice rang out, ''But mine is not.''

All eyes turned to see Winifred, followed by Constance, striding out to the gate. A murmur arose from the baron's troops.

''Who is this?'' Simon asked Nicholas.

Winifred answered for herself. Approaching the men, she said, ''I am Winifred, daughter of Gilbert, baron of Hawse. I can testify that three days ago my father's men seized this woman and brought her illegally to Hawse Castle. Sir Nicholas and Sir Bernard went there to free her.''

The veins on the baron's face seemed about to burst. ''Shut your mouth, you mewling wench,'' he yelled.

Winifred did not flinch. ''Nay, Father. I've kept my mouth shut most of my life, but I'll not protect a murderer.'' She turned to the sheriff. ''I heard my father admit that he killed Arthur Hendry in order to obtain possession of Hendry lands.''

''The doghearted villain.'' The Hendry Hall servants had gathered in front of the house and Nicholas recognized Mollie's voice from the back of the crowd. A number of the others murmured agreement.

Simon took a quick assessment of the volatile situation—the Hendry men in front of him and the Hawse guards behind. He gave a whistle and immediately the Hawse troops were surrounded by the sheriff's men, several with bows drawn.

"The king shall judge this matter himself," Simon said.

Constance stepped forward and the murmurs died as she said with her most regal air, "He shall hear my testimony as well. Hawse deceived my husband into signing away his lands, and Arthur's death was not a natural one. The village healer called it a poisoning." She looked up at the baron, her eyes glistening. "I stubbornly refused to believe that such a thing could be true."

Hawse was looking at Constance with a gaze of pure hatred. "You were ever a fool, madam. You could have had the world with me, untold riches. Now you can enjoy your widow's weeds shriveled and alone."

Simon looked at the three women who had lined up in a defiant row just behind Nicholas and Bernard. "It seems you still have women on your side, Nick," he said with one of his old grins.

"They speak the truth, Simon—" Nicholas began.

Simon stopped his words with a wave of his hand. "The evidence is clear," he said, his voice ringing with authority. He pointed to the baron. "Arrest this man to await the king's justice."

In an instant the baron's horse had been cut off from his guards and surrounded by the sheriff's men. One of the men reached over to relieve him of his reins and another held a sword at his side while a third leaned across his saddle to pull the baron's hands behind his back and tie them.

Simon turned to his old friends. "Aah, lads," he said with a mock sigh. "Do you think you could keep yourselves out of trouble for a month or so?" He turned to Nicholas with a wink. "This time *I've* a lady waiting, Nick."

Nicholas grinned back at him and gave the sheriff a hearty embrace, then stood back as Simon mounted his horse and signalled his men to ride.

The entire family was in the solar, and, to Nicholas's eyes, the room had never appeared so bright. Even the ceiling angels seemed to have a special glow.

Constance was seated next to Beatrice, teaching her future daughter-in-law to stitch a tapestry.

Beatrice looked across the room at Nicholas, her eyes warm. "It'll never be as much fun as a good Latin translation," she said, smiling, "But I'll give it a try."

Owen was playing in the corner of the room with little Nick, who had come to visit. The two boys wore miniature silver tabards with black roses in the corner. They were dueling with mock wooden swords, one straight and one curved like Bernard's scimitar.

"So 'tis time I take my leave, Nick," Bernard said.

"I hope all goes as you hope at Dasset Castle," Nicholas said, his contented expression fading.

Bernard rose to his feet and Nicholas did likewise. "It will. My former liege lord Odo promised me riches and his daughter, and I intend to collect both."

"I would ride with you to help you as you have helped me, my friend, but—" Nicholas looked around the sunny room "—I have a family now."

Bernard grinned. "Aye. Who'd have thought it, Nick? And a right bonny family 'tis. You needn't worry about me. I don't anticipate any problems."

He made his farewells to the ladies, then walked over to the two boys. They stopped their sword fight as he crouched down next to them. "I can see that you are both brave warriors," he said, reaching out to put his hand on Owen's head. "But remember, to be Knights of the Black Rose, you must also be honorable and resourceful."

The boys nodded solemnly, their eyes big and round.

"Good lads," the knight said.

Beatrice rose to accompany the men to the stableyard where Bernard mounted his horse.

"Godspeed, my friend," Nicholas said, and kept his hand raised in salute as the knight rode out to the road and turned south.

"You will miss them," Beatrice said softly. "Your comrades-in-arms."

"Aye. 'Tis a special bond we share." He turned and pulled her against him. "But, in truth, I'm enjoying my new comrade-in-arms more than I ever did the old ones."

She smiled up at him archly. "I'm pleased to hear it."

He leaned down to nuzzle her neck. "In truth, I wouldn't mind having her in my arms right this minute."

"I should get back to my sewing lesson," she said with some regret.

Nicholas grinned. "I had in mind studying of another sort."

He brought his lips to her mouth and teased it open, continuing until she turned soft and pliant in his arms.

But still she protested, "We must wait until evening, my love, lest your mother begin to think me—"

He cut off her words with more kisses. When she made a little moan at the back of her throat, he pulled away, looked around the empty stableyard, then lifted her in his arms.

"Where are you taking me?" she murmured as he started walking toward the stable.

"You heard Bernard. A Knight of the Black Rose must be resourceful. I've prepared a nice hayloft hidden away in the stables for just such a moment as this."

"A hayloft?"

"Aye, milady. Do you object?"

She tucked her head against his neck and smiled. "Nay."

He made his way quickly to the back of the stables and deposited her in a soft bed of hay that he had covered with a quilt. She looked up at him, her eyes shining.

"And do they also say a Knight of the Black Rose must be tender and of noble heart?" she asked.

He lowered himself next to her. "'Tis not the knighthood that bestows those qualities, sweetheart. They come to a man who has found the right woman to love."

Then he took her in his arms and proceeded to show her that he had done just that.

* * * * *

*Bernard Fitzgibbons left for
the Crusades as a lad,
and returned a man.
A man determined to collect
the reward due him—land, and marriage
to his liege lord's youngest daughter!
Be sure to look for*

THE CONQUEROR

by

Shari Anton

The next book in the exciting
Knights of the Black Rose
miniseries.

*Available in April 2000
from Harlequin Historicals*

Take a trip to Merry Old England
with four exciting stories from

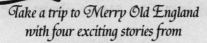

Come escape with Harlequin's new

Series Sampler

Four great full-length Harlequin novels bound together in one fabulous volume and at an unbelievable price.

Be transported back in time with a Harlequin Historical® novel, get caught up in a mystery with Intrigue®, be tempted by a hot, sizzling romance with Harlequin Temptation®, or just enjoy a down-home all-American read with American Romance®.

You won't be able to put this collection down!

On sale February 2000 at your favorite retail outlet.

HARLEQUIN®
Makes any time special ™

Visit us at www.romance.net

PHESC

TAKE A TRIP ACROSS AMERICA FROM SEA TO SHINING SEA WITH THESE HEARTFELT WESTERNS FROM

Harlequin® Historical

In March 2000, look for

THE BONNY BRIDE by **Deborah Hale**
(Nova Scotia, 1814)

and

ONCE A HERO by **Theresa Michaels**
(Arizona & New Mexico, 1893)

In April 2000, look for

THE MARRYING MAN by **Millie Criswell**
(West Virginia, 1800s)

and

HUNTER'S LAW by **Pat Tracy**
(Colorado, 1880s)

Harlequin Historicals
The way the past *should* have been.

Available at your favorite retail outlet.

HARLEQUIN®
Makes any time special ™

Return to the charm of the Regency era with

GEORGETTE HEYER,

creator of the modern Regency genre.

Enjoy six romantic collector's editions with forewords by some of today's bestselling romance authors,

**Nora Roberts, Mary Jo Putney,
Jo Beverley, Mary Balogh,
Theresa Medeiros and Kasey Michaels.**

Frederica
On sale February 2000

The Nonesuch
On sale March 2000

The Convenient Marriage
On sale April 2000

Cousin Kate
On sale May 2000

The Talisman Ring
On sale June 2000

The Corinthian
On sale July 2000

Available at your favorite retail outlet.

HARLEQUIN®
Makes any time special ™

Visit us at www.romance.net   PHGHGEN

COMING NEXT MONTH FROM

HARLEQUIN HISTORICALS

- **THE BONNY BRIDE**
  by **Deborah Hale,** author of A GENTLEMAN OF SUBSTANCE
  Love or money? That is the decision a farmer's daughter must
  make when she sets sail for Nova Scotia as a mail-order bride
  to a wealthy man, and finds the love of her life on the voyage.
  HH #503 ISBN# 29103-5 $4.99 U.S./$5.99 CAN.

- **A WARRIOR'S KISS**
  by **Margaret Moore,** author of THE WELSHMAN'S BRIDE
  In this captivating medieval tale in the *Warrior Series,* a knight
  aspires to make a name for himself at the king's court, but finds
  his plans jeopardized when he falls in love with a woman who is
  a commoner.
  HH #504 ISBN# 29104-3 $4.99 U.S./$5.99 CAN.

- **ONCE A HERO**
  by **Theresa Michaels,** author of THE MERRY WIDOWS—
  SARAH
  A reluctant hero finds himself on a wild adventure when
  he rescues a beautiful woman and loses his heart in
  Theresa Michaels's dramatic return to her *Kincaid* series.
  HH #505 ISBN# 29105-1 $4.99 U.S./$5.99 CAN.

- **THE VIRGIN SPRING**
  by **Debra Lee Brown**
  This talented new author makes her debut with this stirring
  Scottish tale of a young clan laird who finds an amnesiac beauty
  beside a mythical spring.
  HH #506 ISBN# 29106-X $4.99 U.S./$5.99 CAN.

**DON'T MISS ANY OF
THESE TERRIFIC NEW TITLES!**

CNM0300